Let me introduce you.

Actually, Kay-Kay did most of the talking, but I could tell by the little smile on Mother's lips she was enjoying what Kay-Kay had to say: Kay-Kay shops at Landis Lane, the new boutique in town; Kay-Kay works out at Harvey's Gym; Kay-Kay has the sweetest boyfriend, Logan Clark; for Christmas, Logan gave Kay-Kay a tiny diamond pendant (Mother has one just like it); right before Christmas, Kay-Kay was invited to join the Bluebirds (Mother and Aunt Mary were members in high school).

I was so busy listening to Kay-Kay that I dropped an entire box of Goddess nail polish on the floor. The crash was so loud it startled everyone in the shop, or nearly everyone. Mrs. Webb, who's partially deaf, sat unfazed under the dryer. One of the Quilters peered out from behind the *National Enquirer* and crowed, "Good Lord, Rosemary! Be careful!"

Kay-Kay looked at me as if I'd suddenly appeared in the room by some irritating cosmic force. "Does she work here?" asked Kay-Kay.

And do you know what my own mother said? She said, "Yes!" That was all! Just y-e-s! Not, *Oh, let me introduce you, Kay-Kay. This is my daughter.*

Just *yes.*

I stormed off to the basement and made love to a *Snickers* bar.

OTHER BOOKS YOU MAY ENJOY

A Countess Below Stairs	Eva Ibbotson
Aurelia	Anne Osterlund
Cindy Ella	Robin Palmer
Hope Was Here	Joan Bauer
Jerk, California	Jonathan Friesen
Just Listen	Sarah Dessen
My Most Excellent Year	Steve Kluger
Prom	Laurie Halse Anderson
S.A.S.S.: When Irish Guys Are Smiling	Suzanne Supplee
The Truth About Forever	Sarah Dessen

SUZANNE SUPPLEE

Artichoke's Heart

speak
An Imprint of Penguin Group (USA) Inc.

SPEAK
Published by the Penguin Group
Penguin Group (USA) Inc., 345 Hudson Street, New York, New York 10014, U.S.A.
Penguin Group (Canada), 90 Eglinton Avenue East, Suite 700, Toronto, Ontario, Canada M4P 2Y3
(a division of Pearson Penguin Canada Inc.)
Penguin Books Ltd, 80 Strand, London WC2R 0RL, England
Penguin Ireland, 25 St Stephen's Green, Dublin 2, Ireland (a division of Penguin Books Ltd)
Penguin Group (Australia), 250 Camberwell Road, Camberwell, Victoria 3124, Australia
(a division of Pearson Australia Group Pty Ltd)
Penguin Books India Pvt Ltd, 11 Community Centre, Panchsheel Park, New Delhi - 110 017, India
Penguin Group (NZ), 67 Apollo Drive, Rosedale, North Shore 0632, New Zealand
(a division of Pearson New Zealand Ltd)
Penguin Books (South Africa) (Pty) Ltd, 24 Sturdee Avenue,
Rosebank, Johannesburg 2196, South Africa

Registered Offices: Penguin Books Ltd, 80 Strand, London WC2R 0RL, England

First published in the United States of America by Dutton Books,
a member of Penguin Group (USA) Inc., 2008
Published by Speak, an imprint of Penguin Group (USA) Inc., 2009

3 5 7 9 10 8 6 4

THE LIBRARY OF CONGRESS HAS CATALOGED THE DUTTON BOOKS EDITION AS FOLLOWS:
Supplee, Suzanne.
Artichoke's heart / by Suzanne Supplee
p. cm.
Summary: When she is almost sixteen years old, Rosemary decides she is sick of being overweight,
mocked at school and at Heavenly Hair—her mother's beauty salon—and feeling out of control,
and as she slowly loses weight, she realizes that she is able to cope with her mother's cancer,
having a boyfriend for the first time, and discovering that other people's lives
are not as perfect as they seem from the outside.
ISBN: 978-0-525-47902-4 (hc)
[1. Overweight persons—Fiction. 2. Weight control—Fiction. 3. Self-esteem—Fiction.
4. Interpersonal relations—Fiction. 5. Mothers and daughters—Fiction. 6. High school—Fiction.
7. Schools—Fiction. 8. Tennessee—Fiction.] I. Title
PZ7.S96518Ar 2008
[Fic]—dc22
2007028486

Speak ISBN 978-0-14-241427-9

Printed in the United States of America

685102

This book is dedicated to my mother,
Donna Sue Demastus Gibson (1939–2004),
for her life lessons in faith, hope, and God's love,
and to my husband, Scott.

Artichoke's Heart

But a Book is only the Heart's Portrait—every Page a Pulse.

EMILY DICKINSON

chapter one

The Resemblance

Mother spent $700 on a treadmill "from Santa" that I will *never* use. I won't walk three blocks when I actually *want* to get somewhere, much less run three miles on a strip of black rubber only to end up where I started out in the first place. Aunt Mary gave me two stupid diet books and three tickets for the upcoming conference at Columbia State called "Healing the Fat Girl Within" (I'm sensing a theme here). Normally, I'm not a materialistic sort of person, but let's just say this was one disappointing Christmas.

At least Miss Bertha gave me something thoughtful, a complete collection of Emily Dickinson poems (so far my favorite is "I'm Nobody!"), and Grandma Georgia sent money.

Still, all I really needed was to be stricken with some mysterious thyroid condition, a really good one that would cause me to wake up and weigh 120 pounds. Instead of experiencing a newsworthy miracle, however, I spent the holiday in sweatpants, with

Mother and Aunt Mary nagging me to please change clothes. I refused, citing the whole *comfort and joy* argument. The truth was I had outgrown even my fat clothes. It was either sweatpants or nothing.

Once I'd wolfed down enough turkey and dressing and pumpkin pie to choke a horse, I loosened the string in the waistband and plopped down at the computer. Consumed by overeater's guilt, I browsed the Internet and gazed zombie-eyed at the countless and mostly *expensive* ways a person might lose weight (how pathetic to be thinking about this on Christmas night). According to a doctor on one website, "losing weight can be even harder than treating cancer." This uplifting little tidbit was enough to catapult me straight back to the kitchen for two more cups of eggnog—right before bed. When I woke up the next morning, I didn't even have to step on the scale. Still snuggled beneath my bedcovers, I could feel those new pounds clinging to my thighs like koala bears on a eucalyptus tree. The day after Christmas should get its very own italicized title on the calendar: *December 26—the Most Depressing Day of the Year*. With Christmas officially over, I knew there was nothing left to anticipate but the endless gloom of winter, nothing to look forward to except devouring the secret lovers stashed under my bed—Mr. Hershey, Mr. Reeses, and Mr. M&M. I'm convinced Mother must have secret powers because just as I was about to rip open the bag, the phone rang.

"What are you doing, Rosie?" she asked accusingly. "Have you used your treadmill yet? There's a new box of Special K in the pantry. They have that weight loss plan, you know."

"*Mmm*, almost as yummy as packaging peanuts," I replied.

"I'm just calling because we need you at the shop today after all, Rosie," said Mother, ignoring my sarcasm. "I want you to take down the Christmas tree. It's a fire hazard. All dried out and messy needles everywhere." Translation: Mother couldn't take the thought of me eating and watching talk shows all afternoon, so she's dragging me into work. "Miss Bertha'll be over to pick you up in a few, okay?" She said it like it was a question, as if I actually had a choice in the matter.

"O-kay," I said, annoyed. It's not even New Year's Eve, and I already have to rip down the last semblance of festivity and celebration—and *hope*. If it were up to me, I'd leave the tree up all year, but Mother had to shove the manicure station into the closet just to make room for it, and with so many parties right around the corner for New Year's, clients are clawing (ha-ha) for manicures. Mother isn't about to swap good business sense for sentimentality. At least there's time for half an *Oprah* rerun and a few "diet" Reese's cups (they're bite-sized instead of regular).

Several hundred calories later, Miss Bertha picked me up, and since the salon is only a mile or two from my house, we arrived within minutes. Mother was giving Hilda May Brunson blond highlights, and four old ladies from the Hopewell Baptist Church, a.k.a. the Quilters, were sitting under hairdryers, clucking like noisy hens. I was humming "Blue Christmas" (the Elvis version) softly to myself and carefully taking ornaments off the sad, dried-out little tree. Everything was thumping along at the barely tolerable level when I heard Miss Bertha say, "Oh, Lordy, here she comes."

I looked up, and filling Heavenly Hair's entire plate glass window was Mrs. Periwinkle McCutchin, her arms overloaded with a stack of paper plates wrapped in pink-tinted cellophane, her sausage-sized knuckle rapping the glass for someone to help her with the door. I had no other choice; I was forced to let her in.

"Hey, there, Rosemary, I got you some delicious treats today, darlin'!" *Snort, snort.* Big *Hee Haw* laugh. "You'll have to wait till Richard shaves my neck real quick, though. You got time to shave my neck, don't you, Richard?" Richard nodded politely, although I knew for a fact he hated shaving necks, especially Mrs. McCutchin's. "Reckon you can wait that long to get your hands on my goodies, Rosemary?" *Snort, snort.*

Suddenly, I realized Mrs. McCutchin was actually waiting for my reply. "Oh . . . um . . . sure," I mumbled. The Quilters gaped. Hilda May Brunson pursed her thin, judgmental lips together. When you're normal-sized, no one cares what you eat; when you're fat, it's everybody's business.

It took Richard several minutes to shear Mrs. McCutchin like a sheep, and by the time he finished, the Quilters and Hilda May Brunson were standing by the front counter.

"Rosemary!" Mrs. McCutchin called. "Can you help me get some-a this scratchy hair off my back? I won't let Richard put his manly hands up my blouse!" *Snort, snort. Cackle.* (Richard does not have manly hands. In fact, nothing much about him is manly.)

Richard mouthed a *Thank you, God* at the ceiling and rolled his eyes. "Okay," I said, and prayed that the Quilters and Hilda May Brunson would leave before Mrs. McCutchin made another giant fuss over the sweets. Slowly, I brushed the stubby black hairs off her barn-sized back.

"Hurry, sugar pie! Willy Ray and me and the boys is gonna try to make it to Catfish Campus before the rush," Mrs. McCutchin scolded, and then, with everybody listening, she said IT: "Rosemary, I swear you look more like me ever' day. Why, I b'lieve they got you and my little Willy Ray, Jr., mixed up at that hospital. Honey, you are built just exactly like I was at your age."

Heat ran up my face like a scared cat up a tree. The numbers of my morning weigh-in flashed through my brain: 1-9-0. Mrs. McCutchin wasn't a pound under 300.

The next thing I knew, Mrs. McCutchin was trying to pry herself out of the chair. Richard took one side, and I took the other. Somehow, even without the Jaws of Life, we managed to free her and stand her on her feet again. Mrs. McCutchin eyed the heap of treat-covered plates stacked on the worn linoleum and heaved her body forward to grab them. Her polyester skirt hiked up, revealing knee-highs with varicose-veiny fat bulging over. Her pendulous bosom swung in front of her face. Joints crunched. Her cheeks turned a dangerous shade of high-blood-pressure red, and layers of forehead and face and chin and neck pulled toward the ground. For a second, I wondered if Mrs. Periwinkle McCutchin might just turn inside out.

When she was miraculously upright again, the tight little salon expanded with relief. Mrs. McCutchin turned toward me and held up the pile of goodies. I shifted my eyes away from her and caught a glimpse of my reflection in the mirror (the whole salon is nothing but mirrors, unfortunately). It was then that I saw exactly what Mrs. McCutchin was talking about—the resemblance. It wasn't her imagination. It was real.

"I brought tea cakes and blondies and sand tarts just for you, Rosemary!" she went on. "You don't even have to share. And the Piggly Wiggly had pink cellophane. Ain't that the cutest thang!" She grinned proudly and tried to hand me the festive little plates.

All eyes were on me. Every single person in the salon was waiting for my response. In private, I have absolutely no willpower, but in public I wasn't about to fail. "I don't want those things," I said, my voice small and childish. And cold.

"Pardon?" asked Mrs. McCutchin.

"I *said* I don't want them!" Before Mrs. McCutchin could reply or cry, I raced off to the back room and left her standing there, humiliated. It was like shunning Little Debbie or slapping Sara Lee.

According to one of the books Aunt Mary gave me, a person has to be willing to eat differently even if it hurts people's feelings or causes conflict. I guess today I did both, although I was so upset about wounding a woman who has been nothing but nice to me my whole entire life, I came home and ate four chocolate bars and two bags of cheese curls.

Not only am I fat, I'm stupid, too.

chapter two

The Insulator

This morning there was a note from Mother on my bedside table—*Take the day off. It's New Year's Eve!* After what happened with Mrs. McCutchin and her Christmas treats last week, Mother must think it's safe to leave me home alone with food. Maybe she thinks I've turned over a new leaf or something. *Wrong.* I called Miss Bertha to come pick me up. I knew Mother would need the extra help at the salon, it being a holiday and all. Besides that, I knew if I stayed home I'd start eating and never stop.

Last night I dreamed about Emily Dickinson. I must've read a hundred of her poems before bed. I gobbled them up like they were Mrs. McCutchin's sand tarts. In my dream, E.D. and I were sitting together at the school lunch table when nasty Misty Winters walked by and said, "Hey, Fat Artichoke!" E.D. looked at me strangely, as if she could see straight through to my soul, then she said, "Whatever did you do with your dignity, Rosemary?"

When I opened my mouth to respond, all the letters of the alphabet came tumbling out.

The Artichoke name-calling started in sixth grade. All winter long, I'd begged Mother and Aunt Mary and Grandma Georgia (and anybody else who would listen to me for five seconds) for the Insulator. Really it was just a goose-down jacket with arms that zipped in and out. Mother had just purchased the shop. Grandma Georgia was still trying to pay off her lawyer from divorce number three. Aunt Mary hadn't finished paralegal school yet. Basically, nobody had money for the Insulator.

So the gift seemed that much sweeter when it finally arrived that exceptionally warm afternoon in late March, a few days before my birthday. I felt only a mild twinge of disappointment to find the jacket in avocado green with celadon lining. Quickly, Aunt Mary explained, "They were all out of berry pink!" "You'll be an original," said Mother. "You'll set trends," Grandma Georgia promised. I wonder what my adolescence would be like today if L. L. Bean hadn't sold out of berry pink.

All morning long I sweated buckets waiting for the other girls to notice my Insulator. Finally, it was Misty Winters who did. "Oh, my Gawd!" she cried, and motioned me toward her lunch table. Overloaded tray in hand, I made my way across the crowded cafeteria. Finally, *someone* was going to say *something* about my new jacket.

"Did you get your calendar mixed up?" Misty asked.

"What?" I replied.

"Duh!" said Misty sharply. "It's practically summertime outside, and you look just like a sweaty, fat artichoke in that stupid coat!"

I could tell by their dumb, blank faces that most of the kids at Misty's lunch table didn't even know what an artichoke was, but the damage was done, and *artichoke* is a very catchy word for twelve-year-olds. From that fateful day forward, I became the Artichoke, Arti, Chokey, Fat Artichoke. The list of variations is as individual as the name-callers.

Oprah always says, "It's not about the food." But right now, it feels very much about the food. All I do is think about food, try to resist food, give in to food, hate myself over food. I dream about food; even my nickname is a food! Heck, my *real name* is a food, or an herb, at least. Why, this very minute there's a jumbo-sized Hershey bar hidden in my cedar chest, and it's yelling, "Hey, let me out of here!"

Miss Bertha better hurry up.

Mrs. McCutchin came into the salon today. She wanted a wash and set, since she and Mr. McCutchin were going to Country Sizzlin' Steakhouse for dinner. She didn't bring any treats. She didn't smile. She didn't call me "darlin'" or "sugar" or "honey pie." In fact, she didn't even *speak*, at least not to me. Instead, she put on this big act like she wasn't feeling well. "My heart is just a-flutterin' like a little bird," I overheard her say. "My stomach's right queasy, too."

"Peri, you need to call that new doctor who took over Harry Smith's practice. What's his name? I forget," said Mother.

"Aw, naw. Me and Willy Ray's goin' out to eat tonight. I'll call Dr. What's-His-Name next week, after the holidays maybe."

She shifted her weight slightly, and the chair let out an irritable groan.

Mother and Aunt Mary were invited over to Hilda May Brunson's annual New Year's Eve party. Mother said she hated to leave me home alone on a holiday, but New Year's Eve or not, I didn't care. In fact, I was so totally miserable with myself, I actually *wanted* to be alone. Being by myself was certainly better than sitting through another nag session about Special K or listening to a guilt trip about not using my treadmill (*dreadmill*, as I'd started calling it).

After Mother and Aunt Mary left, I clicked through the channels and tried to occupy myself with festive television programs about the shining promise of a brand-new year. Bored, I went to take a peek in the pantry. *It won't hurt just to look at food*, I told myself. I kept hoping the unfortunate episode with Mrs. McCutchin wasn't in vain, that maybe I would start to change— eat better, exercise—*tomorrow*. I stood in the kitchen, closely examining shelf after shelf of canned goods, boxed goods, plastic-bag goods. All of it was boring, the kind of nonperishables people donate to food pantries, as if poor, homeless folks don't have taste buds. All at once, I spotted something promising. It was on the very top shelf, tucked way in the back—hidden from *me*, more than likely, and then forgotten. I climbed on a chair and grabbed the giant bag of Easter eggs.

It seemed way too pathological to start with the Easter eggs (I guess I was still holding out hope that I wouldn't actually consume them), so I began with the Hershey bar from my cedar chest. Slowly, I devoured each happy little rectangle. Just before midnight, I switched stations so I could watch the ball drop in Times Square. It seemed a shame not to toast the New Year with something, so I went to the freezer and found two slices of carrot cake (it was *still frozen* when I ate it). I'm not sure how many calories I consumed, but it was probably more than a person is supposed to have in a whole week. If I were a heroin addict, I'd be in big trouble.

All at once, I got this sinking feeling, a wave of self-hatred so violent, a sense of disgust and regret so crippling, I thought I might die. It was the kind of moment that makes people vow to change things. It occurred to me that right that very second, millions of people all over the world were bracing themselves for resolutions. They were having one last drink, one final smoke. Determined to make January 1 my new day, I ripped open the bag of petrified Easter eggs and swore this would be my last ever indulgence.

After the binge, I turned on the treadmill and sat on my bed watching it move. I wondered how long I'd have to run just to work off the night's calories—from now till morning would probably do the trick. I switched it off again and climbed into bed. I didn't bother changing my clothes. Sweatpants are multifunctional, like those little black dresses they show in magazines that can go from daytime to evening wear (and in my case, back to daytime again). I lay in bed and thought about an Emily Dickinson poem I'd read earlier that day.

Hope is the thing with feathers
That perches in the soul,

And sings the tune without the words,
And never stops at all . . .

E.D., in my opinion, is the perfect (although admittedly slightly
cliché) poet for lonely fat girls. Is that why Miss Bertha gave me
the book? Whatever her reason, I'm grateful. Instead of trying to
fall asleep by counting the day's calories, I squeezed my eyes shut
and focused on that four-letter word: H-O-P-E. I held on to it as
if it were a life vest.

On New Year's Day Mother woke me up with bad news. Mrs.
McCutchin wasn't faking. She had a heart attack right smack in
the middle of Country Sizzlin' Steakhouse. She's barely clinging
to life over at Maury Regional Hospital. Mother says they've
got her on all kinds of machines. Mother also says it's a wonder
Mrs. McCutchin didn't collapse in the middle of Heavenly Hair.
Actually, it would've been better if she had. At least Mother and
Miss Bertha know CPR. The only thing they knew at the steakhouse was the Heimlich maneuver.

That next Friday morning, all the clucking Quilters could talk
about was Mrs. McCutchin. I tried ignoring them. I went to the
back room to fold clean towels. I unpacked and priced new shampoo and conditioner in the basement. I even washed the plate glass
window—from the *outside*. It seemed like everybody, including
the meter maid, was talking about "poor old Mrs. McCutchin"
or "poor old Willy Ray, Sr.," or "those poor little boys soon to
lose their precious mother." I tried not to think about the plate of

goodies she'd brought for me just one week ago, or the expression on her jiggly face when I said I didn't want them.

To make matters worse, school starts back on Monday. I'll have to face Misty Winters and her lunch table filled with teasers and P.E. and my too-tight, ride-up-in-your-crack gym shorts and hall hecklers and locker bangers. If it weren't for learning, school would be hell.

But at least that's two whole days away, and tomorrow Mother is leaving the shop to Miss Bertha, Mildred, our part-time manicurist, and Richard. For the first time since I was twelve, Mother canceled her Saturday clients. Mother, Aunt Mary, and I are spending what's left of Christmas break in Nashville. Maybe I won't even think about Mrs. McCutchin one time while we're gone. Maybe some hope will perch on my soul for a change. I wish it'd perch on Mrs. McCutchin's heart.

chapter three

Hermetically Sealed

*n*ashville has way more stores than Spring Hill, so Mother and Aunt Mary were dying to go shopping first. No one bothered consulting me about what *I* wanted to do first, which was *not* shopping. We started out in the petite section (you can imagine how fond I am of the petite section) at Rayman's Department Store. There was a huge after-Christmas sale going on, and the place was packed.

Mother and Aunt Mary spotted a whole rack of discounted holiday dresses. For what seemed an eternity, I had to listen to Aunt Mary say things like, "Rose Warren, you think I should try the size two in this, or the zero?" To which Mother would reply, "Well, that looks like a mighty big size two to me."

How BIG can a size two be? I wanted to scream.

In the dressing room, I sat on a hard bench and watched as Aunt Mary came parading out of the stall wearing nothing but a black silk skirt and her bra. "You know a lot of these places have surveillance cameras," I reminded her. I could picture a bunch of sweaty men in uniform getting all excited in a back room somewhere. In fact, I'd seen such a thing on television once.

"Well, I hope they enjoy the show!" said Aunt Mary. "Yoohoo, anyone want my phone number?" she said, waving toward the ceiling. Aunt Mary still hasn't recovered from the fact that she didn't have a date for New Year's. "I just don't understand it," she said, and sighed, scrutinizing herself in the mirror.

"Understand what?" I made the mistake of asking.

"Why men aren't just clamoring after me. I mean, *look* at me, Rosie. What is the problem?" She asked the question as if I might actually know the answer. Perhaps I did, but I certainly wasn't going to say anything. Besides, I knew this conversation would veer off in my direction at any second. When Aunt Mary can't fix something about herself, she sets her sights on fixing things in other people. "I have a decent face, good hair, a thin body," she went on. "*I* take care of *myself*," she said pointedly. "By the way, Rosie, how's the new treadmill?"

At that precise moment, a very pale-looking Mother stepped out of the dressing room, a pile of discarded dresses draped over her arm. "She hasn't even turned the thing on," Mother tattled. It was a sore subject between us. "I don't think she's even plugged it in. Have you even plugged it in, Rosie?" asked Mother, stifling a cough. Mother's had the same cold for weeks. In my opinion, she has no business lecturing me about health issues.

"Yes, as a matter of fact, I did plug it in, *and* I turned it on," I said.

"Then what'd you do?" asked Aunt Mary. I glared at her,

refusing to answer. She nodded and pursed her lips together in that know-it-all way she has. "You just watched it run, didn't you?"

"You mean I actually have to get on it?" I asked, being sarcastic, of course. Aunt Mary huffed off into the dressing room, and Mother went to give the rejected dresses to the saleslady. I tried to help her with the heavy heap of clothes, but she tugged them out of my hands again. "I've got it, Rosie!" she snapped.

The whole way back to the car, which was parked about twenty miles from the mall, I had to endure yet another of Aunt Mary's lectures. *Atkins this. South Beach that. Your body's a temple. Don't waste your youth being fat. Blah, blah, blah.* Of course, Mother didn't say a word in my defense. She never does when Aunt Mary, her precious sister, is involved. Mother just walked alongside us and coughed discreetly into a tissue. Just once, I'd like for Mother to tell Aunt Mary to back off and leave me and my thunder thighs and big butt alone, but that's about as likely as the hyperthyroid condition I've been hoping for.

By the time we reached American Eats, the diner down the road from the mall, I'd had enough of my aunt's haranguing and my mother's *I'm-staying-out-of-this* silence. Just to show them both who was boss, I ordered a slab of chocolate cake with a scoop of vanilla ice cream and an extra-large order of curly fries and chocolate milk. I was starving, so it wasn't like I was eating for no reason at all, but even so, the second the cake came, I got this guilty pit in my stomach.

Aunt Mary's mouth flew open. "You're not going to eat all of that?" she asked, horrified by my rebellious gluttony.

I dug my fork into the moist chocolate and delicately slipped the first bite into my mouth. Yes, I felt guilty, but the cake was also very, very good. I didn't bother answering Aunt Mary. My English teacher always says it's better to show than to tell, and in this case, I was definitely showing my aunt who was boss (the cake, clearly).

"Rosie, you are just disgusting! I mean, have you no shame? No shame at all?" Aunt Mary went on.

I blinked at Mother, sent telepathic messages across the table. Your sister just called me, *your daughter*, disgusting. *Aren't you going to intervene? Tell her that's enough?* I slid the cake plate to the side, and squirted a liter of ketchup onto the fries.

"Well, I just don't know how you can stand yourself! You're just ruining your life is all. *And* your health. Rose Warren, aren't you gonna say something? Your daughter's sitting across the table trying to give herself a heart attack, and you're acting like it's no big deal."

Mother seemed at a loss for words, but then at critical moments like this, she's always at a loss for words—*hermetically sealed*, I call her. Vacuum-packed like processed lunchmeat. She sighed and put down her spoon. Her soup was hardly touched, I noticed. "If you two don't mind, I need to use the potty," she said, and slid out of the booth.

"Well, I hope you're satisfied!" Aunt Mary hissed when Mother had gone. "You've all but ruined our weekend!"

My body may be out of shape, but my smart-aleck tongue is

extremely fit. I thought of a million comebacks, but I lacked the energy to use even one. Maybe I am a "disgusting" fat girl, but just once, I'd like Mother to stand up for me, to take my side of things instead of Aunt Mary's all the time. And no matter what my daughter looks like one day, I will never allow anyone to call her disgusting.

chapter four

Delightfully Enormous

I can't believe Christmas break is already over. I was hoping to come back to school ten pounds lighter; instead, I'm ten pounds heavier. This morning my bathroom scale said something it has *never* said before—200 pounds! I was tempted to fake some horrible illness and stay home, since I had nothing in my closet that would actually fit, but I knew Mother would never go for it.

"Rosie, you just missed the bus!" said Mother, clearly irritated. She had slipped up the stairs to my room and was standing there, staring at me in horror, and no wonder she was staring in horror. I had my jeans pulled up to my thighs, and I was duck-walking across the floor, my pathetic attempt to stretch them so I could get them over my butt. "Those jeans are too tight." She sighed.

"Oh, no! Really, they're fine," I lied. "I dried them on *hot*. Dummy me," I said. I stood up and tugged so hard two belt loops broke off.

"They are *too tight*," she said again. Firmly. "How much weight did you gain over Christmas?"

"Oh, Mother, I don't *know*! I'm not obsessed over that whole scale thing like you and Aunt Mary. What difference does it make? I am not defined by size," I said, knowing full well that I'm defined by size.

"Rosie, if you would just try a little." She coughed.

"Mother, you should spend less time focused on me and worry about yourself for a change. Seriously, I'm almost sixteen years old. I could be fat the rest of my life (*dear God, I hope not*). Are you going to nag me for the next forty years if—?" Mother's coughing escalated, so I stopped.

Finally, she gave up talking to me and went downstairs to find the Robitussin. I tugged on my trusty sweatpants, hoping no one would notice that now even *they* are too tight.

Mother's still down at the salon—some sort of plumbing problem. I'm waiting for my sweats to dry and reading an article in the *Raiders' Review*, our school newspaper. Normally, Spring Hill High School news doesn't interest me much. All the popular, pretty people staff the paper just so they can fill the pages with pictures of themselves, but I had already finished my homework and I needed a distraction (there are waffles lurking in our freezer).

The article's about this guy named Kyle Cox. He just transferred into my sixth period study hall. Actually, Kyle was in my honors English class, but he switched to standard after one week with Mrs. Edinburgh. According to the article, defensive lineman

Kyle is "delightfully enormous" and "strapping" *at six feet four inches and 260 pounds.* I wonder if at five feet six inches and 200 pounds I'd be considered "delightfully enormous." Somehow I doubt it.

The waffles in our freezer are homemade. Miss Bertha brought them over yesterday morning, said a good breakfast would build up Mother's bodily defenses a little. . . . If *my* defenses get any more built up, I'll be playing defensive lineman alongside Kyle Cox. . . . The timer just went off on the dryer. . . . It sounds a lot like the *ding* our microwave makes. . . . In the pantry, there's a brand-new jar of microwaveable maple syrup. . . . *How many waffles could I eat and still seem normal? . . . Three? . . . Four at the most?*

I WILL NOT EAT YOU, YOU STUPID WAFFLES!
I WILL NOT! I WILL NOT!

I'm probably the only kid in the whole entire school with a food hangover. Too much partying—*with waffles!* I'm also probably the only kid in *wet* sweatpants. For starters, I left them in the dryer too long last night and they shrank. This happened with a slipcover Mother made once, so she rewashed it, and while it was still damp, she put it back on the sofa. Miraculously, it'd stretched back out again. I figured since my sweatpants and the sofa slipcover are approximately the same size, it was worth a try, but now my sweatpants are wet *and* too little.

At least I have Kyle Cox—*Delightfully Enormous Strapping Boy*—to take my mind off the discomfort. He sits two tables over, and he's so much more fun to look at than Ronnie Derryberry, the only other person at my table. Ronnie's fingernails are so dirty you could grow a row of corn under them. Speaking of food, Kyle Cox is as yummy-looking as Mrs. McCutchin's Heal-a-Broken-Heart chocolate cake. If Shakespeare can compare a pretty girl to a summer's day, I can compare Kyle to chocolate cake.

Tonight after dinner, Mother came upstairs and sat on my bed. She didn't say anything. She just sat there staring at my stupid treadmill, which was overloaded with underwear—it does make a great drying rack. Finally, she started plucking still-damp bras and panties off the treadmill. "They're not dry yet, Mother," I said. My words came out sharper than I'd intended.

"Couldn't you at least try it?" she asked, somewhat pleadingly.

"I have homework."

Mother draped my underwear over a chair and tiptoed back downstairs.

For the rest of the night, I couldn't help thinking how much better off Mother would be with perfect Kay-Kay Reese for a daughter. Kay-Kay's the cheerleader/homecoming court/Miss Spring Hill Beauty Pageant Winner/Bluebird Club kind of girl.

This afternoon, Kay-Kay came into Heavenly Hair. While Mother painstakingly trimmed and highlighted Kay-Kay's perfect blond locks, I restocked the manicure station and eavesdropped on their conversation. Actually, Kay-Kay did most of the talking, but I could tell by the little smile on Mother's lips she was enjoying what Kay-Kay had to say: Kay-Kay shops at Landis Lane, the new boutique in town; Kay-Kay works out at Harvey's Gym; Kay-Kay has the sweetest boyfriend, Logan Clark; for Christmas, Logan gave Kay-Kay a tiny diamond pendant (Mother has one just like it); right before Christmas, Kay-Kay was invited to join the Bluebirds (Mother and Aunt Mary were members in high school).

I was so busy listening to Kay-Kay that I dropped an entire box of Goddess nail polish on the floor. The crash was so loud it startled everyone in the shop, or nearly everyone. Mrs. Webb, who's partially deaf, sat unfazed under the dryer. One of the Quilters peered out from behind the *National Enquirer* and crowed, "Good Lord, Rosemary! Be careful!"

Kay-Kay looked at me as if I'd suddenly appeared in the room by some irritating cosmic force. "Does she work here?" asked Kay-Kay.

And do you know what my own mother said? She said, "Yes!" That was all! Just y-e-s! Not, *Oh, let me introduce you, Kay-Kay. This is my daughter.*

Just *yes.*

I stormed off to the basement and made love to a Snickers bar.

chapter five

A Good Hairdresser

I'm waiting for Miss Bertha to pick me up in her tattered old station wagon. It's left over from all the years she spent raising four girls. Miss Bertha says she's too sentimental to get rid of it, especially now that they've all grown up and moved away. It's not like she has to go very far from her rinky-dink (her description, not mine) house to the salon and back home again. On days when the salon's not busy, Miss Bertha lets me drive. She says I'll pass my driver's test with flying colors when the time comes.

Last summer, Miss Bertha's husband took a job with a trucking company. He's gone most of the time now, so Miss Bertha's life consists of the Mill Creek Methodist Church and all of us at Heavenly Hair. Miss Bertha didn't get her GED until a few years ago, but out of everybody I know, it's Miss Bertha's opinion I respect the most. I bet she's read more books than most of my teachers at Spring Hill High School. Not trashy books either. Miss Bertha prefers the classics—in books *and* music.

The schedule at Heavenly Hair is jam-packed today. Normally, I like it when the salon is hopping like frogs after a summer rain, but tonight's the winter dance, and every girl in town (except for me, of course) is getting her most coveted up-do. They'll be squealing and screaming into their cell phones like tonight's the Academy Awards, and they're all up for Best Actress.

Richard makes fun of the whole scene, calls it a "big rah-rah spectacle." He sneers and says they'll be drunk and pregnant before the last song plays. Richard's bitter. He spent his entire high school career being teased because he's gay. Finally, he dropped out senior year and went to cosmetology school instead.

"Hi, Miss Bertha," I said, sliding into the passenger's seat.

"Oh, Lordy. I've never seen so many silly girls in my whole life. Gum popping, cell phone yacking! Seems like it just gets worse every year. No manners to speak of, and *who* are they all talking to? I thought cell phones were for emergencies." I rolled my eyes but didn't say anything. Miss Bertha has it in for cell phones. "What?" she asked, looking at me. "*You* don't talk on one," she pointed out.

"Exactly who would I call?" I asked. Miss Bertha headed up North Main Street and rounded the courthouse. "Can we stop by Reynolds's Drugstore real quick?"

"Oh, honey, your mama's swamped."

"It'll just take a second. I wanna get a card for Mrs. McCutchin. We're going to see her this afternoon."

"Oh, all right," said Miss Bertha, slinging her boat of a car into a sliver of a parking space.

"I'll be quick," I said, squeezing my way through the tiny space between the two cars.

There was an overwhelming selection of get-well cards, some of them even illness-specific. Funny ones for routine operations, philosophical ones for cancer and other long-term, bleak diseases. There was even a card for a sick pet. Finally, I settled on something short and to the point: *Wishing you a speedy recovery!*

I waited in line at the cash register and noticed a large display:

Pounds-Away Products
—*Buy two six-packs, get the third free!*
—*Drink delicious, nutritious Pounds-Away and watch the ugly fat melt!*

I pictured Mrs. McCutchin on Pounds-Away, but instead of drinking it, the nurses would hook her up to an IV of the stuff. Within seconds, the fat would melt like hot candle wax—sliding down her puffy cheeks and belly and thighs, dripping off the tips of her fingers, soaking the bed sheets, making a mess on the floor. When the process was finally finished, a hazmat crew would clean everything up.

"Are you gettin' that?"

"Huh?" I asked, blinking at the thinnish blonde behind the cash register.

"You was lookin' at that stuff like you might want some," she said, nodding toward the display.

"Oh, um . . . no, thank you. Just the card, please." I paid for my nondescript get-well card and hurried out the door, Pounds-Awayless.

———

Hours later, when the last of the winter dance crowd was finally gone, Mother began packing up a tote bag. "What's that for?" I asked.

"Just a few tools of the trade." She winked and dropped her shears in.

"Mother, you're not gonna shave her neck right there in the hospital!" I protested.

"Oh, no one will know, trust me," she replied calmly. "Now grab that stack of *National Enquirer*s. I reckon the Quilters will have to fight over *Soap Opera Digest* next time they come." Mother was in her efficient, take-charge mode. There was no stopping her.

When we first walked in, I thought Mrs. McCutchin was already dead. The air smelled strange—a combination of bad gas, hospital food, and cleaning solution—and Mrs. McCutchin's eyes were closed, her face the same ghostly color as the sheet. I'd never seen the woman so still or so quiet. If Mrs. McCutchin isn't yammering on and on about peanut brittle or chocolate fudge or a price reduction at Piggly Wiggly, she's singing Shania Twain songs or gossiping about movie stars like she's known them all her life.

Suddenly, Mrs. McCutchin opened her eyes, and I nearly jumped out of my skin. "Well, hidy, y'all," she said hoarsely. She cleared her throat and tried again, but the *hidy, y'all* came out as raspy as the first time. "My voice is a mess from that tube they had down my throat."

I didn't ask. I didn't want to know.

"How you feeling, Peri?" asked Mother. "What do the doctors say?"

"Oh, there's no need to get into all that," said Mrs. McCutchin. "Let's just visit."

Mother looked relieved. "I'll fix your hair if you'd like."

"That'd be nice," Mrs. McCutchin croaked. "I ain't had a thing done to my hair, other than them orderlies trying to wash it. Did you bring your shears?" Mother nodded and raised the hospital bed to the upright position. Mrs. McCutchin smiled up at her as if she were an angel sent straight from heaven. She didn't say a word to me, however.

While Mother worked, she talked. She updated Mrs. McCutchin about the Quilters: Ida Lee Harris turned eighty-nine; Louise Alcott was planning a cruise; Carolyn Wilson had a boyfriend; Laurie Snodgrass quit the church choir. Mother told Mrs. McCutchin all about fixing hair for the winter dance and about Kay-Kay Reese and what a pretty girl she was and how Richard's negative energy was clouding the salon. It was hairdresser magic. Pixie dust and abracadabra all rolled into one.

After an hour with Mother, the color was back in Mrs. McCutchin's cheeks, and she was grinning ear to ear—the TV clicker in one hand, a *National Enquirer* in the other. *So much for modern medicine,* I thought. *Maybe all anyone needs is a trashy magazine and a good hairdresser.*

Just as we were about to leave, I handed Mrs. McCutchin the card. "I'm sorry," I whispered (so softly I'm pretty sure she didn't hear me).

chapter six

The Radical Weight Loss Plan

I can't stop snacking. Last night the scale said 203 pounds. And I do mean it *said* 203 pounds. Aunt Mary saw a talking scale being sold on QVC, and she decided I just had to have it. She even paid extra to have it delivered overnight. The *American Eats* episode must've inspired her purchase.

I just can't believe I've packed on thirteen pounds. *Thirteen pounds!* How did that happen? How can I make it stop? *Why can't* I make it stop? What if it never, ever stops? What if I'm twenty-five and still tortured by talking scales and well-meaning bakers who keep trying to feed the fat girl? What if at my ten-year class reunion I am still the Artichoke?

I can't think about this now. I'll think about something pleasant, like Kyle Cox. *Mmm*, now *he's* pleasant.

Kyle Cox has curly dark hair. His eyes are brown, I think. I wish I could stash Kyle Cox under my bed with the other man in my life—a Mr. Goodbar I have hidden there. I'd devour both of them. Lust is a lot like a chocolate craving.

It's no use. My brain refuses to think pleasant thoughts. It's Tuesday. It's January. It's cold and gray and I'm fat and nothing fits. I will have to wear sweatpants to school, *again*.

A very radical plan has been forming in my head for days. It's a stupid plan—*insane*, actually—but I can't stop thinking about it. It's right up there with my latest fantasy of living in a starving third-world country just so I can lose weight. Mother is in the shower. Maybe if I hurry, I can put my plan into action before she's finished.

I just put a jar of mayonnaise by the very warm heating vent in my room. I tossed a pair of dirty sweats over the top of it just in case Mother happens to come upstairs and gaze with disappointment at my treadmill again.

Tonight it begins. . . .

Kyle Cox just caught me looking at him, but he didn't jerk his head away or act all disgusted like any other Spring Hill High School jock would've done. He smiled. At least, I think he smiled. Was he smiling? *At me?* I feel like passing him a note. *Excuse me*, the note would say. *I need to know, were you looking at/flirting with me? If so, why? Are you myopic? Mentally compromised?*

I'll say one thing for Kyle Cox, I've been observing him rather closely, and he isn't one of the Nucleolus Boys (obviously, I've spent way too much time studying for my biology test). Nucleolus Boys—NBs, as I call them—are the arrogant, popular ones who think they're the center of everything, that the entire *cell* of high school revolves around them.

Even though he's handsome and a jock, Kyle seems more like the centrosome type, close to the nucleus, but not actually *in* the nucleus. Kyle says hello to people. He holds the door open for teachers. He doesn't make fun of fat girls or anyone else, as far as I can tell. I'm more of a vacuole type. I exist in the outer sphere, but I'm still trapped within the cell membrane.

Kay-Kay Reese just came into study hall to deliver a note to Mr. Lawrence. She had on the cutest outfit—slim-fitting jeans, a cool belt, spiky-heeled boots, a crisp white blouse, and a light-blue jacket. Her hair was pulled back into a sleek ponytail, and she had on giant silver hoops. I would give anything to be more like her. *Anything?* I wonder. *Would I toss out the candy under my bed? Climb on that hideous treadmill and actually run? Would I listen to Mother and Aunt Mary? Do what they say for once?*

"Rosie, have you seen the mayonnaise?" Mother's head was stuffed in the fridge, but I knew she wouldn't find what she was looking for. The mayo was still in my room, getting nice and ripe and rancid for later.

"I haven't seen it," I lied coolly.

"Damn!" She stood upright suddenly and stared at me. "You *really* didn't take the mayonnaise?" she asked again.

"Mother, I'm not *that* bad off. Raw mayo isn't exactly my snack of choice!"

"Okay," she said, still clearly puzzled. When she was out of the kitchen, I slipped a can of tuna into my sweatshirt, grabbed a loaf of bread and some Mountain Dew, and headed upstairs to my room again. These were the last of the necessary supplies.

A while later Mother yelled up the stairs, "Rosie, I'm going to Pig's to get some mayo. You need anything?"

"No, thanks!" I said. I heard the front door slam. I listened as she eased her Honda out of the driveway. Originally, I'd planned to wait until Mother was in bed to make my tainted mayo sandwiches, but I decided now was as good a time as any.

I piled globs of slimy, hot mayo on the bread and added some tuna to help with the taste (I wasn't lying when I said raw mayo wouldn't be my snack of choice). I figured two sandwiches would do the trick. I ate them quickly and washed everything down with Mountain Dew. I sat propped up in my bed and marveled at the fact that tainted mayo doesn't taste too bad (no wonder the Quilters poisoned half the Hopewell Baptist Church with their potato salad a few summers ago).

Mother was back. I could hear her in the kitchen opening and closing cabinet doors. "Rosie!" she shouted up the stairs.

"Ye-*es*?"

"Now I can't find the tuna. Did you eat it?"

My stomach clutched up. "Um . . . yeah. Sorry."

"Good Lord! I swear, I spend half my life at that Piggly Wiggly!" I could hear her climbing the stairs. Quickly, I scanned my room for any evidence.

Mother stood at the foot of my bed and frowned at me. "Rosie, is everything all right?" she asked. "I swear, I don't know when I've been so worried about you." She glanced around, and I could tell she was taking inventory of my messy room. Clothes on the treadmill. Shoes piled in *front* of the closet instead of inside it. Random books and hair products and nail polish. "You're sure you're all right?" she asked again.

I thought of spilling my guts (no pun intended), spewing my innermost thoughts all over the room. Instead, I gave Mother her own usual reply. "I'm *just fine*, Mother."

A cloud flitted across her face, and she studied me. I blinked back at her innocently, but already I regretted my comeback. At least when Mother says things are *just fine* it's because she's trying so hard to make them that way. I'd used the words just to mock her, and she knew it. We were in some sort of tug-of-war, Mother and me, but neither of us was exhausted enough to let go of the rope yet.

Here's how the remainder of my *just fine* week went:

Wednesday: Woke up and heaved my guts out. Missed school. Missed work.

Thursday: Still sick. Missed school. Missed work. Wrote up a will just in case (cremate me *and* my sweats).

Friday: Weak but better. Ripped up will. Weighed 190 again.

The Radical Weight Loss Plan was totally not worth the suffering, and if Mother and Aunt Mary find out about what I did, they'll put me in a straitjacket and have me committed to a mental institution for sure. I might just commit myself.

chapter seven

Rolling Fat Girl

Today, I finally went back to school after my tainted mayo calamity. Yesterday was Martin Luther King's birthday, so I had a vacation day on top of all the sick days. There was a little part of me that thought maybe someone would say something like, *Oh, where have you been, Rosemary?* or *How are you feeling, Rosemary?* But the only person who said anything at all was Mrs. Edinburgh. I believe her exact words were, *You have a lot of work to make up, young lady.*

Normally, I would've let the fact that I'm a miserable, unmissed loser ruin my day, but today was different. Right before lunch, I spotted Kyle Cox in the hallway. For a nanosecond our eyes met, and he smiled. At me! This time I'm *sure* he was smiling at me because there was no one else in the hallway. I checked.

All through lunch, I couldn't stop thinking about him. I barely touched my roast beef sandwich and french fries. I didn't even go back for ice cream or chips or seconds and thirds. I drank water instead of soda. The whole time I sat at my lunch table—all by my freakish outcast self—I was at least *thinking* normal things. Instead of lusting after chocolate, I was lusting after Kyle.

Suddenly, I got this shiny little thought: Maybe under all these bulky pounds hides the heart of a normal girl, one who doesn't poison herself with mayo or abuse her body with food. I do have these fleeting seconds sometimes when I think I see her. Like a flash, I glimpse this girl—this other me—out of the corner of my eye. She has friends and a social life and self-confidence. I'm not sure how big or little she is, but I'm pretty sure she's happy. I guess in some ways I am sort of like an artichoke. Maybe I'll have to peel away the layers to get to the good part.

When the sixth-period bell rang, I was the first person out of my seat. Misty Winters and Tara Waters yelled, "Hey, Chokey! What's the rush? Is the ice-cream truck parked out front?" I ignored them and kept going. First, I had to stop off by the bathroom to brush my hair and slap on some lip gloss. I wanted to look my 189-pound best for Kyle. I wanted to hang on to that normal-girl feeling just a little while longer. Right before the warning bell clanged, I slid into my seat. Mr. Lawrence looked up and gave me the *I-hate-fat-people* glare, but he didn't say anything. Sometimes he's as bad as Misty Winters.

Most of the kids around me got busy with something—picking nails or noses or scabs. Lisa Runions, who sits one table over, pulled long, scraggly strands of her bleached-blond hair around in front so she could see to peel her split ends apart. Ronnie Derryberry settled his greasy head on a stack of unopened schoolbooks (I feel sorry for whoever has to use them next year) and fell asleep.

Slowly, I turned my head in Kyle's direction. *Sigh.* Major disappointment. There was only his empty chair. I waited. The late bell rang. Still no Kyle. With a heavy heart, I opened my biology book and resigned myself to cells, *again.* Fat cells.

At 1:32, the library door swung open. In one hand, he carried an overloaded book bag. In the other, he held a bright orange late pass. "Team meeting," I heard him mutter to Mr. Lawrence. At the sound of Kyle's Delightfully Enormous Strapping Boy voice, my heart thrashed around like a cat in a bag. Heat prickled my cheeks. My palms went clammy.

Love is a lot like food poisoning.

To avoid fidgeting, I sat on my hands and waited for Kyle to take his seat. From my chair to his, there was a perfect view, but instead of going to his usual third row, third table, end chair, Kyle took a sharp turn to the left and sat down in front of one of the library computers.

Damn! Damn! Damn! Ronnie Derryberry stirred and looked up at me as if I'd actually said the words out loud. There was only one way to get a good look at Kyle—get out of my chair and walk over to the computer table where he was sitting. *Oh, God.* I'd have to pretend to Google something. Kyle need never know his nanosecond smiles had spawned Stalker Girl.

I waited and watched the clock pulse too quickly toward the end of the period. I thought about how, if you're skinny, walking across the library probably isn't a big deal. In fact, if you're cute and petite like Kay-Kay Reese, it's probably even fun—all that strutting and posing and sticking your good parts out. But, if you're a fat girl, walking clear across the library is like crossing the interstate blindfolded.

I debated. I waited. Finally, I stood. Chairs were wedged too closely together, and the library was warm and packed with kids. Several times, I had to tap people on the shoulder and ask them to scoot in a bit. There were a few irritated sighs but no outright hostility. Finally, I reached a clearing—there was nothing standing between me and Kyle Cox except some ugly stained carpet. I wiped the sweat beads off my upper lip, smoothed out my too-tight black denim skirt (it actually fits again), pulled at my oversized sweater, and aimed my clogged feet in Kyle's direction.

Right next to him was an empty chair. Quickly, before I lost the nerve, I plopped my barn ass into it. Big mistake. Warning! Chair on wheels! Rolling fat girl! Instead of sitting *next* to Kyle, I practically sat *on* Kyle. The computer table shook. Two seniors shot looks of pure hatred across the table. Even Mr. Lawrence glanced up from his newspaper. I sucked in my breath and held it there.

"Whoops," Kyle said, and grinned. With an ever-so-gentle football paw, he slid my chair back to its appropriate position as if I weighed nothing at all!

"Excuse me," I mumbled, mortified.

"No problem," Kyle whispered. "Excuse that chair," he said, and laughed. Then it came—another eye-meeting nanosecond smile. After that, Kyle went back to his work on the computer, which turned out to be checking sports scores on the Internet.

Even though I'll be sixteen in two months, Mother still insists on scheduling my annual check-ups over at Dr. Cooper's office.

Most girls my age have a GYN and a prescription of birth con-trol pills by now; I still go to the pediatrician and read *Highlights for Children* in the waiting room. To make matters worse, at the end of every visit, Dr. Cooper compares this year's weight to last year's weight, then he provides a bunch of bleak statistics on obe-sity (as if he's telling me something I don't already know). Finally, he'll say, "You need to lose weight, Rosemary." *Duh.*

Mother was quiet the whole way there, but I could tell by the way she kept biting her lip and glancing at me sideways that some-thing was up. I didn't want to spoil my Kyle Cox good mood, so I didn't ask her what was wrong. She squeezed into the parking lot and snatched a space next to a behemoth SUV. "Rosie?" she said, shutting off the engine.

"Yeah?" Mother dabbed on some lipstick and checked her reflection in the rearview mirror. "What is it?" I asked.

"Oh, never mind. It was nothing," she said, and hopped out of the car before I could press the matter.

Inside the doctor's office, Mother darted toward the waiting room, and I stopped at the glass partition to give my insurance card to the receptionist. "I'm Rosemary Goode. I have an appoint-ment with Dr. Cooper," I said.

"Dr. Cooper's snow skiing, hon. You're seeing Mrs. Wallace today."

As if on cue, a tall, broad-shouldered woman bustled into the waiting room. "You must be Rosemary," she said, and smiled at me. I glanced over at Mother, but she had her head stuck in a *Field & Stream* magazine.

"Do you have any idea why you're here, Rosemary?" Mrs.

Wallace asked when we were tucked in her office instead of one of the cold, stark examining rooms.

"I *thought* I was here for my usual check-up," I replied.

"I know. I'm sorry about that. I asked your mother to please tell you before y'all came in, but I had a feeling she might not."

"Tell me what?" I asked.

"Well, last week, I ran an ad in the *Daily Herald*. I was looking for candidates to participate in a study I'm conducting for my Ph.D. at Vanderbilt. I'm researching the effects of short-term counseling on weight loss. Your mother was very enthusiastic about signing you up, but she thought you might be reluctant if she pushed the idea on you."

"So she *tricked* me into coming here?"

Mrs. Wallace looked at me apologetically. "I know that must make you angry. It would make me angry, too, but would it be all right if I just told you a little bit about the study and then you could make up your own mind?" I let out an irritated sigh, and she took this as a yes.

"There's been some research that suggests that even a few sessions of counseling can help a person shed extra pounds. You see, food is just a coping mechanism, and like all coping mechanisms, it's used to medicate a problem. A person might feel sad about something, so he or she eats to numb that feeling. Or a person feels empty inside, so he or she eats to fill that void." Mrs. Wallace settled back in her chair and folded her *un*manicured hands across her lap. I could tell she was waiting for me to say something.

"So you're at Vanderbilt?" I asked. Since fourth grade I'd had my sights set on going to what Aunt Mary referred to as a smarty-pants college, and Vandy was my number one choice, even though I'd probably have to sell a kidney to afford it. Mrs. Wallace brightened slightly at my question in spite of the fact that it had nothing to do with coping mechanisms.

"Yep, I'm a Commodore fan all the way. What about you?" she asked.

"I'm not really into sports," I replied. A long uncomfortable silence passed between us. I was trying to make up my mind about whether or not I wanted to be somebody's guinea pig (no pun intended), and it seemed like Mrs. Wallace was trying to help me along by keeping quiet. "So what would we do at these sessions?" I asked finally.

"Mostly we'd just talk. I'd probably ask you to keep a journal. There might be an article I'd want you to read now and then. We'd meet on Monday afternoons for half an hour."

"How involved would my mother be with all this?"

"No more involved than she is right this minute," said Mrs. Wallace. "Listen, you go home and think about it. I'll put you on next Monday's schedule, but if you don't show up, no harm done." She stood and opened the door for me. No pressure. No lecture. I liked this.

On the way home, I didn't yell at Mother. She looked tired and defeated somehow, and I knew she'd tricked me into seeing Mrs. Wallace because she was worried. Frankly, that made two of us.

chapter eight

The C Word

I'm supposed to be folding clean towels and pricing a new line of shampoo, but it's so quiet in the salon this afternoon, I can't stand being here. Normally, this is the busiest time of day—blow dryers roaring, women cackling, the phone ringing off the hook. Today, however, everyone (except Mother) is over at Piggly Wiggly's buying toilet paper. The weather forecast said there'd be a "wintry mix" tonight.

After her last appointment canceled, Mother looked at me and said, "I've got to go. Close up the shop. Miss Bertha'll drive you." Her face was pale and sweaty. For a second, I thought she might faint.

"What's wrong?" I asked. "Let me come with you. Miss Bertha can close up."

"Oh, Rosie, I'm *fine*," said Mother, putting on her happy face. "Everything's *fine*," she said again on her way out the door. Later, when Miss Bertha called to check on her, Mother was *lying on the sofa.* Mother lying on the sofa is about as normal as my going for a jog.

When Miss Bertha dropped me off at home, Mother really did appear to be fine. "I just had a case of low blood sugar," she said, smiling. I swear my mother could lose a limb in a fiery crash and she'd look up at the paramedics and cheerfully say, *Don't y'all worry about me. I am just fine.*

The following morning I heard Mother on the phone—at five-thirty—and I knew there was some sort of crisis. I lay in my warm bed trying to translate the muffled sounds from the first floor into distinguishable words. *Had the pipes at Heavenly Hair frozen again? Was the burglar alarm going off?* I glanced out the window. No "wintry mix" after all.

All at once, I sat up. *It's Mrs. McCutchin,* I told myself. *She's dead.* Quietly, I slipped down the creaky stairs. I sat on the bottom step and pressed my ear against the door. The kitchen was just on the other side, and I could tell Mother was making her morning tea. I could also tell by the way she was talking that Aunt Mary was on the other end of the phone line.

"He just said I needed a lung X-ray," said Mother. "And he wants to run tests." The teakettle started to whistle. Mother rattled cups and saucers. "Hold on a minute," she said.

A lung X-ray? Why? What sort of tests? I wanted to burst through the door and ask my questions all out in a rush, but I didn't. Instead, I crept up the stairs and climbed back into my still-warm bed. Mother wouldn't tell me what was really going on anyway. She'd talk to Aunt Mary for sure, but not to me. When I ask Mother *why* she won't tell me things, her standard answer is "Rosie, I'm the parent. You're the child. It's my job to do the worrying." I know this protective attitude is supposed to make me feel all safe and warm, but it doesn't. It just makes me feel left out.

According to Grandma Georgia, Mother and Aunt Mary weren't always so close. Grandma Georgia says once upon a time they were like two dogs trying to piss on the same tree. They fought over everything back in high school—clothes, shoes, boys, friends. After Mother got pregnant with me (at age seventeen!), Aunt Mary thought she'd finally have Spring Hill High School all to herself—Bluebirds, cheerleading, drama club—but it didn't turn out that way.

Mother became the topic of choice on the high school rumor mill: *I heard she's getting her GED. I heard she's putting that baby up for adoption.* At first, Aunt Mary tried to squelch the rumors with the truth: *Yes, she's coming back to school. Yes, she's keeping the baby.* But the talk persisted and the rumors raged. Soon, my aunt avoided the gossip altogether—she skipped Bluebird meetings, missed cheerleading practices. She didn't even audition for the spring musical.

The way Grandma Georgia remembers it, Mother was furious when she learned her sister was hiding out in shame. "Just act like everything's fine and ignore them!" Mother ordered. So typical. Grandma Georgia says Mother never missed a beat when she found out she was pregnant. Apparently, she reorganized her dreams the way some people clean out closets—threw out the old ones and hung new ones in their place.

The following afternoon things were humming right along at the salon. Miss Bertha was politely trying to discourage Hannah Pierce, a friend of hers from the Methodist church, from getting hair extensions, and Richard was totally livid. He had his heart set on the 15 percent tip (hair extensions are $400). Apparently, when Mrs. Pierce called to make the appointment, Richard had answered the phone. She does have a very young voice; Richard had no idea that the woman was a retired granny living on Social Security.

Mother mysteriously disappeared, although it wasn't really a mystery. I knew she'd probably gone to have the chest X-ray. To distract myself, I played around with Richard's old hairdresser dummy. I renamed her Misty and gave her a fabulous mullet.

Around five, Richard left in a huff. "Good-bye, *Rosie*," he said too sweetly and let the door clatter noisily behind him.

"Good-bye to you, too," Miss Bertha mumbled under her breath. "The very idea that he was going to give that poor lady extensions. I mean, really! Can you imagine if old Hannah showed up at church on Sunday morning with hair trailing down her back? I did have a hell of a time talking her out of them, though. I hope she's not starting to lose it a little. She barely scrapes by on Social Security and a flimsy pension. How on earth could she justify hair extensions? Unless Richard didn't tell her how much they cost. That'd be just like him, don't you think, Rosie? Not to tell her, I mean."

The sufficiently mulleted hairdresser dummy was propped up at Richard's station, and I was poking her vacant polystyrene foam eyes with bobby pins.

"You're mighty quiet this afternoon, hon. Cat got your tongue?"

"Mother went for a chest X-ray," I said. Miss Bertha stopped closing out the register and looked at me. "I know you probably already know about it. I overheard her on the phone with Aunt Mary yesterday morning."

"So what do *you* think it is?" Miss Bertha asked. I could tell she was relieved in a way to be talking about it. I shrugged and sighed and jammed the bobby pin in harder.

"Hon, Richard still uses that dummy once in a while."

"I don't know what it is, but it's not like Mother to go home from work early and lie down. Whatever it is, I'm sure she'll never tell me about it. She could be dying and I'd be the last to know."

"Rosie! Hush your mouth!" Miss Bertha scolded.

"It's just a figure of speech. I mean, she's not *dying*. Is she?" I asked, wondering if Miss Bertha knew things I didn't.

"Oh, of course not! It's just bronchitis, is my guess. Pneumonia at the worst."

"That's what I was thinking," I replied.

That night at home Mother seemed strange. She was pale again and coughing. She barely touched her dinner, and she was quiet. No *Have you used your treadmill, Rosie?* or *When will you clean up that messy room?* I hung out with her awhile, but I could tell she wanted to be alone. Finally, I went upstairs. I knew better than to ask about the X-ray I wasn't even supposed to know existed.

Just before nine, the phone rang. Mother picked up downstairs. I picked up upstairs (as if anyone would be calling for me). "Hang up," Mother snapped. Just as I was about to, I heard a man's voice on the other end of the line. *Dr. What's-His-Name? What doctor calls patients at nine o'clock on a Friday night? Shouldn't he be finishing up dinner at the country club by now? It was bad news.* "Rosie, I said *hang up*," Mother insisted. Obediently, I pressed the button on my phone.

I fumed. I paced. If I had more nerve, I'd eavesdrop or pound down the steps and demand the truth. Instead, my imagination turned to food—an off-limits bag of nachos and a jar of salsa, snacks for Mother's downtown merchants' meeting.

It would be so nice to have my own refrigerator, to buy my own groceries. I could eat anything I wanted then, without scrutiny and judgment. Without warning. Without stopping.

I will not eat. I will not think about eating. A person eats to numb sad feelings or fill a void, I heard Mrs. Wallace say.

I fell on my soft bed and closed my eyes. The sound of distant tires on asphalt whispered through the pale blue walls. The next-door neighbor called the dog in from his nightly pee. I slipped between the cool, clean sheets and thought about Kyle, which was sort of like fantasizing about a hot fudge sundae. I knew I couldn't have either one. Finally, I gave up and went to take a bath.

I filled my claw-foot tub with water and lavender-scented bubbles. Mother remodeled my bathroom several years ago. She replaced the cracked tiles, painted the walls a lovely shade of lavender, made toile curtains. We got the old tub at a junk stand on the side of the road. I thought Mother was crazy when she brought it home, but one of her clients reglazed it for free, and now it's good as new. It's the kind of glamorous tub that *should* make a girl feel pretty when she's in it.

Just as I was about to climb in, I heard a voice. I turned to look, although I already knew what it was. It belonged to the sneaky full-length mirror hanging on the back of the bathroom door. "You're an idiot, Rosemary Goode," it said.

"You should be more tactful," I whispered, poised to hang a towel over the ill-mannered thing, but I stopped myself. I stared at my glob-like reflection—bumps and lumps and dimples everywhere. Not even a nanosecond smiler who appears to be without the sadistic Y chromosome that afflicts so many other high school boys could stomach that, a bulging, hulking, out-of-shape body. The mirror might be caustic, but it's correct just the same.

After my bath, I headed downstairs. I was ready to devour the leftovers in the fridge, snarf up the Ben & Jerry's Chunky Monkey, feast on Mother's chips and salsa. I was just about to start. I had my nose shoved in the carton, and I was inhaling the ice cream like one of those addicts who sniffs aerosol cans. I took a deep breath. I closed my eyes.

I thought of Kyle again and his lovely smile. I thought of Kay-Kay.

Quietly, I scraped everything into the garbage, neatly tied up the bag, and tossed it into the outside trash can. Mother would be pissed, of course, but not as pissed as if I'd eaten everything. It was my own private victory, right in my very own kitchen, the least likely place for me to experience victory of any sort.

Mother had been holed up in her bedroom since dinner. Through the walls, I could hear the monotonous droning of some woman on HGTV. This was not at all like Mother. Mother's a go-to-bed-early, get-up-early kind of person. On Friday nights, she's asleep before ten because on Saturday mornings—her busiest day—she's at the salon by six o'clock.

For the first few years after I was born, Mother chugged along like the Little Engine That Could (Grandma Georgia's description, not mine). She worked for Mrs. Avery, the previous owner of Heavenly Hair, saved every dime she made, built up a loyal clientele, and when it came time for Mrs. Avery to retire, Mother bought the shop. Right from the start, she was ambitious; her goal was to fix every head of hair in Maury County, male or female. She advertised. She did mass mailings. She put ads on the local radio and cable stations. She participated in every community event and even sponsored a softball team. Within two years of buying Heavenly Hair, Mother had doubled its profits. Mother would never stay up this late on a Friday night.

I tiptoed to her door and debated whether or not I should knock. "Come in," said Mother. "I know you're standing out there."

Mother was in bed and still wearing her work clothes. "Sit down," she said, patting the bed. The mattress sagged beneath my weight. The HGTV topic was slugs. Garden Lady scooped up a fat slimy creature and held it closer to the camera. Mother muted her.

"I went to the doctor this afternoon," she said without my even asking. I held my breath and cursed myself for dumping Ben &

Jerry. There'd be no lovers to comfort me later. I tried not to look at the dark half-moons under Mother's eyes. *How long have they been there? A month? Six months?* Mother drew in a ragged breath and let it out again. "Normally, I wouldn't burden you with something like this, but . . . well, Spring Hill is a small town. People are bound to notice certain things," she said.

"Notice what things? What's wrong?" My heart pumped furiously. *Bronchitis,* I prayed. *Pneumonia, please!* I could feel blood pulsing toward my face.

"I had some tests this afternoon. I don't have a bad cold. It's something called Hodgkin's disease," said Mother flatly. She took my hand and squeezed it hard. Two syllables formed the dreaded word. "It's can-cer," Mother whispered. I tried to breathe, but my throat closed up tight. "Don't worry, Rosie." said Mother quickly. "Everything's going to be just fine. Even the doctor says so." Mother kept on talking—*the lymph something or other . . . white blood cells . . . trial versus standard treatments . . . the most curable kind.*

I struggled to listen, to make myself believe the positive spin Mother put on the C word. When she'd finished talking, I mustered a smile and a *You'll be okay,* but I knew she wasn't okay. A part of me wanted to confront her with the cancer truth—chemo and radiation and suffering—so we could both deal with it honestly, but mostly I wanted to comfort her, to be the first person she needed instead of Aunt Mary. For a long while, we just sat there in the quiet darkness, still holding hands. Mine was sweaty and warm, hers clammy and cold. I could almost feel the fear pulsing back and forth between us.

chapter nine

Healing the Fat Girl Within

*L*ast night was the Healing the Fat Girl Within conference. I didn't want to go. It just didn't seem right to be preoccupied with calories and meaningless fat girl issues when my mother has cancer. *Cancer* is definitely an uglier word than *fat*.

Mother said, "I'll still have Hodgkin's disease whether we go to the conference or not." Aunt Mary had complained that she'd already paid $150 for our tickets. The money was nonrefundable. Needless to say, Aunt Mary got her way.

My first clue about the unscrupulous nature of things should've been the registration area. They were serving hors d'oeuvres—buffalo wings, cheese and crackers, sausage rolls, artichoke (ha) dip, and—*get this*—pigs-in-a-blanket. You'd think a sensitive fat girl like myself might have taken offense to pigs-in-a-blanket being served at a fat girl conference, but I couldn't stop eating them long enough to consider the political incorrectness of it.

Mother and Aunt Mary stood on the sidelines of it all, delicately sipping Diet Cokes. I knew they were grossed out by the gluttony, but I didn't care. For once, Mother and Aunt Mary were the outcasts, significantly outnumbered by plus-sized females who'd come from as far as Knoxville to participate in tonight's "big" event. Even if it was a fat girl fest, it felt nice to actually fit in someplace. At first.

It wasn't until our plump bodies were packed in Columbia State's noisy gymnasium that I realized this fat girl "conference" was nothing more than a giant sales pitch. Every diet from A Lot to Lose to Zodiac Weight Loss was being peddled by chattering, smiling sales representatives: Hollywood Hills, Catfish Soup (no, I'm not kidding), Citrus Fruit, Herbs for Loss, Nutri Management, and Soy Solutions, just to name a few.

The first speaker was an overweight, middle-aged woman from a company called Trim 'n' Glam. Before she even opened her mouth, I knew her product wasn't any good; otherwise, she would've been skinny herself.

Next, a crunchy-granola type took the stage and spent twenty minutes showing slides about an herbal colon cleanser. Aunt Mary was so grossed out she went to wait in the lobby. After that, the director of a place called Dairy Details took the podium. "At Dairy Details we explore the effects of calcium on fat," he explained. "We have a tightly controlled setting where we monitor very closely what goes into our clients' bodies and what comes out of their bodies."

What comes out? I elbowed Mother. "What does he mean by that?" I whispered.

"I don't care to know," Mother mumbled.

Finally, in the middle of a sermon (and I mean that literally) about a weight loss plan called Thin for God, Mother motioned toward the door. "You wanna go?" she whispered. I nodded vigorously.

The drive home was quiet. Sullen Aunt Mary stared at the road and said nothing to Mother or to me. I could tell she was furious that she'd wasted her money. She pulled up in front of our house. Quickly, Mother got out of the car. "Thanks, Mary," Mother called, waving her sister off as she headed toward the door. Obviously, Mother is much better at reading her sister's bad moods. Fool that I am, I lagged behind. Even though I resented Aunt Mary for buying the stupid tickets in the first place, and I had tried to tell her we shouldn't go, I knew she couldn't afford to waste $150 on nothing. "Thanks for trying, Aunt Mary," I said. "Sorry you wasted your money."

Aunt Mary rolled her eyes and tapped the steering wheel with her pointy red nails. "Do you realize I could've had Tom Cruise declawed with that money?" she said. Tom Cruise is Aunt Mary's cat. I couldn't help thinking Aunt Mary should've had herself declawed. "Why can't you just lose weight, Rosie? I mean, is it so hard just to stop doing this?" she asked, moving her hand back and forth from an imaginary plate to her mouth.

"So it's *my* fault the conference was a rip-off?" I replied.

"No. But it's your fault we had to go to a conference in the first place. I'm not saying I don't understand why you gained weight.

I mean, your life hasn't exactly been perfect. No father, a young single mother who works too much . . . but you could just get a grip on yourself, you know, find a *hobby*." The *h* in *hobby* came out as if Aunt Mary were loosening something stuck in her throat. I no longer cared that she'd wasted her precious money. I just wanted her to drive away into the darkness and never come back.

"Rosie, come on inside!" Mother called from the porch.

"You're not so perfect yourself," I said. "But you don't see *me* criticizing *you* all the time. Those hideous plastic nails, for one thing. I could say plenty about those. And your love life. I mean, I'm fat, so it's obvious why I don't have a boyfriend, but what's your excuse?" Aunt Mary's jaw dropped.

"You're disrespectful," she said. It came out in a whisper.

"So are you," I replied. For all her dishing out, Aunt Mary certainly couldn't take it. I had plenty more to say, but I stopped myself. Instead, I slammed the car door and stormed off toward the house. Aunt Mary zoomed up Stewart Street and squealed tires as she made the left onto Third Avenue. *"Idiot,"* I mumbled under my breath. Mother was standing beneath the porch light, her face an eerie shade of jaundiced yellow in its glow. She didn't say anything, but I knew she was disappointed in me.

"Sorry," I said when we were inside.

"You should go a little easier on her," said Mother. "She loves you, after all."

"She loves having someone to criticize," I corrected. "Maybe you're lucky I'm fat. Otherwise, all Aunt Mary's attention would be focused on you. Do you know what it's like to be under constant scrutiny? At school people stare at my lunch tray. At the salon old ladies actually come right out and ask how my diet's going. At home I'm harassed over a treadmill that I never asked for in the first place."

"Okay," said Mother quietly. I could tell she wasn't in the mood for fighting. "Are you going up to bed?" she asked. I shook my head.

"I'm gonna hang out down here awhile." Mother opened her mouth to speak, but I stopped her words with my eyes. She was about to tell me not to snack before bedtime, but she clamped her mouth shut and drifted off down the hallway to her room.

I thought of going upstairs, but it was too depressing to go to bed before ten o'clock on a Saturday night. Instead, I slipped off my shoes and lay down on the slipcovered sofa. The living room was the nicest room in the house, yet we barely ever spent any time there—blue walls with shiny white moldings, a fireplace we'd only used once (Mother preferred candles to real flames), a pretty floral rug purchased at a discount store that looked anything but discount, elegant striped draperies with pinched pleats that stretched from ceiling to floor (a trick Mother claimed made the smallish windows appear bigger). I gazed up at the beautiful bookcase wedged in between two windows. The massive structure was a perfect contrast to the draperies and walls. It *popped*, according to Mother.

I switched off the lamp and lay staring at the shadows on the walls. "Stop," I whispered at the ceiling. "Please just help me stop."

————

If possible, Monday was even worse than Saturday. Mother had a consultation with a specialist in Nashville, a Dr. Prescott Wheeling, some fancy Ivy League Hodgkin's expert guy. Did Mother take me, her only child, with her to this important appointment?

No. Only Child went to school.

Did Mother take Aunt Mary?

Yes.

The two of them picked me up at Spring Hill High School on their way back from the doctor's. I could tell by Aunt Mary's polite coolness she was still mad about Saturday night (that made two of us). Without a word, I squeezed into the backseat of Mother's Honda and listened as Aunt Mary rattled on and on about Hodgkin's and chemo and radiation as if she were now some kind of expert after accompanying Mother to *one* doctor's visit. Aunt Mary's talking must've annoyed Mother, too. She shot through two traffic lights on the way to Aunt Mary's apartment.

"Rose Warren, why in God's name are you in such a hurry?" Aunt Mary snapped after Mother zipped through the second light. "I'd prefer not to be maimed in a traffic accident today."

"Rosie's due at Dr. Cooper's," said Mother. "I don't wanna be late."

"We're not going to see Mrs. Wallace *today*, are we?" I protested. Truthfully, I'd forgotten all about my appointment.

"Why wouldn't we be going *today*?" Mother snapped. "You know I hate it when my clients just don't show up. I refuse to do that to somebody else. And I had a doctor's appointment this afternoon, not a heart transplant. I wish you *both* would just stop talking about this!" Mother scowled at me in the rearview mirror.

"Both?" I said indignantly. "She's the one—"

"That's enough!" Mother shouted—at me.

Aunt Mary got out of the car. "Call me if you need anything, Rose Warren," she said sweetly, then tossed a dirty look my way. I pretended to be engrossed in an English paper I'd gotten back from Mrs. Edinburgh that morning, and I made sure the A+ was in plain view. Neither of us said good-bye.

"Mother, I never agreed to see Mrs. Wallace," I said after we drove away.

"Do you really have a choice, Rosie?" Mother asked, her voice strained and tired.

"Of course, I have a choice! This should be entirely my choice! Even Mrs. Wallace said so!" I yelled.

Mother slammed the brakes and shoved the gear into Park. "Do *I* have a choice, Rosie? *Huh?* What if I just decide to ignore this cancer? You think it'll go away on its own?"

At the doctor's office, Mother settled herself by the fish tank with a *People* magazine, and I paced around the empty waiting room. When Mrs. Wallace appeared in the doorway, she looked happy to see me. "I'm glad you're here, Rosie." She smiled and patted me on the back. It was the nicest thing anyone had said to me all day.

After a few polite comments, a heavy silence descended on us. I'd listened to Mother's cheerful hairdresser chitchat a million times, yet the gene to fill silent air with polite small talk had passed me by. Mrs. Wallace and I stared at one another, as if in a game of Who'll Blink First.

Finally, I gave in. "My mother has Hodgkin's disease," I announced. Mrs. Wallace's face was a wide-open window, but she didn't say anything. "We just found out today she has to have chemotherapy," I went on. "Then radiation. Mother's chances of survival are good, according to my Aunt Mary."

"Your aunt's a doctor?" asked Mrs. Wallace.

"No, just a know-it-all," I replied. The corners of Mrs. Wallace's mouth turned up ever so slightly, but it was hard to tell if she was actually smiling. I made a few more sarcastic comments about my aunt, then Mrs. Wallace and I sat in silence again.

By the end of the half-hour, I couldn't stand it another second. I was missing *Oprah* for this woman. I don't miss Monday *Oprah*s for anyone (Monday is the only time I can watch the show, since the salon is closed that day). "I don't mean to be rude, but could you tell me what I'm supposed to do here?" I asked.

"This is the one place, Rosie, where you're not really *supposed* to do anything. You can say whatever you like, feel whatever you like. Silence is okay, too. In fact, it's kinda part of the process."

"But silence probably won't help me lose weight," I pointed out.

Mrs. Wallace smiled at me. "I think considering what you've been through these past few days, it's pretty impressive that you came today at all."

I stared down at my ample lap, which took up the entire chair and spilled out over its sides. Mrs. Wallace was a nice woman. I liked her easygoing demeanor. Talking to Mrs. Wallace had to be better than colon cleansers or tainted mayonnaise diets (which, after the fat girl conference, I realized wasn't all that crazy an idea, after all). "So should I come the same time next week?" I asked. Mrs. Wallace nodded and shook my hand. Her palms were rough but warm.

After dinner, Mother went to bed, and I headed upstairs. I couldn't wait to tuck myself in bed and watch a gastric-bypass special on the Health Channel. While listening to the stories of surgical hell and sipping a bottled water, I tried to imagine myself going through such a grisly procedure. Judging from the patients on television, I'd probably have to gain more weight just to be a candidate. Peanut butter cups danced through my head like sugar plums, but I resisted (okay, so I didn't have any). Instead, I closed my eyes and pictured the post-gastric-bypass-surgery Rosemary. She was thin. She would never have to worry about being fat again. She had no choice but to be skinny. Sadly, there was no more comfort food in her life either, just an endless supply of pro-tein shakes and prepackaged astronaut food and big scars.

Fast-forward fantasy. I'm post gastric bypass and skinny. I'm also post the grieving-over-food stage. In fact, I'm completely over food. Food no longer matters to me. Why should it when I have Kyle Cox? We go to parties, to movies, to restaurants, to malls. Kyle even takes me to his parents' house for dinner. "Hey, Dad. Hey, Mom. This is Rosie. You'll have to liquefy her pot roast in the Cuisinart," Kyle explains. "Her stomach's the size of a walnut."

Fantasy not working. Rewind. No gastric bypass. Miraculously, I'm just a thinner, more disciplined, better-controlled Rosemary

Goode. My once-lumpy body is now smooth. There's me panting on a treadmill (my barn ass is not jiggling repulsively). There's me holding up an old pair of fat jeans, like that Jared Fogle guy. There's me slow-dancing with Kyle Cox.

chapter ten

The Velveteen Rabbit

Mother had a late appointment (she almost always does), so Miss Bertha drove me home from work. On the way, I asked her to stop off at Reynolds's Drugstore again. "Buying another get-well card?" she guessed. I nodded, although this was a lie. It hadn't even crossed my mind to buy a second get-well card.

"I'll just be a minute," I said.

"Take your time, sweetie. Nobody's waitin' for me at home but Jem and Scout." She winked. Miss Bertha had recently purchased a pair of birds, *finches* to be precise.

The same blonde stood smacking her gum behind the counter. "Hidy," she said and smiled at me.

"Hi," I replied, glancing around for the Pounds-Away display. As it turned out, it'd been replaced with Valentine's gifts—boxes of chocolate, stuffed teddy bears, fake long-stemmed red roses, heart-shaped trinkets.

"Can I help you?" the woman asked.

"Oh, um . . . I'm just looking," I replied, and headed toward the back of the store. Finally, I found it, although the sale was clearly over—$8.99 for a six-pack and no buy-two-get-the-third-free special either. I debated—$8.99 was way more than I made in an hour at Heavenly Hair. The last thing I needed was to blow my money on diet products I might not even use.

"Them thangs really work," the blonde said. She had followed me and stood smacking her gum at the end of the aisle.

"Really?" I asked.

"Oh, hell yeah. Why, after I had my third kid, I like to never took that weight off. Seemed like it was just stuck right to me, you know?" I nodded. I did know. "Anyways, them thangs worked like a charm. Well, that and chain smoking, but I don't recommend you start *that*. I got to chew this nicotine gum now, too," she said, showing me the wad on her tongue. "It's always one thang or nuther, ain't it?" I nodded again.

Carrying a six-pack of Pounds-Away, I followed Darlene (according to her name tag) to the cash register. "Thank you, Darlene," I said, and smiled at her. "If this works, I'll be back."

"You do that, hon, but my name's not Darlene. I forgot my name tag, so I just put this'n here on. It's more personal somehow even if it ain't the right name. Anyways, Darlene quit 'bout a year ago, which wasn't no great loss, if you ask me. I'm Charmaine. Charmaine Chumley."

"I'm Rosemary Goode," I replied.

"You any relation to Rose Warren Goode?" she asked.

"I'm her daughter."

"Oh, your mama's real nice. She comes in here sometimes. You have a good night now, hear. Let me know how this stuff works out."

The Spring Hill town clock clanged noisily, and the tiniest spits of rain-snow trickled down from the dark sky. I felt it then, a remote wave of hope, no more substantial than those snow-flakes, which were sure to melt the second they hit the sidewalk. Faint as the feeling was, I was grateful for it. I knew it came from Charmaine Chumley. It's amazing how much better you feel when anyone, even a random stranger in a drugstore, shows you the slightest degree of kindness.

That night, instead of devouring the roast that had been cook-ing in Mother's crock-pot all day, I drank a Pounds-Away shake. Not an easy thing when the whole cozy house smells like meat and vegetables. But somehow I managed it, then retreated to my room again. By nine o'clock, I was ready to gnaw the varnish off my bedpost. Instead, I took a bath and briefly considered Char-maine's chain-smoking tactic, but I decided one cancer patient in the family was more than enough.

Finally, with my stomach raging and grumbling, I climbed in between the sheets and distracted myself with Kyle Cox fanta-sies. Around midnight, I woke up again. Hunger churned in my belly, and dread held my brain hostage. Mother was just coming in from the shop. I could hear her rattling around in the kitchen. I wondered if she'd notice that I hadn't eaten anything. More than likely she'd stayed at the salon extra late to make up for all the work she would miss tomorrow (today, actually). Her first chemo treatment was in ten hours.

Mother says she's tired, but otherwise fine. *"Fine,"* she says with her happy face firmly fixed. Mother shrugs off four hours of chemo like it was a bikini wax. If you ask me, toxic chemicals coursing through your veins and a lymph system filled with cancer is not *fine.* If I had cancer everyone around me would know how miserable I felt. I don't think I'd be the type to hold it all inside.

I just spent two hours online researching Hodgkin's disease instead of doing my homework. There's almost too much information on the topic. Hodgkin's is a kind of cancer called a "lymphoma," and it's "uncommon." According to one website, "it accounts for less than one percent of all cancers." Mother's of ripe Hodgkin's age—the fifteen-to-forty category. One site I found said that a diagnosis of Hodgkin's is "preferable" to being diagnosed with other types of cancer. I say not being diagnosed with cancer at all is preferable!

The scariest part is where Hodgkin's goes. It's cancer of the lymph system, and the lymph system is all over the body—the neck, the chest, armpits, liver, spleen, groin. Mother's Hodgkin's is mostly in her chest, which explains the nagging cough she's had forever.

I have to stop thinking about this for a while. Too much and I'll go crazy.

Today in the cafeteria, Misty Winters sat down beside me. "What's it really like?" she asked.

"What's *what* really like?" I replied, trying to hide my overloaded lunch tray. After Pounds-Away for dinner last night, and Pounds-Away for breakfast this morning, I had to have real food, lots of it.

Before Misty could explain, Tara Waters walked up. "Are we sitting with *her*?" she asked, obviously disgusted at the thought.

"No, Tara *Tard*! Just give me a minute," Misty snapped. "Artichoke, I'm doing a story on adolescent obesity for the school paper. I need a subject. Now what's it like? Give me a good sound bite."

Before I could open my mouth, Kay-Kay Reese plopped down in the chair right beside me. "You work at Heavenly Hair," said Kay-Kay cheerfully. "I just love that salon. Don't y'all love it, too? You're so lucky to work there." The girl rambled on as if we were all best friends. I glanced at the tiny bluebird pin on her sweater. All the fledglings wore them. Obviously, being one of the newest members, Kay-Kay was not yet in tune with the Bluebirds' customary hatred of fat girls.

"I don't know how Artichoke works anyplace carrying all that extra poundage around. In case you haven't noticed, Kay-Kay, this is not a social call. I just need an authentic source for my fat-kid article. We're not actually sitting here!"

"Oh," said Kay-Kay. She blinked her blue eyes at me, then stared down at her tray, as if fruit salad, yogurt, and bagel chips were suddenly mesmerizing.

Misty pulled a notepad out of her fake Kate Spade bag and cocked her head to one side like a parrot. "Okay, shoot," she ordered. "I still have to eat lunch."

"Misty, I have an idea for you," I said, easing my way to the edge of the chair so I could make a fast break for the cafeteria hinterland. "Why don't you do a story on vacuous girls with a propensity for dark roots? That way, you can be your *own* authentic source." I snatched up my tray and squeezed through the too-tight space. As I swish-swished away, I heard Kay-Kay Reese laugh and say, "Guess she told you, Misty."

Big mistake, Kay-Kay, I thought to myself. Instead of chiding Misty, Kay-Kay should've cracked a fat girl joke loud enough for me to overhear. Even *I* knew that was standard Bluebird protocol. At the rate she was going, Kay-Kay Reese wouldn't stay a Bluebird for long.

The week seemed to drag by, and I had absolutely nothing to look forward to. Instead of frozen waffles dripping in melted butter and hot syrup or powdered, sugary donuts or multiple Pop-Tarts with frosting, I drank a Pounds-Away for breakfast. At lunch, there were no school cafeteria french fries dripping in grease and smothered with ketchup, no pizza coated in sauce and stringy cheese, no sloppy joes or ice-cream sandwiches. Just a single can of misery! I dragged my weak-with-hunger self from one class to another, so starved I couldn't even manage a Kyle Cox fantasy.

This changed in the first five minutes of study hall, however.

There's nothing like another person's misery to take your mind off your own, and Kyle Cox was clearly suffering. He blew his nose repeatedly and hacked like someone in a tuberculosis ward. In his giant hand was one ratty, overused tissue, nothing more than a clump of wet lint. Quickly, I grabbed a pack of fresh tissues from the bottom of my backpack and scanned the path between my chair and Kyle's. As far as I could tell, there were no too-tight spaces, Bluebirds, or Nucleolus Boys. *All clear*, I thought.

I stood. I glanced over at Mr. Lawrence, but his head was stuck in some giant history book. I tugged at my shirt to make sure it was covering the fat and not stuck in between any rolls. It's a five-second walk from my chair to Kyle's, but I felt as though I were about to swim the English Channel, attempt the Iditarod, climb Mount Kilimanjaro.

Slowly, I walked over. "Here. Take these," I whispered, extending my trembling hand.

Kyle glanced up at me. His brown eyes were red-rimmed and tired, his nose was chafed and specked with bits from the tissue. He took the package and looked at me gratefully, which was when he said IT. Actually, he whispered IT, hoarsely.

"Thanks, Rosemary."

Safely back in my orange plastic chair and watching Ronnie Derryberry's REM-stage eyelids flutter, I replayed the scene over and over. *Thanks, Rosemary. Thanks, Rosemary. Thanks, Rosemary.* Kyle Cox had said my name. He actually *knew* my name.

At the salon, I was still reeling from my Kyle Cox miracle. I got right to work—no afternoon snack, no fantasies of crock-pot chicken (our usual dinner on Thursday nights), just cleaning and folding towels, and chitchatting happily with Richard and Miss Bertha and Mildred and Mother. As pathetic as it sounds, I felt a little like that velveteen rabbit right after he discovered he was real.

Miracle number two happened around four-thirty when a disheveled-looking walk-in banged through the front door. I heard Miss Bertha say, "Oh, we'll make time for you, don't worry." Miss Bertha is a big believer in walk-ins. She says walk-ins become loyal clients if you're polite to them and somehow squeeze them in that first time. Richard vehemently disagrees. He says accepting walk-ins is a sign you're a low-rent salon. Thankfully, Richard's not the boss, or Mother and I would probably starve. Of course, for me, that'd be a good thing. But I digress. Richard was smack in the middle of a blue hair repair, so Mother took this particular client.

"Welcome to Heavenly Hair," said Mother. "I'm Rose Warren Goode. What are we doing today?"

The woman sighed as she looked at herself in the large mirror. "Oh, I don't really care," she said. "Just do something. If you can," she added. She wasn't what you'd call fat, just stocky, built like a tree stump or a barrel. She was also middle-aged and "poorly styled," as Richard would say. Her clothes weren't awful, at least not awful for old lady clothes, but they were wrinkled, as if plucked from the hamper instead of the closet.

"You want to leave everything up to me?" Mother asked, her face stretching into a smile. Mother loves it when clients leave everything up to her.

"Do whatever you want, just not too fussy," said the woman, pointing her finger at Mother. "I have three kids and a fourth one they call a husband. I don't have time for too much girly stuff."

Mother went to work. The color was a light honey brown with a few highlights mixed in the front. The cut was like something off

Style Network—a classic but slightly modernized bob with a few wispy bangs. "Now don't style your bob under," Mother shouted as she blow-dried. "Flip it out this way, so it looks more stylish. It's easier to turn it out than under, and it makes all the difference in how the cut looks."

"Sure thing," the woman agreed. Her face was brighter, and I could tell she liked what Mother had done. Without getting in Mother's way, I swept hair out from underneath the chair.

"I wouldn't go more than six weeks on the color," Mother went on. "If you touch up those highlights they'll last a lot longer. You'll need a trim by then, too, if you want to keep the style."

"Oh, I'll keep it up," said the woman. "That was my New Year's resolution, to look better, to take better care of *myself*."

"I know I've seen you over at the Piggly Wiggly," said Mother. "I apologize for not knowing your name."

"Oh, honey, I wouldn't *expect* you to know my name. Of course, everybody in town knows yours. Why, every person I asked said the same thing. 'Go see Rose Warren Goode over at Heavenly Hair. She'll fix you right up.'" Mother smiled, although people were *always* saying things like that about Mother. "I'm Roberta Cox," said the woman. Right away, my ears perked up at the last name. "Husband's Fred. He owns the lumberyard out on the Nashville Highway."

"Oh, of course," said Mother. "When I did some work on my house, that's where I bought the lumber. A very fair place," said Mother. "You have boys, don't you?"

"Three," said Mrs. Cox. "Kyle, Chris, and Kirk. Sixteen, thirteen, and ten."

I nearly dropped my broom.

"They play football, don't they?" I was always amazed at the number of details Mother kept stored in her brain. I fought back the urge to squeeze Mrs. Cox and introduce myself as her future daughter-in-law. Instead, I memorized her every detail.

"Oh, they all play everything," Mrs. Cox went on. "The oldest one, Kyle, is the one in the papers all the time. He could use a social life. For him it's sports and nothing else. I keep telling him to find a nice girl to go with, but nobody listens to me."

Sweat prickled under my arms. My cheeks felt red. I couldn't decide if I wanted Mother to introduce me or not. Finally, I decided *not*. I slipped off to the back room where I could still hear and see, but not be heard or seen. From behind the curtain, I scrutinized the woman who had given birth to Kyle Cox.

In a strange way, I was thankful she was frumpy and kind of overweight and wrinkled. Maybe Kyle wasn't too picky about physical things. Maybe *that* was why he gave me nanosecond smiles. He was used to a big woman, after all.

chapter eleven

The Perfect Shade of Blue

Since Thursday, I've had nine Pounds-Away shakes, two Pounds-Away protein bars (Darlene-Charmaine talked me into buying them), and absolutely nothing else. This morning when I stepped on the scale, I'd lost a whopping five pounds. If a tornado ripped smack through my bedroom, I might actually move an inch or two.

I think Mother is feeling the effects of the chemo. This morning, when I asked her how she was, she smiled and said *fine*, but there were tears in her eyes when she said it. Of course, she was mixing up color for Nancy Guthrie, so I guess the tears could've been from the chemicals.

Tonight is Nancy Guthrie's surprise fortieth birthday party, which Mrs. Guthrie knows all about (that's why she was getting her hair done). Aunt Mary talked Mother into going to the party with her.

Right after Mother and Aunt Mary pulled out of the driveway,

Grandma Georgia called long-distance from Florida. When she asked how Mother was doing, I did my best Mother imitation. "Just *fine*," I trilled cheerfully.

Right away, Grandma Georgia *got it*. *"Oy vey,"* she groaned. Since retiring to Florida three years ago, my grandmother has taken up a second language. Her first language is Southern; her second, Yiddish. "How are *you*?" she asked.

"Not fine," I said. "Scared. I'm really scared." It felt good to say it.

"Me, too, Rose Garden," said Grandma Georgia. "I expect your mama is, too. Deep down. It's her genes that won't let her admit it. She takes after your damn grandpa. God rest his soul," she added quickly.

"What do you mean?" I asked.

"He lived in a musical! I used to call him Oscar Hammerstein. I'd bring up some real-life thing that needed doin' or fixin' or some late bill that *had* to be paid, and your grandpa would start whistlin'! That was his response. *Whistling!* When I married him I thought some of that positive attitude would rub off on me, but it didn't. It just rubbed me plumb raw, like sandpaper on a sunburn. Between his whistling and his toenails, I *had* to get out."

"Toenails?" I asked.

"He never clipped them! Gouged me every single night when he climbed into bed. Toenails and toothpaste caps and toilet seats and whistling. It may sound like small stuff, but it looms large in the marriage bed. Don't let nobody tell you different."

"I'll keep all that in mind," I said, trying not to laugh.

"And you keep *trying* to talk to your mama, Rosie. I think it'd be good for both of you if you talked about it." Grandma's voice was serious now.

"I will," I said, uncertain whether or not I would actually keep my promise.

"This Hodgkin's thing . . . you know it's pretty serious, right?"

"I know, Grandma. I found out a lot of stuff on the Internet."

"So did I," said Grandma Georgia. "Don't be too hard on your mama now, hear? I was kvetching about your grandpa, but your mama's different. She's a responsible person. She doesn't completely ignore her troubles the way he always did. She just doesn't talk about them."

"Maybe," I said.

"Well, Rose Garden, this long-distance bill will cost a fortune if I don't hang up. You call collect if you need to. Hear?"

"I will, Grandma," I said.

The night felt eerie after I hung up. The whole house was so quiet it was like white noise in my ears. I put on an old Bonnie Raitt CD and lay on my bed, staring at the blue ceiling. It was painted several shades darker than my walls—"to make the room feel cozy," according to Mother. She'd tried four different hues before she finally got the right one. A mother who would paint the ceiling four times had to love her daughter an awful lot. I closed my eyes and pictured Mother standing on the rickety ladder in my bedroom, her face dotted with paint spatters. "I think I got it, Rosie!" she'd said after coat number four was applied. "It's perfect! Finally!"

"Cool," I remember saying. Personally, I couldn't tell the difference between blue number one and blue number four, but Mother certainly could, and she would've put *ten* coats on the ceiling just to get the color right. I wish I could go back to that day, when Mother was perfectly healthy. I wish I could go back and say something nicer than *cool*.

chapter twelve

Fat Girl Goes Bad

Technically, you could say I'm *on* the treadmill. I don't know why I'm sitting here. Just restless, I guess. Every five seconds, I either have to poop or I have gas that feels like it may or may not be a poop. *Gross*, I realize, but my stomach's so twisted up, I feel like there's a whole Boy Scout troop in there—working on their knot badges with my intestines.

Today at lunch, I felt the need to masticate. The liquid diet was making me insane. My teeth needed to crunch and chew! And there'd been too much misery all weekend—my depressing phone conversation with Grandma Georgia, surfing *more* Hodgkin's websites. And to top it all off, Mrs. McCutchin had another heart attack yesterday. Every problem must've been thumbtacked to my face, because right in the middle of a unit test, Mrs. Edinburgh leaned down by my desk and whispered, "Are you okay, Rosemary? You don't look like yourself."

"I *wish* I didn't look like myself," I mumbled. Mrs. Edinburgh cocked her head to one side. "Only joking," I lied. "I'm fine." I smiled up at her just the way Mother would've done. Thankfully, Mrs. Edinburgh didn't ask any more questions.

At lunch, I ate like a *Survivor* contender who'd just been kicked off the island. I grazed my way through three lunch shifts— two barbecue sandwiches, french fries, chocolate pudding, ice cream . . . I sat in the hinterland, my back to the world, and ate away the success of the last several days. If I'd been slashing my skin with razors or shooting up, someone would've stopped me. There would've been interventions and meetings. As it was, the fat girl was eating. What else was new?

By the time the episode was over, I was thirty minutes late for study hall. I didn't have a late pass. I didn't care. The whole waddle down the empty hallway, I thought about Kyle Cox. I wondered if he'd missed me the way I always miss him when he's late to study hall. *Yeah, right. When pigs fly out of my ass!* I thought (and considering what I'd consumed during lunch, this wasn't entirely unrealistic).

The library door squeaked loudly when I opened it. Every head turned toward me, then jerked quickly away. Just once, I'd like to know how it feels to walk into a room looking like Kay-Kay Reese—the lingering eyes, the longing glances, the envious hearts. *Fat chance.*

Mr. Lawrence sat grading papers. I held my breath and waited for his scolding, but he just rolled his pointy black eyes at me and wrote something in his grade book. Points off for tardiness, more than likely. I didn't look in Kyle's direction.

Ronnie Derryberry was asleep and drooling on his books again, but for once his fingernails were clean and neatly trimmed, a sharp contrast to my own, which were now dirty and sticky with barbecue sauce and chocolate. I settled into some pre-calculus homework and tried to forget myself. Impossible. My overloaded stomach was *killing* me.

"*Pssst*! Hey, Rosemary." It was Kyle (his cold sounded better). The shame of having gorged my way through lunch was lodged in my throat, and my gut rolled like that giant bingo barrel down at the American Legion building. I kept my eyes locked on the blurred page of my textbook. I didn't want to see Kyle's friendly brown eyes or Kyle's million-dollar nanosecond smile. Kyle would never belong to me, and there was little point in torturing myself. "*Pssst!*" he hissed again.

Quietly, I closed my book and stuffed it into my backpack. I slid my purse over one shoulder and my backpack over the other. Thunder thighs swishing together, I walked out—no hall pass—no acknowledgment of Kyle's *pssst*s. I did not tell Mr. Lawrence where I was going.

FAT GIRL GOES BAD! WANDERS HALLWAYS WITHOUT A PASS! That'd be the headline for Misty Winters's next big Spring Hill High School story. The corridors were empty. I passed the teachers' lavatory, then turned back again. My stomach rumbled like Mount St. Helens.

Inside, the cherry-scented disinfectant made me light-headed. My mouth watered. I sat on the floor and leaned my head against the cool cement wall, but the sick feeling wouldn't pass. Before I knew it, all my lunch was back up again. Floating in the blue toilet water were bits of pork, a lump of foamy ice cream, some nuts from a Snickers bar, and lots of unrecognizable things. *How could stuff that tasted so good thirty minutes earlier smell so sour now?* I flushed the toilet, washed my face and hands, rinsed my mouth out, and spritzed Binaca on my tongue. *I have to stop this. I have to get control over myself! I have to change!* My desperation was practically palpable.

When I pushed open the door, Mrs. Edinburgh was standing on the other side. We both glanced at the sign that read FOR TEACHERS ONLY. I didn't wait for the scolding. Rudely, I brushed past her. "Rosemary," she called after me. I kept walking. "Rosemary!" she tried again.

The bell rang just as I was about to open the library door. Kyle and I ran smack into each other. "Rosemary!" Kyle smiled and looked surprised. "Are you okay? I saw you race out of study hall."

"Oh, um . . . I'm okay," I lied. Truthfully, my throat felt like I'd swallowed a package of thumbtacks, but at least the nausea was gone.

"I wanted to give you something," said Kyle. He pulled a pack of tissues from his coat pocket and handed them to me. "Thanks for the rescue the other day. I thought my nose was gonna run right off my face. Where you headed?" he asked.

"Related arts," I replied. Having a conversation with Kyle Cox was like riding a bicycle for the first time—once I realized it was actually happening, I fell off. My tongue got all tied up (those damn Boy Scouts again). Kyle said something, but I was too busy staring at the tissues he'd given me. "I'm sorry. What?" I asked, looking up at him. We were standing close. *Thank God for Binaca.*

If only Kyle knew I'd had my head in a public toilet ten minutes earlier.

Kyle smiled, cleared his throat, and rubbed his large bear paws (minus the fur) across his faded jeans. "You like basketball?" he asked, flashing that smile. Several NBs crowded the hallway. One crashed into me, but kept going, no apology. "I was thinking how I never see you *out* anyplace," Kyle went on. "You should come to our basketball game Friday night." The warning bell sounded. "Oh, God! Another unexcused late and I'll have to sit out a game!" said Kyle. "Bye, Rosie," he called over his shoulder.

I stood at the bottom of the stairs and watched Kyle bound up them effortlessly, two at a time. His butt was a nice, wide, manly football butt, not exactly the basketball build. In fact, Kyle was on the stocky side. I stared at the small package of tissues he'd given me—little red hearts were printed on them. For exactly two seconds, I actually considered going to the game. It would be worth it just to get a look at Kyle's thick legs, to watch his muscles strain.

"Get to class, Miss Goode!" I heard Mr. Lawrence shout from behind me. "Climbing a few stairs won't kill you!"

Two thoughts pulsed through my head simultaneously:

(1) What would become of all the fat girls in the world if people just treated them nicely?
(2) The only people who call me Rosie instead of Rosemary are the ones who love me.

Kyle had just called me Rosie.

After my confusing pig-out–barf-up–heart-tissue day, I went to see Mrs. Wallace. We didn't talk about Mother or Hodgkin's or Mrs. McCutchin or Aunt Mary. I wasn't about to get all shrinky today. Instead, I spent the whole entire thirty minutes obsessing over Kleenex. "Do you think it's just a coincidence that there were little hearts on them?" I asked. "And *why* is he being so nice to *me* when he could have a Bluebird? Maybe they were just some old tissues his mother already had. Maybe he didn't even *notice* the hearts," I went on.

Mrs. Wallace seemed glad to have me talking, even if it was about tissues. She didn't provide any answers. She just kept responding with more questions.

"Next week I want you to come up with some reasons why Kyle might prefer a girl like you over a Bluebird," said Mrs. Wallace.

"That should be one short assignment," I joked. Mrs. Wallace didn't laugh.

"May I disclose something about myself, Rosemary?" she asked, leaning forward a little.

"Sure," I replied.

"I was at my very fattest when I married Joel, my husband."

"You were *fat*?" I asked, surprised. Mrs. Wallace wasn't skinny by any means, but she wasn't fat either, just tall and *big-boned*, as Grandma Georgia would say.

"Oh, I was more than just fat. I was o-bese," said Mrs. Wallace, "way bigger than you. Three hundred and fifteen pounds, to be exact," she said. "Joel loved me, though." She handed me a picture. In it, Joel, who was normal-sized and normal-looking, smiled and held a dog on his lap. "I just want you to know, Rosemary, that it's possible to be fat and still be loved. You don't have to wait until you lose weight to have a life."

I glanced at Joel's picture again and wondered what was wrong with him.

chapter thirteen

Life Force

Ginny Cronan came flying into the salon, acting all solicitous over Mother's health. "Oh, honey, me and Hank's been down in Florida. You know we spend most winters there now," she bragged, dangling her left hand just right so her fat diamond would catch the light. "I just heard about the *cancer*." She whispered the last word, giving it more emphasis.

Richard looked up from his *GQ* magazine. I stopped scrubbing the paraffin tub. Like matching copperheads, the two of us were prepared to strike. It's Spring Hill common knowledge that Ginny Cronan hates Mother (something to do with high school cheerleader tryouts). No doubt the *real* reason Ginny stopped by was to see if Mother's hair had started to fall out yet.

Miss Bertha hung up the phone. She'd been talking to some long-winded client about various straightening methods. "Rose Warren, Mrs. Simms just parked her car out front. You better get her color ready. She'll be in a hurry today on account of her carpool."

"Oh, yes. Well, you take care, Ginny," said Mother briskly. With that she disappeared down the basement stairs.

Before I could take a breath, Ginny rested her hateful blue eyes on me. I suppose if she couldn't slam Mother, I was the next best thing. "My, *you've* certainly filled out," she said, her face plain and wide and speckled like an Appaloosa's behind. Her thin, straight hair was cropped just below her ears, a style a five-year-old might wear. Richard eyed me. He was waiting for my verbal dropkick.

"You know, Mrs. Cronan, if all your freckles ran together, you'd have a tan," I said. Richard's face went red. He nearly swallowed the bobby pin he'd been chewing (his latest tactic to quit smoking). I waited for Ginny's next insult, but she bolted out the front door, nearly knocking Mrs. Simms over.

Miss Bertha had an emergency budget meeting at her church, so I stayed late and helped Mother get the salon ready for the next day. For a long while, the two of us swept up hair and straightened work stations and folded still-warm towels in silence. Mother's face was drawn and pensive. She hadn't been the same since Ginny's unexpected visit.

"Don't worry about that woman," I said finally.

"Oh, I'm not worried about *her*!" said Mother.

"Then how did you know which *woman* I was talking about?" I couldn't keep myself from saying it out loud. Mother smiled slightly.

"She's had it in for me ever since I made the Spring Hill cheer-leading squad and she didn't. Somehow she decided *I* was the one who cost her a slot, which is ridiculous. Considering we had fifteen girls and two alternates, it could have been any one of us who prevented her from making the team. She's one person I hope I never lay eyes on again. If she went to Florida and never came back, I'd just love it."

"That makes two of us," I replied. "Why do you think girls like her are so mean?" I asked, but Mother didn't hear me. While dusting her station she'd caught a glimpse of herself in the mirror.

"Oh, God. I look sick. I *look* sick," she said again. "Why, that damn gossip Ginny will tell every soul in town how awful I look. She'll have me at death's door in no time! What if people think I'm too bad off to work? Why, this stupid disease could ruin my business! She'll see to it! That's probably why she came!"

"Mother, clients aren't going to desert you because you have *cancer*," I said. A tiny gray feather had come loose from Mother's duster. It swirled around on the linoleum floor as if empowered by a mysterious life force instead of the heating vent, which had just clicked on again.

Mother straightened her narrow shoulders and smoothed her hair out with her fingers. "Everything will be just *fine*," she said. Her mouth was tight and angry now. "Damn it, it *will!*" she hissed under her breath.

Instead of going home and eating (or drinking) a nutritious dinner (or shake) and getting some sleep, we stayed at the salon until midnight. Somehow the threat of Ginny Cronan had ener-gized Mother. She washed the front curtains and rearranged the chairs in the waiting area. She had me call Doris's Florist to order a bouquet of freshly cut flowers to be delivered first thing the next morning (I had to leave a message, since sane business owners are home by that time of night). Just when I thought Mother was finally finished, she decided to give herself a facial and a vegetable hair treatment. After that, she made me do her nails.

Hope is the thing with feathers.

chapter fourteen

The Biggest Error

I haven't eaten one bite of real food since Monday's barf episode, just nine Pounds-Away shakes in three days. No one knows. I haven't said a word to Mother about Pounds-Away. I know she wouldn't approve of my method, but for some reason getting off food completely for a while seems like the right thing. This morning, I weighed 181.

Encouraged by my progress, I put Mr. Hershey, Mr. Goodbar, Mr. Nestlé, and Mr. Reeses out with the trash. Actually, I stuffed them into a gift bag and left them for the garbage collectors with a note thanking them for their dedicated service (fat girls and garbage collectors have similar disadvantages in this image-obsessed world). Besides, it was twenty degrees out. I figured they could use a few extra calories just to stay warm.

Mother was expecting a package, so instead of going to the salon this afternoon, she had me stay home to sign for it. Right in the middle of *Oprah*, Miss Bertha called. "I know you're watching your show, Rosie, but I wanted to let you know a man just called for you."

"What?" I asked, lowering the volume. "A *man*?"

"He asked for your number, but I told him I couldn't give out the home numbers of employees without their permission first."

"Miss Bertha, you can put my number on a billboard if you want! What did he sound like? Young or old? Did he have a sort of raspy jock-type voice?" I asked. A girl is allowed to fantasize, after all.

"Honey, I got to go. Richard just spilled a drop of hair dye on his new shirt, and you'd think somebody poured acid in his eyes the way he's carryin' on about it." With the sound of Richard screaming in the background, Miss Bertha hung up.

"Damn! Why didn't she just give out my number?" I was so focused on happy Kyle fantasies it took a minute for it to dawn on me. This could be a fat-girl prank. Misty still hadn't retaliated for my insult in the cafeteria that day. Surely she wouldn't let me off that easy. Fear soon replaced excitement, so I turned up the volume slightly on *Oprah* to distract myself.

Two seconds later, the phone rang. I sat there staring at it. After the second, no-I'm-not-a-loser ring, I picked up. "Hello," I said, trying to *sound* skinny, just in case.

"Can I speak to . . . *garble* . . . *garble* . . . *static*?" The mysterious caller had a bad cell connection.

"Hello? Hell-*o*?" I tried. Dead air. Silence.

"Do you have anything in . . . *garble* . . . *garble* . . . ?"

"I can't hear you. Hello?" I was about to hang up, but suddenly the voice came through clear as a bell.

"I *said*, 'Do you have anything in *green*?'" a male voice shouted.

My heart sank. I recognized Kyle's voice, and he'd just said something about *green*. *Green* is the color of artichokes.

"Sorry," Kyle laughed when he realized he was coming through loud and clear. "I didn't mean to bust your eardrum." No, just my heart, I felt like saying. "The reason I'm call—"

"I *know* why you're calling, Kyle. You're not the first person to crank call me."

"Crank call you?"

"Go ahead. Make your little *green* comment."

"Well, what I was . . . um . . . about to say was that I just wanted to see if you'd come to the Raiders game tomorrow night."

"What does that have to do with green?" I asked.

"Our school colors. They're green and white. A lot of people wear green to the game."

I could just imagine Misty Winters or one of the NBs sitting next to Kyle, giggling into a pillow.

"I have to work," I replied.

"Oh. Well, uh, some other time then." Without a good-bye, Kyle hung up.

Either I had just made the biggest error of my high school career, or I had just avoided making the biggest error of my high school career.

chapter fifteen

To Be Continued

By some miracle the salon was quiet, except for the rain pounding the metal roof like noisy nickels. Richard had three no-shows in a row (no one wants to get their hair done in a deluge). Mildred had four (apparently, no one wants their nails done in a deluge either). Mildred threw a cover over the manicure station and went home early. Mother left for a hair show in Murfreesboro even though, as Grandma Georgia would say, she looked like death on a cracker.

While Miss Bertha and I updated client information cards, Richard spun round and round in his chair and ranted about the inconsiderate behavior of clients. "They don't call when they're not coming! They don't say thank you half the time! They just take me for granted, completely and absolutely for granted! And the tips! Don't even get me started on the—"

"You could go on home and enjoy the rest of your afternoon," Miss Bertha interrupted. She might as well have suggested he play a game of rugby. Richard lives alone. He needs

an audience when he vents. Unless we could think of some way
to divert his attention, his tirade was likely to continue until closing time.

"I could use a haircut," I offered, which was true. It had been
six months since my last trim, and that one I'd done myself at
home with a pair of nose hair scissors.

"When did we do you last?" asked Richard, instantly perked
up by the idea.

"Six months ago," I confessed (I knew better than to tell him
about the nose hair scissors).

Richard stared at me in horror. "Six months?" he asked. "Six
months! Oh. My. God." Richard strode over to the shampoo chair
and patted its seat as if he were coaxing me to the operating table.
"Right this way, please," he said. "And FYI, Daughter of Hair
Salon Owner. It's not a hair *cut*. I'm not Floyd down at the barber-
shop. It's called a hair *style*."

Obediently, I sat down at the shampoo station. Richard sang
a Sting song falsetto while he lathered me up, and when he'd finished, he led me to his chair.

When Richard was done combing and cutting and pulling at
strands to check the lines and blow-drying and styling, he twirled
me around to face the mirror, but I could barely look at myself.
"You have the hair of a goddess!" He clapped his hands together
like an overly excited child. "I swear, you could be in shampoo
commercials, Rosie!" I stared at Richard. His smile was wide and
flashy. His skin, flawless. His cornflower blue eyes, full pouty
lips, and Steven Cojocaru spiky haircut made him look like something out of a Calvin Klein ad (I suspect Richard would be very
good at pouting and writhing around in his underwear).

"*You're* the one who should be in commercials," I corrected him.

"Oh, puh-*leassse!*" Richard protested, but I knew for a fact he thought the same thing. He was always talking about becoming a model. "Rosie, let's do some makeup." Richard's reflection was talking to mine, and my reflection made an unpleasant face in response to his suggestion. "Come *on*! You'll look great, I swear, honey. Just a tad to accentuate your features. You need to *work it* a little, girlfriend. Know what I'm sayin'?" he said, using his sista voice. Miss Bertha let out a cackle.

"Okay. Okay! Just a little," I agreed, mainly to make him stop. "But if I end up looking like some character out of a John Waters film, you're in big trouble."

I settled back in the chair again and closed my eyes. Richard hummed an old Rod Stewart song, and I could tell by the light strokes that he was, in fact, taking it easy. There's only one thing worse than being a regular fat girl, and that's being an overly made-up fat girl. A blush brush is not a liposuction wand.

The concealer and base went on first, and Richard blended it with a sponge wedge. Next, he applied eye shadow and blush and eyeliner and mascara. He dusted my face with a coat of sweet-smelling powder, and I knew when he smudged my lips with gloss, he was finished. "You can open your eyes, Rosie," he whispered.

"No."

"Come on. *Look* in the mirror," Richard insisted.

Reluctantly, I opened my eyes. The dark chestnut hair was sleek and shiny, as if it might belong to some really pretty, skinny girl. It certainly didn't seem to belong on *my* head. The makeup was faint, an enhancement instead of a cover-up. Minus the extra person I was lugging around under my skin, I might've actually been pretty—brown eyes, small nose, full lips.

"Well?" asked Richard.

"I love the hair," I said, which was true. "And the makeup isn't bad."

"Isn't *bad*! Are you kidding me!"

"I love it!" I said, hugging him quickly. With Richard you have to make amends fast or he develops a grudge, and Richard-grudges can last months. He was just coming out of one with Mildred because she'd used his hair dryer on a client's fingernails without asking. "I love this eye shadow and the way you contoured it in the corners here. And the blush! What's this color called again?" The words came out so fake I reminded myself of a Bluebird.

"Berry Glow," he replied flatly, putting all his brushes away. "Miss Bertha, will you clock me out. I'm all done here."

"*Richard.*" I tugged at his sleeve. Thankfully, the phone rang and distracted Miss Bertha. With Richard I could tell the truth about my lack of self-esteem. He wasn't exactly brimming with the stuff himself, but I didn't want Miss Bertha to overhear. "Richard, you did a great job. I love my hair. I'd love the makeup, too, if it were on another head, a less fat one. Please don't be mad, okay?"

"I'm not mad. It's just a sucky Valentine's Day eve is all." He glanced at himself in the mirror. "God, my hair is one giant frizz ball!" His hair was perfect, so I knew he wanted to change the subject.

Richard left, grudge-free, thankfully, but I knew I'd been the final thing to tip his rotten-mood scale. Sometimes the bad feelings I have about myself rub off on other people.

Miss Bertha dropped me off in front of my dark, empty house a little after five. The rain had stopped, and the street had that Krispy Kreme glaze about it. "We have a church supper tonight," said Miss Bertha. "I'd love it if you'd come." Miss Bertha always feels guilty dropping me off at an empty house.

"No, thanks," I said. I squared my shoulders and bounded up the sidewalk with as much fake cheerfulness as I could muster. On the way home I'd started obsessing about Kyle's basketball game invitation again. Maybe his invitation was real. But even with nice makeup and a new hair *style*, attending a basketball game alone on a Friday night was too much. I just didn't have the courage.

"When I find myself in times of trouble, Ben and Jerry come to me . . ." I was creating blasphemous lyrics and staring into our empty freezer when I noticed the red light flashing on the answering machine. *Probably Richard*, I thought and pressed the button.

Message one: *Beep.* "Hi. It's Kyle again. Just wanted to let you know the game starts at seven-thirty. In case you decide to come." *Beep.*

Message two: *Beep.* "It's a home game, by the way." *Beep.*

My heart hammered in my throat. I glanced over at the fridge. The door hung wide open, and its interior light cast a haunting glow across the kitchen. I slammed it shut and looked up Melvin Plunkett's Cab Service in the phone book. Quickly, before I lost my nerve, I dialed the number.

"Hi, uh . . . Mr. Plunkett, this is Rosemary Goode over on Stewart Street. I need a ride to Spring Hill High School tonight. I'm going to the basketball game," I announced, as if Mr. Plunkett might comprehend the magnitude of this social stride.

I banged through the gymnasium door hideously early. According to the clock on the wall, which was protected by a metal cage, it was six-forty. The only other people there that early were a few of the overly involved parent types and their elementary-age kids. A brunette chattered animatedly about an upcoming fruit sale while her children slid up and down the sidelines and got their socks dirty.

Kyle stood at half-court. He was bulky-looking in his basketball uniform—thick arms that were not entirely muscle, beefy legs, a rounded middle. Right away, he smiled and waved. A basketball smacked him right in the mouth. "Eyes on the ball, Cox!" Coach Lord yelled. I jerked my head away and pretended not to notice the mishap.

The climb to the top and very isolated (just to be on the safe side) row of the bleachers made my heart pound. My deprived stomach growled. My low-blood-sugar head spun. The Pounds-Away I'd downed in Mr. Plunkett's cab did nothing to stave off my hunger. I settled on my hard seat and watched Kyle practice.

The spectators trickled in slowly at first, then all of a sudden the gymnasium was filled, and the game started. Clearly, anybody who was anybody sat on the lower bleachers—Bluebirds, NBs, miscellaneous popular kids—SGA officers, homecoming and winter dance stars (queens and kings were elected at both). I sat in the loser nosebleed section unnoticed, of course, which wasn't all bad. Being unnoticed was way better than being spotted and subsequently tortured. Besides, I could stare at Kyle openly without feeling like some weird stalker chick.

For such a big guy, Kyle was in great shape. Effortlessly, he bounded up and down the court. He blocked shot after shot. He stole the ball. At halftime, I watched a parade of Bluebirds file out to the concession stand. Diet Cokes in hand, they filed back in again just as the buzzer sounded.

Kyle started the second half, too. Machinelike, he passed and shot and dribbled and rebounded. I didn't know who to be more proud of—myself, for simply showing up, or Kyle, for playing so well. Finally, with only ten minutes left on the clock, Enormous Strapping Jock Boy came out for a break. We were a solid twelve points ahead, but he didn't sit down. Instead, he paced the sidelines and gulped water. With five minutes left, Coach Lord put him back in again.

At Kyle's return, Kay-Kay Reese and the other cheerleaders went wild. "Hey, hey hey," they chanted, "another one bites the dust." The bleachers vibrated. The scoreboard flashed. It struck me then that people did this every Friday night. While I was home with my head in a bag of peanut butter cups, the world went right on turning. Without me. I thought of Aunt Mary's mantra: *Don't waste your youth being fat.*

The Wildcats, our opponents, tried and failed to score. Thirty seconds. Fifteen. At ten, the crowd started counting down. The victory horn sounded. The Spring Hill Raiders won! I felt myself leap to my feet and cheer right along with everyone else. For that shimmering, victorious moment, I was a Spring Hill High School Raider. Not a fat-girl Raider or a misfit Raider, but a regular Raider.

I watched as Misty Winters led the other Bluebirds out the door. More than likely, they were off to some postgame keg party. After everyone was gone (except for the clean-up crew), I made my way down the bleachers. It struck me then that I didn't have a ride home, so I headed to the lobby and dialed Mother from a pay phone.

"Hey." I felt a tap on my shoulder. "You came," he said when I turned around. A freshly showered, still somewhat sweaty, but smiling Kyle towered over me. *He is delightfully enormous,* I thought to myself. *And handsome. God!*

"Great game," I managed to say.

"I had a feeling if you came you'd bring me luck." He smiled.

Mother picked up. "Hello? Hell-*o*?" I held up a just-a-minute finger to Kyle.

"Mother, can you pick me up at school?" I spoke as if I were making the most normal request in the world.

"School? What are you doing at school? You didn't ask me if—"

Kyle was mouthing something I couldn't hear. "What?" I asked him. "No, not you, Mother. Hold on a sec."

"I can take you home," Kyle whispered.

My heart doubled in size and banged against my rib cage. "Are you sure?" I asked.

"Sure," said Kyle, licking the small cut on his lip.

"Never mind, Mother. I'll be home later. Bye," I said, hanging up before she could ask questions.

Kyle's ancient blue and white Suburban smelled of wet dog and mildewed athletic equipment. He hoisted a set of golf clubs over the seat, then tossed a pair of cleats, a basketball, and several mysterious padded items into the way-back. "Sorry." He grinned. "We have a lot of jocks in our family. I mean . . . um . . . athletes," he corrected himself.

Smokey Robinson's "Cruisin'" played on the oldies station, and Kyle sang along, *loudly*. His voice (Kyle's, not Smokey's) was slightly off-key, but I liked his easygoing, sing-out-loud confidence.

All too soon, we reached my house. Kyle shifted the gear to Park and turned to face me. "Did you do something to your hair?" he asked. I nodded. "It looks nice."

"Thanks," I replied. "I work at my mom's salon. One of the stylists there talked me into getting it done."

"Kay-Kay told me you worked there."

"Kay-Kay Reese?" I asked, even though there wasn't another Kay-Kay in the whole town as far as I knew.

"Yeah. She says you have a great shop. Or your mom does."

"Oh. Yeah, we do. Or she does." The fact that Kyle Cox and Kay-Kay Reese had actually engaged in a conversation about *me* left me stuttering.

"Kay-Kay dates a football buddy of mine. Logan Clark. You know him?"

"I know of him," I said, which was sort of like *knowing of* Brad Pitt.

"Me and Kay-Kay went to kindergarten together. Brown Elementary. I went to private school for middle school, then transferred to Spring Hill last year. Sports were lousy at Kessler, the private school."

"I went to Riverside," I replied. "And to Spring Hill Middle School." The air grew heavy with silence. I racked my brain for something interesting to say, but I'd run out of alma maters.

"Big plans for Valentine's tomorrow?" asked Kyle.

"Oh, definitely," I lied, trying to sound impressive. The truth was I'd be tucked in bed by eight o'clock, watching a rerun of *Golden Girls*. A car whispered past us; its taillights cast a red glow on our faces. All at once it struck me that perhaps Kyle wasn't asking about my plans for the sake of conversation; maybe he'd wanted to ask me out! I swallowed hard and tried to think of a way to backtrack, but Mother flicked on the porch light. I could see her pacing around in the living room. "I guess I'd better go," I said reluctantly. "Thanks for the ride and for inviting me to the game."

"You have an open invitation, you know." He flashed a teasing smile, and I thought I might wet my pants. Actually, I'd had to pee since halftime, but I'd been too afraid to climb down the bleachers and walk past the Bluebirds.

"I'll keep that in mind," I replied. I smiled and dragged my eyes up to meet his. I had no clue what flirting was, but I hoped it was some involuntary-response kind of thing, like migration or mating calls. I climbed out of the big, clunky car and watched Kyle ease up the street.

chapter sixteen

Her Terms

I tried not to dwell on my missed Valentine's Day opportunity, but it was hard, especially since Mother and Aunt Mary had plans for the night. The downtown merchants were hosting a Valentine's Day dance at the Elks Lodge, and from the sound of things, the entire adult population of Spring Hill planned to attend. Mother had ordered a dress off the Internet, and she'd found a great pair of strappy black heels on sale over at Landis Lane. Mother and Aunt Mary didn't have dates (they never have dates), but Aunt Mary claimed there might be some nice single men there.

Early Saturday morning, I was awakened by sobs. I tiptoed downstairs and stood outside Mother's bathroom door, debating whether or not to knock. Finally, I did. "Yes," said Mother. Gently I pushed open the door.

"What's wro—?" I stopped myself. Mother held a brush so thick with hair it looked like a small rodent.

"Get a paper bag," Mother ordered.

"A paper bag?"

"I'm saving it," she said flatly.

"Saving what?"

"My hair. I'm saving every strand of it!" she snapped, as if I were somehow missing the logic in this idea. Once her hair was safely tucked in the paper bag, Mother left for work, and I began to notice the familiar warning signs.

My swinish gluttony never attacks without warning signs. As I showered and dressed and styled my hair and drank my very last Pounds-Away, I noticed my palms were sweating. While I waited on the front stoop for Miss Bertha, guilty food fantasies darted around in my brain like bats. My heart had that heavy, pulling-down feeling, the kind you get when you've just failed a test or lost something valuable (or consumed an entire Domino's pizza by yourself).

Miss Bertha and I were almost to Heavenly Hair when I blurted out, "I need to buy another get-well card!" I couldn't tell Miss Bertha about Pounds-Away any more than I could tell Mother. They'd both vehemently disagree with my drastic weight-loss measures.

"Honey, the salon's real busy this—"

"I won't take long, I promise. I swear if you don't stop, I'll—"

"Oh, all right, calm down! You and Richard have *got* to stop spending so much time together. His dramatic streak's startin' to rub off!" she scolded. Miss Bertha turned her car around in the Dairy Queen parking lot, and my eyes locked on the giant ice-cream-cone sign out front.

"Hurry," I said, as if contraband Pounds-Away were some powerful antidote to the Dairy Queen.

That night Aunt Mary showed up at our door wearing a black silk dress and a bright red wrap. She did look very stylish. "Mother's in the bathroom," I said, letting her in. "She'll be out in a minute." I didn't bother telling Aunt Mary that Mother'd spent half her day sobbing in the Heavenly Hair bathroom.

Mother sobbing is practically an oxymoron.

"Rosie, do you *ever* wear anything besides sweats?" said Aunt Mary. "You know they add at least ten pounds."

I ignored her and tried to return to focusing on my homework. Usually, I do homework in my room, but since Mother would be gone, I'd brought everything downstairs.

"It just kills me—that sour, puffed-up look you get every time I come around," Aunt Mary went on. "A respectful niece would *answer me* instead of sitting there with her head in a book. I can tell you're not really reading, Rosie. Your eyes aren't moving. When people read their eyes move."

I was just about to let my tongue off its leash when Mother, still wearing her slippers and bathrobe, scuffed into the living room. Around her head she'd wrapped some red fabric that was supposed to be a turban. I think.

"What on earth, Rose Warren? You do realize we're due at the Elks Lodge in fifteen minutes? Why aren't you dressed? And what's that awful thing on your head?"

"I tried to call you on your cell," said Mother.

"Tried to call me for what?"

Mother looked ready to cry again, and I could tell she was having a hard time getting the words out.

"Aunt Mary, her hair is falling out!" I said sharply, a distinct tone of *duh* in my voice. Mother's face crumpled, and she dashed toward the kitchen. Aunt Mary shot me a look as if I were somehow responsible for the side effects of doxorubicin and followed her. I didn't bother going after them. I knew I'd just be relegated to the sofa again. Similar scenes had been played out repeatedly in my life: There is a crisis of some sort; Mother and Aunt Mary huddle together and whisper about it; I wait just out of earshot and try to figure out what might happen next.

A few minutes later a somber Aunt Mary headed out the front door. I listened to her heels click down the sidewalk. She didn't say good-bye—not that I cared. I heard Mother's bedroom door snap shut. She didn't say good night.

Around midnight I needed some air, so I went to get the soggy newspaper off the front lawn—it'd been out there all day. In order to put the paper in the recycling bin, I had to go into the kitchen. And since the bin is right next to the pantry, I opened the door and peeked inside. On the shelf was a fresh bag of innocent nacho chips. Just next to it was an entirely vulnerable jar of mild salsa. This time Mother had labeled both with a pink sticky note: PLEASE DO NOT EAT OR THROW AWAY.

I grabbed a Coke from the fridge. A person couldn't very well consume spicy salsa and salty chips without something to drink. My heart raced, and I could feel the rush of prebinge adrenaline. *The point of no return*, I thought. *This is it. Right here. This is that point where you put the Coke back in the fridge and the chips and salsa back on the shelf. You go upstairs, wash your face, brush your teeth, go to bed.* Kay-Kay Reese would've done this. Aunt Mary and Mother and Richard would have done this, too.

In a game of *he loves me, he loves me not,* I put the chips back, picked them up again, put them back, picked them up. I got all the way to my room with the Coke and the chips and the salsa, glanced at the treadmill, then hurried downstairs again. Carefully, I reattached Mother's note and put everything back where it belonged.

This afternoon, Mother dropped me off at Dr. Cooper's for my appointment with Mrs. Wallace. "You're not staying?" I asked when she pulled up to the curb. She shook her head, which was covered with a blue velvet hat, a gift from Miss Bertha (so much better than the turban).

"I'm gonna run over to the hospital and see Peri for a minute. I won't be long. I just want to say hidy and drop these off," she said, patting the stack of *Enquirers* on the seat.

"Are you gonna fix her hair?"

Mother shook her head. I knew this meant Mrs. McCutchin was too sick to have her hair fixed or her neck shaved.

I hadn't even warmed up the ripped vinyl chair in Mrs. Wallace's office before I started spilling my guts. I told her about going to the basketball game alone. I told her all about my almost date with Kyle Cox. I told her about Mother's sudden hair loss and the completely freaky, weird, saving-her-hair-in-a-paper-bag thing and the subsequent sobbing attacks. I *almost* told her about Saturday night's salsa dance, but something held me back. Instead, I pushed out a fake cough and handed her my homework—the one reason I could think of that Kyle Cox might actually like me: *I have nice hair.* Kyle said so.

Mrs. Wallace glanced at my so-called list. Clearly, she wasn't impressed. "We'll discuss this next session," she said, slipping the paper into her Rosemary file. "First, I want to hear more about what happened with your mother."

I took a deep breath and let it out again. "Well, Mother has seemed fine up to this point. I mean, she didn't say all that much about the cancer, but with my mother, the roof could fall on her head and she'd say she was fine. That's just how she is."

"I see," said Mrs. Wallace. "So she's not opening up about her feelings yet."

"*Yet?* No, you don't understand. There is no *yet.* Rose Warren Goode doesn't ever open up about anything." I thought about what Grandma Georgia had said. *She reorganized her dreams the way some people clean out closets—threw the old ones out and hung new ones in their place.*

"So she *never* talks to you?"

"Oh, she talks. I mean, she'll tell me what's for dinner or talk about her decorating ideas for the house. . . ."

"But she doesn't talk about her problems."

"My mother doesn't have problems," I said sarcastically. "Look, it's not like I want every gory detail of her life. But I'm fifteen, about to turn sixteen. There are things I need to know, especially now. And if she's . . . you know . . . really sick, then . . ." The words caught in my throat.

Mrs. Wallace waited, but I couldn't speak. "You'd like to comfort her," she finally filled in for me. I nodded and grabbed a tissue.

"Sounds like you and your mother want things from each other that neither of you is willing to give at the moment."

"What do you mean?" I asked, wiping my nose.

"Well, your mother bought you a treadmill. She's tried to help you lose weight, but—"

"What's *that* got to do with anything?"

"Rosemary, what's it like for you when your mother and aunt pressure you to diet and exercise?"

"It's like I'm not good enough just the way I am. Like all the other good things I do in life—good grades and working at the salon—like none of that counts because I'm fat."

"And does their nudging make you lose weight?"

"Obviously not."

"What I'm saying is your mother's battle with cancer is somewhat like your battle with weight. She'll have to handle it on *her* terms."

chapter seventeen

Poopy Head

I'm so hungry I could lick envelopes just for the glue. Mother's working late, and there's a new box of Cheerios in the pantry. Cheerios might not sound like much of a threat, but when you've been on a liquid diet . . . Well, let's just say I could crunch my way through an entire box, which would work out to about 2,850 calories, if you include the skim milk.

If I were going to consume 2,850 calories, I would not waste them on Cheerios. Since I only like Cheerios in a very mild way, I would use up those precious 2,850 calories on something I really love, like a massive hot fudge sundae or or whole cake. But, if I ate the cake and/or sundae, I'd feel defeated and depressed. And when I'm defeated and depressed, I turn to food, so I'd wind up eating the Cheerios anyway. This is where one tiny, seemingly harmless bowl of Cheerios would lead me—down the twisted path of Fat Girl Logic. This is also why I refuse to go off Pounds-Away.

Instead of eating anything, I read Mrs. Wallace's "Coping Mechanisms and Weight Loss" brochure. First on the list of positive coping mechanisms was exercise.

Guiltily, I glanced at my treadmill, and I could sense its dark disapproval. I walked across the room and turned it on. The damn thing still worked. I turned it off again and climbed on its slightly tilted slope. I tried to imagine myself running every single day for the rest of my life, *uphill.*

The math was too difficult to do in my head, so I jumped off the treadmill and grabbed a calculator. If I lived to eighty, I'd have approximately 23,725 days of exercise ahead. If I exercised five days a week instead of seven, that would still work out to 16,900 days. If I took the last ten years off and worked out five days instead of seven, that'd still be 14,300 days.

I climbed on the treadmill again. Half expecting confetti to fall from the ceiling, I turned it on. I tried to remember the motion of *r-u-n-n-i-n-g.* Within seconds my heart was pounding. My lead-like legs ached. The stitch in my side was so severe, I felt sure it was appendicitis. Sweat poured off me and I envisioned it as calories. The fantasy sundae and/or cake and Cheerios were magically *gone* (in reality, I'd burned off half a Pounds-Away shake at best). Finally, after fifteen excruciating minutes, I turned the treadmill off again.

The thought of doing this every single day for the rest of my life made me want to die—*soon*, like early tomorrow morning perhaps.

The real reason I got on the treadmill in the first place was because Kay-Kay Reese came bounding in the shop today, and I do mean *bounding*. She moves off the sidelines the same way she moves on them—in a constant state of perpetual cheerleader bounce. She must burn 3,000 calories a day just being Kay-Kay. Anyway, I kept my head down and swept around her chair while Mother trimmed her hair. I listened while the two of them chatted pleasantly about the new spring collection at Landis Lane. Right in the middle of Kay-Kay's diatribe on synthetic blends, she glanced at me and smiled. "Hey, Rosie," she said, interrupting herself.

"Oh . . . *hi,* " I replied, pretending I'd only just noticed her that very second. For some reason, having a girl like Kay-Kay Reese smile at me (even if she is a Bluebird) made me feel like a million bucks.

"Yoo-hoo," Miss Bertha called to Mother from across the salon. "Rose Warren, it's Hilda Brunson on the phone. Her highlights have gone green again."

"I'm sorry, Kay-Kay," Mother apologized. "I have to take this call," she said, hurrying across the salon. Mother tired easily, and her skin was dry, additional side effects from the chemo, but as far as I knew, she hadn't cried once in the last several days, *and* she had a whole collection of new hats and scarves, gifts from her clients, a sure sign of their unwavering patronage.

Kay-Kay shot me a look of fear. "Green?" she asked.

"Oh, don't worry. Mrs. Brunson has too much copper in her well water and very porous hair. Mother'll just put a rinse over it," I explained.

"Thank God!" said Kay-Kay. "That happened to me one year at camp. I swam every day that summer, and my blond hair turned the color of pea soup. I guess it must've been the chemicals or something. Anyway, school was starting up the very next week."

"Oh, no!" I said, sympathizing. I knew exactly what Kay-Kay was talking about. During the summer months, Mother gets a frantic call from some towheaded kid's parent for that very reason at least once every few days.

"For the entire fourth grade year, I was known as Poopy Head."

I tried to imagine a girl like Kay-Kay Reese being called anything other than beautiful. "What did you do when somebody called you that?" I asked, scooping a clump of blond Kay-Kay hair into the dustpan and dumping it into the trash. Given my last session with Mrs. Wallace and my own nickname, I was interested in Kay-Kay's *coping mechanism.*

"I cried every day and sat in the back of the class with"—she smirked when she said this—"Kyle Cox." I stopped sweeping and looked at her. "The two of us were a real pair," Kay-Kay went on. "Poopy Head and . . ." She stopped herself.

"And what?" I asked.

"Oh, well . . . I probably shouldn't tell *you* of all people." She grinned, and her teeth reminded me of the tiles in Mother's bathroom, a perfectly even row of gleaming white porcelain.

"Why not tell *me*?"

"Because Kyle *likes* you, silly. He wouldn't want you to know his hideous old nickname." All of a sudden, I felt like I was having one of Miss Bertha's hot flashes. "You're *blushing*," Kay-Kay singsonged. "That must mean you like him, too. Oh, all right, I'll tell you, since you already like him anyway. Kyle was known as Bacon."

"Bacon?"

"Because he was . . ." Kay-Kay looked at me nervously.

"Because he was *fat*?" I asked, filling in the blank for her.

Kay-Kay nodded. "That's why he went to Kessler for middle school. They have sucky teams there, so he was able to make junior football, which is how he eventually dropped the weight and became such a great athlete."

Before I could reply or ask more questions, Mother was back and snipping the ends of Kay-Kay's hair again. For the rest of the afternoon, I floated around Heavenly Hair on a cloud of hope—with a little hair mixed in, of course.

chapter eighteen

The Box

Today was crazy busy at the salon. We've had springlike temperatures for the past two days, which makes everyone want a new hairdo. I offered to stay till closing (on Saturdays, I only work ten to one), but Mother insisted Miss Bertha take me home. "Go enjoy the day," said Mother. "Maybe get a little exercise."

On the way to my house, Miss Bertha stopped off at the park. She wanted to eat her lunch in peace before going back to the Saturday afternoon chaos—four perms, two highlights, three manicures, and walk-ins. I agreed to keep her company, provided she wouldn't let me eat anything.

Miss Bertha unpacked her lunch, and I stared out the window: babies wailed in strollers; bigger kids squealed on swings; a couple lay kissing on a faded quilt. I pretended not to notice The Kissers. "So how are you, Rosie?" asked Miss Bertha. "We've been so busy I've hardly spoken to you today."

"My grades are good," I replied, distractedly. Kisser Boy had his hand on Kisser Girl's breast now, and he was kneading it like bread dough.

"Well, I'm glad about the good grades," said Miss Bertha. She took a swig of sweet tea, stifled a delicate belch, then slipped a stray piece of ham into her mouth. The Kissers had pulled the blanket on top of them. "Good Lord, I do wish they'd show some dignity!" Miss Bertha snapped. "I feel like yellin' *Get a room!* out the car window."

"Please don't."

"Oh, I'm just teasing, Rosie. I won't, but don't you think that's disgusting?"

"Well, sure," I said. This was a lie, however. Personally, I was glad *somebody* was having teen sex. Miss Bertha started the car, eased it forward a few feet, then turned it off again. Now all I had to look at was a rusty swing set. I knew better than to suggest we go sit at the picnic table a few feet away; Miss Bertha's convinced public places like that are crawling with germs.

"So what have you got planned for tonight?" she asked, studying me over the top of her drugstore half-glasses. I rolled my eyes. Miss Bertha knows I *never* have plans. "How about spending the night at my house? We have another church supper." I rolled my eyes again. "I could pick you up *after* the supper," she tried. I watched while Miss Bertha packed up her assorted pieces of Tupperware as if they were fine bone china.

"I have homework," I replied, which was true. Mrs. Edinburgh had given out an extra-credit assignment (although with a 95 average, I didn't really need it).

I thought back to when I used to spend the night with Miss Bertha on a regular basis. It was always fun—partly because she'd kept her daughters' old Barbie dolls, and partly because she made real chocolate fudge, from scratch, without burning it. As good as her fudge always was, I never once overate it. Miss Bertha and I were always too busy talking—or rather *I* was too busy talking. Other than Grandma Georgia, Miss Bertha was the only person who made me feel like what I had to say was important. She'd nibble her piece of fudge, dress a Barbie, and listen to me talk like I was the most interesting person on earth.

"Well, you can always change your mind later," she said, switching on the ignition. Smokey Robinson's "Cruisin'" eased out of the speakers. Miss Bertha had the dial set on the oldies station, the same one Kyle and I had listened to on the way home from the game. I thought back to what Kay-Kay had said about Kyle's liking me.

"Rosie? *Rosie?*"

"Huh?"

"Good Lord, you're far away. Why don't you drive so I can fix my face before I get back to the shop."

I got out of the car and went around to the driver's side, and Miss Bertha slid across the seat. I glanced back at The Kissers, but they were gone. It struck me then what Smokey was talking about with all his *oh, oh, babes*. The lovers in the song weren't just driving around town. They were cruisin' *away from here*—probably so they could go get a room. The whole distracted drive back to my house I fantasized about Kyle wanting to get closer and closer—*ooooooh, ooooooh*.

"What on earth are you thinking about, hon? You've been smiling for the last ten minutes, and I ain't said a thing funny!" said Miss Bertha.

"Oh, no reason," I lied. "I'm just in a good mood is all."

At home, I went straight to my room, but it was hot and stuffy upstairs. I cracked the window open a little and sniffed the air outside. Even though it was only the last day of February, I could actually smell spring. It was distant and faraway, but there just the same. I glanced at the treadmill. It was free of damp bras and panties (only because my hamper was overflowing), ready for use, but I couldn't stand the thought of climbing on it. Instead, I decided to go for a walk. Yes, I said *walk*.

I reached the end of my street and took a left onto Third Avenue. I kept going until Carter Street and made another left toward my old elementary school. At Riverside Drive, I took a right. The Duck River Bridge had a pedestrian walkway, which I had never in all my life used. Back when I was little and actually rode my bike and went for walks, I wasn't allowed on the bridge. Timidly, I stepped on the walkway and glanced down at the muddy water coursing below. The river's nickname was the Muddy Duck, and it reminded me of that chocolate river in *Willy Wonka and the Chocolate Factory*, a movie that'd always scared me with its disappearing kids and freaky parents. I sped up and climbed the steep hill on North Main and headed toward the courthouse.

My thighs screamed. Sweat poured off me. My barely broken-in tennis shoes rubbed watery blisters on my heels. The clock tower clanged three times. I kept walking. Shops lined both sides of the street, but I avoided looking in their windows. Hope was perching on my soul again, and a glimpse of my reflection would surely kill it. I rounded the corner toward Reynolds's Drugstore. Even from a distance, I could see Charmaine was at the cash register (her bleached-blond hair is impossible to miss). I stared at my feet and kept walking.

"Hey, Rosemary!" Charmaine stuck her head out the door and called after me.

"Hey," I panted and waved.

"Hon, we're having another special on that Pounds-Away. Look in tomorrow's paper for the coupon, okay?" I nodded and tried to catch my breath. "Go on, doll. I didn't mean to interrupt you."

"It's okay," I half gagged. "Thanks."

"Don't forget them coupons now! You can use more'n one. I'll just ring ever-thang up separately," she said, and went inside the store again. I leaned over, hands atop my knees, just the way I'd seen athletes do after a race. Blood thumped noisily in my ears, and I wondered if this was how Mrs. McCutchin felt just before her heart attack.

"Well, hey there! I didn't know you were a runner!" Kay-Kay wore neon-yellow running shorts and a pink sports bra. Delicate beads of perspiration glistened on her slightly tanned skin (a visit to the tanning bed, no doubt).

"Oh, I'm not a runner. I'm barely a walker," I explained.

Kay-Kay let out a laugh. It seemed to come from someplace deep within her flat six-pack abdomen. "Great about the Raiders last night, huh?" she said, still jogging in place. "Kyle played amazingly well. You really should come to his games. Hey, you know, we should run together one of these days. I get so bored doing this all by myself. It'd be fun to have somebody to talk to!"

I could barely talk and stand still, much less talk and run with Kay-Kay. I struggled to catch my breath. "Sure," I managed to croak.

"Well, I'd better go for now! You come to those games, hear?" Kay-Kay winked at me and smiled. I watched her sprint off toward the Episcopal church. Her body was a tight, efficient machine. Nothing jiggled except her ponytail. Without thinking, I glanced at myself in the plate glass window. The girl staring back at me was a sweaty, fat mess—lumpy thighs, chunky middle, hair stuck to her head, and a big fat face. It hit me then what another win for the Raiders meant. More away championship games. More endless study halls *without* Kyle.

The second I got home, I called her. "Miss Bertha, I changed my mind. I think I will spend the night at your house tonight, if it's still okay."

"Why sure, honey! You know it is. I'd skip the church supper, but I'm in charge of the dessert table. I'll try to get out a little early, though. Unless you've changed your mind and want to come with me?"

"Uh, no thanks. Just pick me up after, okay?"

"See you round seven-thirty then," she said, and hung up.

Miss Bertha didn't make her famous fudge. She didn't even *offer* to make fudge. Instead, we watched *Pretty Woman* and ate hot-air popcorn (no salt, no butter, no taste, no calories), and I had a Diet Coke. I knew these were special purchases for my benefit.

Miss Bertha never drinks anything besides sweet tea, and pop-corn kernels get stuck in her bridgework.

"What do you think the odds are that he stayed with her?" I asked. Secretly, I was comparing Julia Roberts's chances of snaring Richard Gere with my own for dating Kyle Cox.

"I think it's highly unlikely that some tycoon would wind up with a prostitute, but crazier things have happened, I reckon. We all need a fairytale happy ending now and then."

"We sure do." I sighed. It was getting late, and I knew Miss Bertha liked to turn in early. "I think I'll go to bed now."

"Wait just a minute, hon. I got something I been meanin' to give you." Miss Bertha disappeared for a minute and came back with an old shoebox. It was decorated with magazine cutouts and Spring Hill High School stickers. It looked like something that might belong to me, but I knew it didn't.

"What's that?" I asked.

Miss Bertha took a deep breath and let it out again. "Your grandma left this with me when she moved. It's some of your mama's old stuff. I tried to give it to Rose Warren, but she wouldn't take it, said for me to pitch it." Miss Bertha handed the box to me.

"So what is it?" I asked, feeling squirmy all of a sudden.

"Just a bunch of old pictures. Stuff most mothers would want their daughters to see."

"My mother is not *most mothers*," I reminded Miss Bertha.

"I know that, and don't you dare tell her I gave it to you. She'd have a fit."

"I won't," I promised. I was just about to head up the stairs when Miss Bertha stopped me.

"Rosie, now that I think about it, maybe things did work out for that Julia Roberts and Richard Gere. They were both just alike—two desperate people doing desperate things they regretted later on. I guess they probably had a pretty good understandin' of one another."

"I guess so," I agreed.

In the privacy of Miss Bertha's tiny attic, which serves as a guest room/craft area, I opened the box. The first thing I saw was a five-by-seven photograph of Mother and Aunt Mary. Obviously, they were at some sort of school-sponsored event, a formal one at that. Mother's face was slightly chubby, and she wore a pale blue strapless chiffon dress, pearls, and dyed-to-match pumps just barely visible beneath the floor-length hem. Aunt Mary had on a similar dress except it was pink *with* straps, and she wore a silver necklace instead of pearls. Mother clutched a small beaded bag and faced the camera. Aunt Mary clutched Mother's arm and leaned into her, as if shielding her somehow. I glanced at the back of the picture.

"Oh, my God," I whispered, noticing the date. I was born just one month before the picture was taken. I studied Mother's face again. She wasn't chubby. She was postpartum. And this wasn't just some school function, it was the prom. It had to be. Spring Hill High School didn't have any other formal year-end events. No wonder Aunt Mary stood so close to Mother; they were sticking together. I could only imagine the scandal—high school girl gets pregnant, boyfriend bolts, small town talks and talks and talks, ruined girl has the nerve to try to reclaim her old life . . . and go to the prom.

In other, larger, more sophisticated towns, none of this would've been a big deal, but in Spring Hill, Tennessee, it was huge. I stared at Mother's face and wondered if *this* was why she worked so hard. Years and years of toiling away at Heavenly Hair, at home, at raising me. Maybe Mother was still trying to prove she was a good girl. Maybe that's why she was so desperate for me to lose weight. Maybe she thought my fatness made her look like a failure.

There were various other mementos in the box—yellowed newspaper clippings, wrinkled photographs. In one, Mother accepted the Best Spirit award at cheerleading camp. In another, she took the first-place ribbon for the literary magazine's poetry competition. There wasn't a single mention of my biological father. It was as if Mother had conceived me all on her own; certainly, she'd done everything else for me that way. I tried to imagine what it would be like, getting pregnant in high school. In some pictures, Mother wore the happy expression of an uncomplicated girl. In others, she appeared careworn—Before Me and After Me pictures.

Carefully, I tucked the artifacts back into the box, switched off the lamp, and pulled the covers up around my neck. Spiky tree branches danced on Miss Bertha's attic ceiling until the lady next door switched off her porch light. I lay in the darkness and tried to imagine Mother's seventeen-year-old life. Mother had reorganized her dreams because I'd given her no other choice.

chapter nineteen

Fatty

Kyle was not in study hall—*again*—but at least I got to see him in the crowded hallway for one fleeting, albeit wonderful, moment. It was early in the day, just after homeroom announcements, and I was headed to English. "Rosie! Hey, Rosie! Wait up!" he called. I turned to see Enormous Strapping Jock Boy headed straight toward me. I sucked in my stomach and tried to stand up straight. "Hey," he said when we were face to chest (Kyle's so large he even makes me feel small).

"Hey," I replied.

"So there's, like, a game tonight in Murfreesboro, and the pep bus is only five dollars. I think there's still room if you wanna come."

Why can't the Raiders just lose? Pep bus equals sharing close quarters with Bluebirds and NBs—no place to run, nowhere to hide. No way, I thought. "Well, I would love to come, but Mr. Sparks has one of his infamous ruin-your-GPA tests tomorrow. I *have* to study tonight," I replied.

Kyle shrugged. "It was worth a try." I struggled to think of something encouraging to say. Certainly, I didn't want Kyle to think I didn't like him. Just then, a noisy group of Bluebird fledglings rounded the corner. They squealed and cackled and shoved one another playfully. Kay-Kay wasn't among them, I noticed. Kyle rolled his eyes.

"What was that for?" I asked.

"What was what for? Oh, I wasn't rolling my eyes at *you*!" he said, clearly alarmed.

"I know. You were rolling them at those Bluebirds."

Kyle shifted his weight uneasily. "Sorry. You're not about to become one, are you?" he asked, knitting his thick brows together. I shook my head. "Good, 'cause they . . ." He stopped himself.

"'Cause they *what*?" I asked, blinking up at him.

"'Cause they scare me." He laughed, but I was pretty sure he was serious.

For the first time, I looked at Kyle, *really* looked at him, and he gazed back at me. "Well, if it makes you feel any better, they scare me, too. Probably a lot more than they do you. Thanks for the pep bus offer. Sorry I can't go," I said.

After this self-esteem-enhancing exchange, I was practically gliding down the hallway—until the freight train hit.

A pack of NBs were shoving each other. The tallest one slammed into me so hard my teeth rattled. Did jerk NB say "Excuse me"? No. He looked me square in the face and snarled, "Why don't you go on a diet, fatty?"

Anger shot right through me, and before I could stop myself, I stuck my clogged foot in front of him. He was too busy flipping his shaggy, in-his-face hair (and being amused by his cruel remark) to notice the obstruction, and he fell flat—a major face plant to the cold, hard floor. Books scattered, and pages of his notebook fluttered off down the hallway. His buddies roared with laughter. I slipped into the crowd and ran toward Mrs. Edinburgh's room.

For the rest of the morning, no matter how hard I fought against it, pre-pig-out symptoms plagued me. Even in biology, where we were forced to watch Mr. Donahue dissect a rat, I struggled with wacko food fantasies. Just tell me this: How can a girl, even a fat one, think about food while watching a rather unattractive, slightly-on-the-greasy-side biology teacher stick pins in the skin of a giant dead rat? Recently, I'd been wandering the hallways in between fifth and sixth periods (I know where Mrs. Edinburgh keeps the spare pass), but Mr. Lawrence caught me and threatened a month-long stint in detention if I didn't go to the cafeteria like everybody else.

There was only one way to avoid overeating at lunch—sit close to the Bluebirds. Obviously, this kind of radical measure is social suicide for me, but at least I knew there was no way I'd succumb to temptation with the Bluebirds close by.

All the way to the cafeteria, I sharpened my tongue, prepared myself for the harassment that would surely come. I'd already taken down an NB, after all. Certainly I could handle a few overly perfumed, hair-tossing mean girls. As if headed to my own execution, I made my way up the narrow aisle, squeezed through the too-tight space, and sat down. It was several seconds before I remembered to breathe. I stared at my tray, which could've easily belonged to Kay-Kay: small salad, yogurt, and a box of raisins (there was no way I'd drink a Pounds-Away in public). I cracked open my water bottle and glanced over at the Bluebirds, but they didn't even notice me. Not a single one of them realized I was even there, a close-range target, a sitting-duck fat girl.

They were too busy shunning Kay-Kay Reese to notice me. Shunning Kay-Kay Reese! I was shocked, yet all along I'd predicted it for numerous reasons:

1. Kay-Kay Reese is too glamorous for the Bluebirds.

2. Kay-Kay Reese isn't mean enough to be a Bluebird. After all, she speaks to me.

3. Kay-Kay Reese doesn't maintain the proper level of respect for Misty Winters. This is likely the *real* reason she's being shunned. Misty has a way of eliminating any serious competition.

I took small, slow bites of yogurt and watched the teenage drama unfold. Kay-Kay stood next to her usual chair, which was occupied by a rather plain-looking and unsuspecting freshman. "What's going on?" I heard Kay-Kay say. "How come y'all didn't save my seat?" Clattering silverware, banging trays, cold silence. "Hell-*ooo*," Kay-Kay tried again. "What *is* the matter?" Kay-Kay laughed, but I could see she was getting nervous. Her voice was tight. Twice her empty plastic cup clattered to the floor. Twice I picked it up and handed it back to her. The Bluebirds refused to look at her. Quietly, like robots, they ate their low-fat lunches and sipped their Diet Cokes. It seemed Kay-Kay'd gone invisible.

I thought of Julius Caesar at the senate, about to be stabbed to death by his so-called friends. Only that morning in Mrs. Edinburgh's class I'd read Caesar's stunned words: *Et tu, Brute?* Across the narrow aisle, I sent telepathic warnings to Kay-Kay: *Don't grovel, just give them the giant, defiant screw-you. Casually find another table. Act like you don't care.*

Message received. The next thing I knew, Kay-Kay Reese was halfheartedly munching a bright green salad (no dressing) in the chair right across from me.

Every once in a while, just to enhance Kay-Kay's torture, the Bluebirds pressed their brassy, dark-rooted heads together and looked straight at her while they whispered back and forth. I made an effort not to stare at my unlikely lunch partner, but with her tragic blue eyes and anguished berry-colored lips, it was difficult not to.

When the bell rang, Kay-Kay and I waited for the dreaded flock to leave. We walked toward study hall together, although I knew Kay-Kay's class was in the opposite direction. "Thanks for letting me sit with you, Rosie," said Kay-Kay when we reached the library. I'd never seen her look so *un*perky.

"No problem," I replied.

"Would you mind if I ate with you tomorrow, too?" she asked. "Maybe at a different table? Far away from them?"

"Not at all," I said, "just as long as you don't talk so much." Kay-Kay hadn't said a word the whole lunch period. She forced a polite smile at my lame joke and headed off down the long empty hallway. Alone.

chapter twenty

My Lucky Day

Mother and I had a huge fight this morning just before she left for Heavenly Hair. You'd think an argument about tuna casserole would be pretty lame, one of those silly fights you take too seriously in the beginning, but end up laughing about later, but no.

At five forty-five, according to my clock radio, Mother pounded up the stairs. "Rosemary Goode, did you eat that casserole or throw it away?" She stood over me, hands on her thin hips, lips tight and angry. She hadn't covered her head yet, so I wasn't quite sure who she was when I first woke up. With her pale skin and even paler scalp, my once-pretty mother resembled an alien.

"Huh?" I asked, squinting against the light.

"That casserole was for Willy Ray McCutchin and his boys. Peri goes to the rehab center today, and I made it thinking it would save them some time and money. Do you ever think about anybody besides yourself? And please don't tell me you threw out my good Pyrex dish just to hide your tracks!"

"Mother, I have no idea what you're talking about," I groaned, and covered my head with a pillow. Mother snatched the pillow off my face and glowered. It hit me then what was different about her—her eyelashes and eyebrows were gone now, too. *When did this happen? How did I not notice?*

Mother stormed across my room and snatched up the window shade. Angrily, she plucked damp laundry off the treadmill. "And the next pair of panties I see drip-dryin' on this $700 machine . . . well, they're just going straight to the trash!" I wondered who had sneaked into our house in the middle of the night and replaced my real mother with this raving lunatic.

"Mother, what *is* your problem? I didn't eat any tuna casserole! I've lost weight, not that anyone around here has noticed!"

"And what exactly is going on with that anyway? One minute you're eating everything in sight, the next you're pitching perfectly good food in the garbage can! They don't give pot roast away at the Piggly Wiggly, Rosemary Goode! I have to buy it. And another thing while I'm gettin' this stuff off my chest. You are to be nice to your Aunt Mary, hear? I'm not kidding. I'm sick of your constant bickering with her."

"*My* bickering with *her*?" I asked, incredulous. "What about—?"

"Hush! I mean it! Your aunt has done a lot for you over the years. She's done a lot for *me*. You are to treat her with respect, do you *understand*?" I was fully awake now and angry. It was Saturday. I didn't have to be at work until ten. And I hadn't eaten any stupid casserole *or* thrown it away! Mother turned to go downstairs.

"I didn't eat your damn casserole," I mumbled under my breath.

"I heard that!" Mother whirled around. "Rosie, surely, to the good Lord in heaven, if I can fight cancer cells you can fight fat ones!"

"Well, if I could take chemo to fight my fat cells, I would! And another thing, I can't stand Aunt Mary!"

"You take that back!" The blue veins in Mother's neck were bulging now.

"No!" I slung the covers off my bed, stormed into the bathroom, and slammed the door.

"Fat cells are a whole lot easier to cure than cancer cells!" Mother shouted. "Self-restraint is the only drug you need!"

"That's not what the Internet says!" I flushed the toilet and turned on the shower to drown Mother out. Finally, she gave up and went downstairs.

While I took a shower, I thought about what Mrs. Wallace would say about our fight. "Why were you and your mother *really* angry with one another? Was your argument about Willy Ray McCutchin's casserole, or was it about something else?" I knew it was probably about something else, but I couldn't put my finger on exactly what it was.

Mother and I didn't talk the rest of the day, which wasn't all that difficult. The salon was like Grand Central Station—people coming and going and talking and laughing. Mildred had added on a bunch of manicures without telling Miss Bertha first, so she was double-booked. Mother had to pitch in and help Mildred with the manicures, which meant Richard had to take over Hilda May Brunson's highlights. Richard doesn't *do* nails.

Because of the ongoing well water problem, Mrs. Brunson

decided to go with red highlights this time instead of blond ones (red doesn't show the green cast the way blond does), but she and Richard couldn't agree on the shade. "You'll look brassy as hell with light copper!" said Richard.

"Well, medium copper makes me look sallow," Mrs. Brunson argued back.

On days when the salon is buzzing like a hive, I am the official mess-picker-upper. I clear away soiled towels and toss them into the wash, empty trash cans, and sweep up hair. When the wash cycle is complete, the towels go into the dryer, then they're folded, and the whole thing starts all over again.

By the end of the day, I was nothing but a giant fur ball. Hair was stuck to my skin, my clothes, my shoes, everything, even my lips! I was fantasizing about a shower and my trusty sweatpants when the bells jangled on the front door again.

"Oh, good God! Don't these morons ever call first?" Richard hissed under his breath.

I glanced toward the door. "Oh, my God," I whispered. "That's *her*."

"Who?" Richard asked too loudly.

"*Shhh!* She's the Bluebird, the mean one I was telling you about."

Richard's jaw dropped. "Well, *I'm* not touching her! Honey, she's got some serious disulfide-bond issues, the little slut! What *does* she condition her hair with? Battery acid? Gasoline?"

"I'm going to the basement," I whispered.

"You will not! It's your shop, not hers!"

"Come get me when she's gone," I said, and slipped down the creaky stairs.

I felt like I'd been in the musty basement for hours. More than likely, Misty was long gone; Richard was probably just paying me back for being such a coward. He hates it when I don't stand up to my tormentors. Usually, I have to remind him that when it came to dealing with his own tormentors, he quit school.

Finally, I trudged up the stairs again. It had been a very long day, after all, and I just wanted to go home. I opened the door and came around the corner. To my horror, Misty was *still there*, although her hair did look better, unfortunately. It shone in the recessed light just above Miss Bertha's head, no brassy roots, no damaged cuticles. Mother had given her highlights, a deep-conditioning treatment—and a trim, no doubt. Misty shifted her weight from one trendy-shoed foot to the other while Miss Bertha totaled her bill. I hid behind the magazine rack and kept very, *very* still.

"Wait! I think I've changed my mind," I heard Misty say. "I need a wax real quick, too."

"Oh, I'm afraid there's no one to do a wax this time a day," said Miss Bertha. Mother darted out of the back room suddenly. She was fumbling through her purse instead of looking where she was going and crashed right into me. A pile of *Soap Opera Digest*s flew off the rack and smacked the floor.

Misty turned around and saw me standing there. I cringed. I waited. I glanced around for Richard, but he'd already gone for the day. His station had been cleared, and his Madonna key ring was missing from the hook. Misty's cold snake eyes rested on me, but her expression never changed. It was as if she'd seen nothing, just the blank wall behind me. I don't know why, but having Misty Winters ignore me made me angrier than if she'd insulted me.

"Well, she did my hair. Can't *she* do the wax, too?" Misty asked, nodding toward Mother.

"Oh, I'm so sorry," said Mother. "Normally, I would, but I'm in a rush today. I have a casserole to make."

"A casserole?" said Misty, irritation seeping into the fake-nice tone of her voice.

Oh, dear God, Mother! Please, whatever you do, don't tell Misty Winters you think I ate your casserole! Mother shot me a look, and I nearly choked on the air I'd inhaled. "It's a long story," said Mother. "Come back Tuesday, and I'll even give you a discount."

"I don't *need* a discount. I need a wax!"

"I'll do it," I interrupted, just to prevent any further casserole talk. Misty looked startled by my offer. "Really, it's no trouble at all. I'd be happy to do it." I gave Misty one of her very own, you-better-watch-out, fake Bluebird smiles.

"Oh, just never mind!" she said. In a flash, she paid her bill and flew out the door.

"Lord, that girl is something," said Miss Bertha. "You know her?"

"Not really," I lied.

"Well, I'm off to Piggly Wiggly," said Mother. "That tuna casserole isn't gonna make itself, and I wanna get it to Willy Ray before suppertime. Can you take Rosie home?" Mother asked this question as if I weren't standing two feet away from her (and as if Miss Bertha didn't take me home every day anyway).

"Gladly," Miss Bertha replied.

"Rosie, I don't know what you've been doing in that basement, but every trash can is overflowing, and dirty towels are everywhere. And you can change out the Barbicide again while you're waiting for the towels to dry. At *every* station," she added on her way out the door.

Angrily, I hauled the trash out back and hurled it into the big Dumpster. Under normal circumstances, Mother wouldn't have made me change the Barbicide twice in one day. I knew she was just trying to get back at me for the casserole. I was beginning to think maybe I *had* eaten the damn thing, like in my sleep or something. Maybe my body was so deprived of real food, it was staging a covert rebellion. For a second I considered telling Mother about the Pounds-Away. At least then she wouldn't waste her money, but I decided against it. She would never understand my inability to eat sensible portions of regular food. I didn't even understand it myself.

I went back inside just in time to see Mr. McCutchin and his two little boys file through the front door. They were a morbid trio, beaten down like characters straight out of *The Grapes of Wrath*. Slump-shouldered and flat-eyed, they stood at the reception desk, their mouths pulled downward as if stitched that way. Mrs. McCutchin's health was taking a toll on everyone, it seemed. Mr. McCutchin was clutching his wife's familiar Tupperware container, the one she used especially for cakes. "I wuz lookin' for Rose Warren. She here?" he asked.

"I'm 'fraid she's gone for the day, Willy Ray. I think she was coming to see you later," said Miss Bertha, confused.

Mr. McCutchin's frown lines deepened to furrows. "Well, I come to thank her for that tuna casserole. It wuz mighty good of her to make it, bein' so sick and all." He held up the cake container. "We brung angel food cake. I cain't bake like Peri. Me and my boys picked this'n up at Pig's. Seemed like a good choice, considerin' what a angel Rose Warren's been to my wife."

"You mean you already got the casserole?" asked Miss Bertha.

"Aw, yeah. Her sister brung it to us las' night. It was kindly late when she come. It 'uz mighty good, though."

Aunt Mary took the casserole! Once again Mother sides with her instead of me! The same old story over and— In the middle of my mental tuna tangent, I noticed the McCutchin boys, *really* noticed them.

The youngest one, a dark-haired, heavy-set child of no more than five or six, put a hand on his father's coat sleeve and held it there awkwardly. The older boy dug his toe into the floor. Their normally close-cropped hair had grown shaggy, and I could tell it hadn't been combed all day. Their usually clean, starched clothes were mismatched and wrinkled, their pant legs streaked with mud, their noses crusty. Mrs. McCutchin would've had another heart attack if she'd seen them out in public that way.

Here I was thinking about revenge and vindication over such trivial matters, and these boys were standing right smack in front of me, two crushing reminders that sometimes sick mothers don't get well. All at once, my throat squeezed up so tight I felt like I was having an allergic reaction.

After they'd gone, I headed for the snack machine. For the price of one, *two* Snickers bars hit the metal tray. *It must be my lucky day*, I thought glumly. Guiltily, I polished off the first candy bar and stuffed the second into my pocket for later. A setback, I told myself. That's all this is.

It was nearly seven o'clock by the time Miss Bertha dropped me off. It would've been even later, except Miss Bertha insisted on taking all the dirty towels home. "I'm not spending what's left of my Saturday night doing laundry at Heavenly Hair when I've got a perfectly good washing machine at home," she said.

The house had that quiet, empty feeling, although Mother's car was in the driveway, so I knew she was home. On the kitchen island was a brand-new Pyrex dish with a freshly made tuna casserole inside. It was still warm and covered in aluminum foil with a note attached.

> *Gone to bed. Heard about the mix-up. Sorry for accusing you.*
> *Mother*

My Saturday night was all planned out suddenly—a warm shower, a heaping plate of dinner, another Snickers bar, and angel food cake. The perfect ending to a stressful day. Besides, I was out of Pounds-Away anyhow. What my body needed was real food.

Just as I stepped in the shower, the phone rang. I considered letting the machine pick up, but I knew it would wake Mother. And it was probably my aunt, the casserole kidnapper. I raced to the phone and snatched it up. "Hell-*ooo*," I said (*not* in a nice way).

"Oh, um . . . did I catch you at a bad time?" he asked. "It's Kyle. We lost."

"Oh . . . um, no! You didn't catch me at a bad time," I lied. I was naked and shivering and dripping water onto my rug. The shower was still running. "Well, that's terrible that you lost. What was the score?"

"You don't wanna know," said Kyle. "There were hardly any Spring Hill kids there. The game was too far away, I guess. That's what hurt us, I think. Not enough fan support."

"That's too bad," I said, wrapping myself in my comforter.

"So I was wonderin' if you'd help me drown my sorrows in a pitcher of Coke and a slice of pizza?"

"You mean tonight? Right *now*?" I asked.

"I know it's short notice, but—"

"No. I mean *yes*! I'd love to," I said.

"I'll pick you up in fifteen minutes," he said, and hung up before I could protest the time frame.

I jumped around my room and did a silent scream. Finally! *Finally!* A real date with Kyle Cox! I raced to the bathroom. "My, aren't you just the picture of loveliness," the wicked mirror hissed at me. "It would take a whole army of Richards, as in Richard *Simmons*, to fix you up!"

"You're just jealous because I have a date and you're stuck hanging around here all night!" I laughed at my corny joke, but the mirror was right. Aside from my usual fat issues, my hair was wet and still unwashed, mascara streaked down my cheeks, and I had Snickers bar smudges in each corner of my mouth, and all of it had to be resolved in *fifteen minutes*!

chapter twenty-one

Beautiful Vision

I basically had two minutes to decide what to wear, so of course I went with black: black denim skirt, black T-shirt, oversized black sweater, black suede clogs, black tights (legs too fat and pasty for au naturel). For a pop of color, I wore silver hoop earrings (I have *got* to go shopping). My hair was still wet from my almost shower, but instead of washing it, I blew it out, rolled it in hot curlers for about sixty seconds, spritzed it with sweet-smelling product, then threw it in a clip—*messy but stylish* was the look I was going for.

Richard would've been proud of my makeup application. I used his D-C-S technique—eyeliner for Drama; a hint of eye shadow and blush for Color; lightly tinted lip gloss for Shine. My nails were a mess, but I filed them down and slapped on some clear polish—more Shine.

With a minute to spare, I went downstairs and stood outside Mother's bedroom door. I debated whether or not to wake her.

For a second, I debated whether or not to even go. *Aren't daughters supposed to tell mothers when they're going out, especially with a boy? Aren't daughters supposed to stay home and take care of cancer-stricken mothers?* I went into the living room and switched on the lamp in the front window, and the porch light, too, just in case Kyle had forgotten which house was mine.

In the dim, cool quiet, I paced back and forth and thought about the reality of the situation. Even if I stayed home, Mother was asleep. And even if she woke up, she would never allow *me* to take care of *her*. I pictured Kyle Cox's Hershey bar brown eyes, his strapping-boy physique, his nanosecond smiles, his unexpected interest in me, and the decision to go was suddenly easy. I left a quick note, just in case Mother woke up, then bolted out the door.

The Suburban's dank odor of mildew and boy sweat had been slightly masked by the wooden evergreen tree hanging from the rearview mirror. Kyle (or someone) had cleared away all the athletic equipment. I could hear it rolling around in the way-back. "Do you like old music?" Kyle asked, fastening his safety belt.

"Sure," I said, settling into the cold seat.

"Good," Kyle said, and grinned. He pulled to the stop sign at the end of my street and shifted the gear to Park. Quickly, he flipped through a suitcase-sized CD catalog and popped in his selection. Aretha Franklin's slinky voice eased out of the speakers.

"Oh, I *love* her," I said.

"You do?" asked Kyle, surprised. I nodded and tried to seem

at ease. "So tell me you like deep-dish instead of thin-crust, too." For a second, I wondered if the pizza comment was directed at my taste buds or my thunder thighs. "Aw, let me guess, you're thin-crust all the way?" he said.

"No. Actually, I like deep-dish the best."

The Pizza Palace is less than a mile from my house. In a matter of seconds, Kyle was pulling into the lot and looking for a place to park. Quickly, I scanned the row of cars. It was Saturday night, and Pizza Palace was a popular place with the Spring Hill High School crowd. I feared Misty Winters and her crew might show up. "So do you think a lot of your friends will be here?" I asked. I tried to sound casual, but my heart was beating wildly.

"Not likely. There's a big keg party out on Glen Mill Road." Kyle looked at the clock on his dashboard. "My guess is those Bluebirds are downing wine coolers and slinging their hair around by now." I wondered how Kyle had read my mind. I had inquired about *his* friends, not the Bluebirds, yet somehow he'd known what I was thinking. My heart slowed a little, and I took a deep breath and followed Kyle inside.

After our Pizza Palace meal of fully loaded, deep-dish pizza and a pitcher of *Diet* Coke (my idea, not Kyle's), Kyle seemed at a loss for what to do next. We drove all over Spring Hill while I listened to Kyle talk about basketball and football. He rehashed the Raiders' losing game in the play-offs. He discussed the specifics of last fall's homecoming game. Then he explained the Titans' practice drills. Just when I thought he'd exhausted the sports topic, he launched into his *brothers'* basketball and football programs. Finally, Kyle said, "You wanna go to my favorite place?"

"Not the football stadium," I said, without thinking. A concerned look flitted across Kyle's face. His cheeks turned pink.

"I talk too much about sports. I know. It's a habit. Mama says no girl will—" Kyle stopped himself.

"Will what?" I asked.

Kyle sighed. "Mama says no girl will ever want to go anywhere with me unless I learn the art of conversation." Kyle stopped at a red light and stared at me. The light turned green, but he didn't go. "I've seen your name on the gold honor roll. I bet you've made straight A's your whole life," he said. His mother had also probably told him the best way to steer a conversation in the right direction is to talk about the other person.

I shrugged and nodded. I *had* made excellent grades my whole life, but there was no point in bragging about it. "You must make good grades, too," I said, "or you would never have gotten into Mrs. Edinburgh's honors class. Why'd you drop that class anyway?" The light turned yellow, then red again.

"Mrs. Edinburgh's too hard," said Kyle, "and if I fail a class, I don't get to play sports, and if I don't play sports, I *die*."

"As in an enchanted curse?" I asked.

"Pretty much." Kyle flicked on his blinker and turned into the Exxon station. "This is it," he said.

"This is what?"

"This is my favorite place."

"The *gas station* is your favorite place?"

"No, the car wash," said Kyle, as if it were the most normal favorite place in the world. He looped around to the wide door, fed the code box some quarters, and eased the Suburban forward until a red light flashed Stop. "Let's listen to Van Morrison," he yelled over the whirling brushes and water jets. Kyle inserted a new CD, pushed the button to song number four, then reached for my hand.

My stomach clenched up as if I'd just bungee-jumped off the Duck River Bridge. My hand began to sweat and tingle. SPRING HILL HIGH SCHOOL FAT GIRL HAS STROKE ON FIRST EVER DATE! When the song and the car wash ended at precisely the same time, Kyle let go of my sweaty, tingling hand and lowered the volume. "Why is this your favorite place?" I asked.

"When I was little, me and my dad used to come here every Saturday, even if it rained. It was the only thing we ever did together—without my brothers taggin' along. It's like you're suspended in some other reality when you're in here. It's all noisy and quiet at the same time. A paradox." He grinned.

For the first time all night, our eyes met, and neither one of us looked away. I got the strangest feeling all at once. It was almost like Kyle and I didn't need to *get* to know one another because we already did. "You keep using big words like *paradox* and Mrs. Edinburgh will drag you back to honors English," I said, just to break the awkward silence.

"I might go willingly if I get to sit next to you," Kyle replied without missing a beat. There wasn't a hint of disgust or disappointment behind his eyes; Kyle Cox looked at me the way I *longed* to look at myself.

We headed toward Riverside again, and for exactly three minutes, the two of us sat parked in front of my house. I glanced at the windows and wondered if Mother had even missed me. Probably not, considering how hard she'd worked all day. It was doubtful she'd even rolled over. I also wondered if Kyle might kiss me good night.

"So do you have plans next weekend?" he asked.

"No," I said quickly.

"I was thinking it could . . . you know, be fun to go to the Sundown Drive-in Saturday night. Wanna come?"

"Sure," I replied, worrying only slightly about who would be there. Bluebirds for sure.

"Seven okay?" I nodded and tried to position myself for the kiss just in case it came.

"Um, sorry to say this, but . . . um . . . I have a curfew," said Kyle. "I only have seventeen minutes to get home." The clock on the dashboard glared 11:43.

"Oh, *God!*" Sorry!" I swung open the squeaky door and hopped down to the curb.

"*I'm* the one who's sorry," said Kyle. "I'd stay out later, but Mama would have a SWAT team looking for us, and all those helicopters might disturb your neighbors."

Inside, I switched off all the lights, grabbed a bottled water from the fridge (the tuna casserole and angel food cake and extra Snickers bar weren't even slightly tempting now), and climbed the stairs to my bedroom. The smell of perfume and Dove soap with a hint of nail polish still lingered in the air, and I breathed it in, wondering if *this* was how I'd smelled to Kyle.

Maybe he was driving home right this second, listening to song number four on the Van Morrison CD again, and thinking how his car still carried the scent of Rosemary Goode (which is a whole lot better than old sweat and mildewed athletic equipment, mind you). Maybe he was thinking about how much fun we'd had or how he couldn't wait to see me in study hall on Monday or that next Saturday night seemed a long, *long* way off.

I logged on to my computer, and in seconds found the Van Morrison lyrics. *Beautiful vision—stay with me all of the time.* . . .

chapter twenty-two

Thank You

Just a few minutes before ten, I arrived at the shop. Miss Bertha dropped me off at the front door, then drove around back to park. I hadn't been at work two seconds when helmet-haired Crystal Lamay came pressing through the front door in a cloud of thick, sweet perfume.

"Hi, sugar!" she said, as if we were long lost friends. In fact, we hardly know each other. Crystal is *not* a client of Mother's. She prefers to save money and do her own hair, a fact she announces loudly every time she enters the salon. Of course, she doesn't need to announce this fact; her whole head screams "fine-tooth comb and Aqua Net." "Hey Rich*aaard*!" she called across the salon. Richard gave her a hi-there-now-go-away nod and turned his back toward her. "Oh, he's just always so busy, ain't he?" said Crystal, clearly dazzled by Richard's aloofness. "Didn't he train in New York or something?"

"Or something," I said. Just then Mother stuffed Ida Lee Harris under the dryer and headed our way.

"What can I do for you, Crystal?" asked Mother. She was looking at Crystal's giant, plastic hairdo the way a dentist might eye rotten teeth. She was just dying to get her hands on it, I could tell.

"Now, honey, you just mize well take your eyes off my hair. I do it all myself," she said, and glanced around to see if anyone had overheard. Apparently, no one had. "Well, anyways, I'm here about the pageant. It's that time a year again. The Miss Fireworks pageant'll be here before we can say jackrabbit." *Jackrabbit*, I mumbled in my brain. "I'm shore hoping you'll recommend all your teenagers apply. The pretty ones, of course," she whispered to Mother, and glanced sideways at me. "The Jaycees is sponsorin' it, as they do ever year, and the winner will receive a condo down in Gulf Shores and all kinds of local prizes, donated by fine merchants like yourself." Clearly, Crystal was giving her spiel now.

"The winner gets a free condo at the beach? Last year all she got was a color television," I pointed out.

"No, sil*ly*," said Crystal. "Just a weekend is all. Now, Rose Warren, we could use a donation from you, too. Like maybe a full-day spa treatment and a complete makeover."

"Why would she need a makeover?" I interrupted. "I mean, she did just win a beauty pageant, after all." Crystal rolled her eyes.

"Rosie, the buzzer went off on the dryer again," said Mother, trying to get rid of me.

I left Crystal to her soliciting and went to get the towels. I knew no matter how many smart-aleck remarks I hurled, Mother would still give Crystal a generous donation in spite of what happened last year. "You give to the community and the community gives to you," Mother always said, which was the case for most contributions Mother made, but not this one. Last year, Mother donated a $300 gift card to the winner, and Crystal never even bothered to send a thank-you note, not to mention the fact that Miss Fireworks sold her gift card for $150 at a yard sale. And when the retired school bus driver showed up to redeem her prize, Mother actually honored it!

Normally on an insanely busy day, which pretty much describes every Saturday, I offer to stay late and help. Mother usually turns me down, but at least I offer. Today, I didn't even offer. I didn't want to stay. For once, I had better things to do. It was the first official day of spring and crazy warm—seventy-six degrees! Plus, I had my date with Kyle Cox to get ready for. It would take hours just to decide which black outfit to wear.

I climbed the stairs to my room and glanced at the treadmill. An urgent, pressing feeling clumped up in my chest. I needed to run, to sweat, to burn off more calories, but I was so very tempted to do other things—change the filter in the coffee pot, clean the lint screen on the dryer, put a new bleach tablet in the toilet tank. Kay-Kay Reese jogged through my brain and smiled and waved. *Hi, Rosie! We should do this together sometime!* I heard her say. I was half tempted to call her up, but then I pictured her toned, tight, stretch-markless body in athletic shorts and a sports bra. The image of us running side by side was too humiliating.

It was too hot for sweatpants, so I rummaged through my closet until I found a large plastic box labeled Summer Clothes. Inside were two pairs of black shorts and a lime green tube top. The shorts were too loose, and the tube top was, well . . . a tube top. Wearing my lovely little ensemble, I climbed aboard the treadmill, set the Projected Workout Time for one hour, then switched it on. I vowed not to look at the angry little calorie counter or its matching clock. I threw a towel over the numbers, locked my eyes on the blue wall in front of me, and ran.

My thighs jiggled, my butt jiggled, my boobs bounced all around (okay, a tube top is probably not the best choice for high-impact exercise), and I could hear the wicked mirror laughing hysterically all the way from my bathroom. "Shut up!" I yelled. My shins ached, my feet felt as if they'd gone to sleep, my thighs protested, and my lungs were positively asthmatic.

After what seemed an eternity, I peeked under the towel—ten minutes, forty-eight seconds. "Oh, my God! That's *all*?" I threw the towel over the screen again and vowed not to look at it until the timer went off. At 15:46, I peeked, then changed my Projected Workout Time from one hour to thirty minutes. At 17:51, I changed my workout time to twenty minutes. At 19:46 I climbed off. Those last fourteen seconds might possibly have killed me.

Kyle picked me up promptly at seven. This time he actually met Mother briefly, and I could tell by the expression on her face she was surprised by his good looks. She was also self-conscious. She wasn't wearing her wig, and she kept pulling her blue cap down over her ears.

"Your mother has cancer, right?" Kyle asked when we got to the car.

"Hodgkin's disease," I corrected him. "It's cancer, but a different kind. *Very* curable. She's gonna be fine," I said, as if Mother's illness were no big deal (perhaps Mother isn't the only one trying to make everything seem perfect).

Kyle looked at me. "I hope so," he said, turning the ignition. The doubt in his voice annoyed me. "Hey, do you mind if I listen to the end of a game real quick?" he asked. Before I even had a chance to respond, he'd raised the volume. The game crackled noisily over the AM station.

"Actually, I *do* mind," I replied. Kyle stared at me.

"I swear it's almost over," he pleaded.

"I'm kidding."

Kyle grinned and turned the Suburban toward the Sundown Drive-in. I settled myself in the seat beside him and watched as he shouted and pounded the dashboard every time his team scored or didn't. I tried to think of something in my own life that generated such enthusiasm, but all I could come up with was Kyle himself or the baked goods aisle at Piggly Wiggly.

The Sundown was like some scene from *Ferris Bueller's Day Off* or *Animal House*—wild teenagers, loud music, steamed-up car windows. A timid little thrill rippled through my stomach. *Escape from Alcatraz*, an ancient movie starring Clint Eastwood, was the featured film.

"I'm going to the concession stand. Wanna come?" asked Kyle.

"Oh, no, thanks," I replied, for various reasons. Aside from the usual food temptations, I dreaded walking through the Sundown parking lot. Misty Winters and the other Bluebirds were surely lurking. "Can I bring you anything?" he tried. I smiled and shook my head.

It was twenty minutes before Kyle made it back with a jumbo-sized bucket of popcorn and two bags of peanut M&M's. He'd stuffed two straws in his super-sized Coke, but I resisted and chewed my now-stale stick of sugarless gum.

"Do you know where the bathroom is?" I asked finally. Ever since we'd arrived, I'd been denying my full bladder.

"Over there," said Kyle, pointing to a mile-long string of females. "Some girls just go back there, though. See that row of pine trees?"

I laughed. "I don't think so."

The moon was full, so there'd be no hiding in the shadows. Instantly, I spotted familiar faces from school—Margaret Abernathy, head cheerleader; Peggy Wells, homecoming queen; Rolanda Davidson, student council president. I actually *heard* Misty Winters before I saw her. She and Tara Waters were toward the front of the bathroom line, laughing their highlighted heads off—thanks to Mother, Misty's highlights were perfect. Luckily, there were at least ten girls in between us. I turned my back to them and prayed they wouldn't notice me (there *are* advantages to an all-black wardrobe).

Tara and Misty's cackling grew louder. The queue inched closer. Surreptitiously, I tried to see what they were laughing at. Suddenly, I realized it wasn't a *what* but *who*. Pretty, tiny Kay-Kay Reese sat slumped against the cement block building, her stylish white capris and bright blue halter top streaked with something pink. Kay-Kay was drunk. Falling-down, puke-your-guts-up drunk.

If I stepped out of line and tried to help her, Tara and Misty would surely notice me. In fact, they were sure to do more than just notice me. Already I could feel their sharp tongues sinking into my flesh, but in the scheme of things, what was one more Bluebird insult? I walked over and stooped down to Kay-Kay's level. "You all right?" I whispered.

"No," Kay-Kay groaned. Her breath was a sweet yet sour combination of alcohol and vomit. "I think I might be sick again."

"Well, look who it is! Hey, Artichoke!" Misty yelled at my back. "Concession stand's the other way!" I didn't bother acknowledging her. I pulled Kay-Kay to her feet and pointed her in the direction of the pine trees. "You better be careful, Kay-Kay!" Misty shouted after us. "Old Arti might get you in those pines and *eat* you for dinner!"

Carefully, I eased Kay-Kay onto the soft brown needles. Moonlight filtered through the trees, making it easy for us to see each other. "How much did you drink?" I asked, squatting down beside her.

"Three wine coolers," she replied. "Oh, *God.* I think I'm . . . I think—" Quickly, Kay-Kay turned away from me. Vile gag, scary splatter, grotesque belch. I fumbled through my purse for some tissues and tried not to gag.

"Are you here with your boyfriend?" I asked when she'd finished.

"Soon-to-be *ex*-boyfriend," Kay-Kay whimpered, and wiped her mouth. "He's so mad. . . ."

"Logan?"

Kay-Kay nodded. "He said if I puked in his car one more time—" Kay-Kay gagged, but this time it was only a dry heave. "One more time, and he'd break up."

"How many times have you puked in his car already?" I asked.

Kay-Kay's face crumpled again, and fresh tears slid down her mascara-streaked cheeks. "Three times since I got shunned." Kay-Kay looked up at me. Even a drunken mess, she was still beautiful. "They're so mean," she whispered. I nodded. I knew *firsthand* just how mean. "Mean and *stupid*," said Kay-Kay childishly.

"And jealous," I added.

"Jealous?" asked Kay-Kay.

"Who *wouldn't* be jealous of you? You're pretty much perfect as far as I can see—well, *most* of the time anyway." Kay-Kay smiled slightly. "Do you think you can walk back to the car?"

She nodded. "I have to pee first, though."

"Me, too," I said. The two of us squatted side by side, our behinds undoubtedly resembling a Jenny Craig Before and After.

The Bluebirds must've moved their party from the bathroom to the car. By the time Kay-Kay and I were back at Logan's car, there wasn't any heckling. Logan didn't even acknowledge his girlfriend's return. He just stared straight ahead, clenching and unclenching his jaw. "Good luck," I whispered. The second I closed the door, I could hear the two of them arguing through the thick, closed windows.

After the movie, Kyle drove through the Maury County Park and stopped at the Kiwanis shelter. He shoved an old Police CD into the player and cracked his knuckles. "Good for gripping the ball," he laughed. *How about gripping me,* I thought, but didn't say. For a while, we sat in silence and listened to Sting's hypnotic voice. "So what do you wanna be when you grow up?" asked Kyle. It was a very out-of-the-blue sort of question, and it caught me off guard.

"A size two," I replied, without thinking.

"No, seriously," said Kyle, ignoring my idiotic response. "I worry about this sort of thing."

"You worry about what I'm gonna be?" I asked.

"Well, no, but I like to ask smart people this question. I figure the smarter the people are, the more likely they are to have a plan. My only plan is to play football."

"So you want to be a pro?" I asked.

"It's not the most realistic goal in the world," he pointed out.

I debated on whether or not to say what was on the tip of my tongue. Finally, I just said it. "My being a size two isn't very realistic either," I replied. For some odd reason, I needed to put the whole fat girl issue out there. I needed to see how Kyle would respond.

"I'm not sure I'd like pro ball even if I could do it, you know? All that time on the road and the pressure. The injuries. Sometimes I think I won't last past college in the sport. What makes you want to be a size two?" he asked.

My heart stopped midbeat. I froze. My tongue stalled out, and I couldn't think of one single smart-ass thing to say. Kyle was giving me that look again, the one that said he already knew my answer, the one that told me he wasn't the slightest bit afraid of the topic—*if* I wanted to discuss it. I inhaled his inviting smell of Dentyne breath and spicy grocery-store-brand shampoo (much too harsh for his thick shiny curls, in my opinion). Without warning, I leaned in close and kissed him. It was part Enormous Strapping Jock Boy attraction; it was also part thank you.

chapter twenty-three

A Giant Leap

I have the worst gas ever—a known Pounds-Away side effect. There should be a warning on the label: May cause uncontrollable flatulence. At least I can jog on my treadmill and fart my brains out—there's no one around to hear. I can't very well have an active social life with chronic gas and painful bloating, which is why I've given serious thought to going off Pounds-Away completely and for good, but I'm just too scared.

First of all, I can't trust myself with round-the-clock, real food just yet, not when I'm making such progress. And, second, I *so* don't want to be fat this summer. What if Kyle is still asking me out then—in the season of shorts and *bathing suits*? No, I can't go off Pounds-Away, not now.

Ever since my date with Kyle, I've been acting like one of those starry-eyed teenagers you see in the movies. I sing to myself for no reason. I actually cleaned up my room without Mother nagging me. I was nice to Aunt Mary when she called. *And* I have a giant test in Mr. Sparks's history class tomorrow that I haven't bothered to study for (okay, so all the Kyle side effects aren't positive), but it's difficult to study for history when you're busy trying to make it: FAT GIRL LANDS JOCK BOY—ONE SMALL STEP FOR WOMAN, ONE GIANT LEAP FOR WOMANKIND!

I know myself, though. In the end, I'll stay up till all hours studying because there is no way I'll give Fat-Person Hater, Mr. Sparks, the satisfaction of seeing me get anything less than an A. Mrs. Wallace seems to think one of the reasons I'm obsessed with getting good grades is to defy the fat-girl stereotype—society's false perception that we're all lazy or sloppy or stupid.

In spite of my recent good mood, everything hasn't been completely rosy since Saturday night. I had lunch with Kay-Kay today—lunch for me included bottled water and sugarless gum (I'd already consumed my Pounds-Away earlier that morning, *in a restroom stall*). I so wanted to tell her about kissing Kyle. I so wanted to tell anybody who would listen to me for five seconds, but Kay-Kay was way too depressed about her own love life for me to launch into the details of my romantic triumph.

"Logan broke up with me yesterday, *officially*," Kay-Kay announced the minute we sat down. Her blue eyes filled with tears, and one spilled down her nose and plopped into her salad.

"What happened?" I asked, handing her an unused napkin.

"He agreed to give me one more chance, but then yesterday"—Kay-Kay wiped her eyes again—"yesterday, I went to his mother's for Sunday brunch. I was so hungover I could barely eat anything, but then I had some grits. Next thing I knew I was barfing in Mrs. Clark's powder room."

"And Logan broke up with you?" I asked. Kay-Kay nodded and fanned away more tears. As if on cue, Misty and Tara swooped right over.

"We thought you might need this," said Tara, shoving a pamphlet on teen alcoholism into Kay-Kay's hand.

"And we have big news," said Misty. "Logan already has a date with"—she paused for effect—"Marta Pitts." Kay-Kay's mouth fell open, and she stared at them. Marta Pitts, a.k.a. Marta Tits. The girl has the most sought-after breasts at Spring Hill High School. Just when I thought Tara and Misty had finished their torture, they turned to me. Misty narrowed her eyes. "Everyone knows you're just Kyle Cox's fat screw. Boys like him *never* date girls like you," she said, her upper lip curling slightly to express her utter disgust of me.

Before I could think of some equally awful thing to say back, the bell sounded, and Misty and Tara slithered off like a pair of eels. I dumped the multiple gum wrappers off my tray, forced a smile at the cafeteria lady, and followed Kay-Kay out of the lunchroom. "See you later, Kay-Kay," I said, trying to act like none of it was any big deal.

"Yeah. Okay," she replied, and drifted off toward her class like a zombie.

I pushed through the study hall door, and Kyle and I instantly locked eyes. My stomach rolled (from nerves, not gas), and I smiled at him and waved. He seemed genuinely glad to see me, but I couldn't let go of Misty's words. I thought back to our Saturday night kiss and wondered if the Bluebirds knew something I didn't.

I opened my notebook, but I couldn't bring myself to work on anything. A bird was squawking in my head. *Fat screw! Fat screw!* it cawed. I glanced up at Ronnie Derryberry, and for once he wasn't asleep. In fact, he was looking straight at me. Quickly, he scribbled something on a scrap of paper and passed me the note. *You lost weight*, it read. I smiled at him, and he smiled back, then he plopped his head on his books and went to sleep like always.

chapter twenty-four

Fat Birthday

Rosie, I can't take this another second!" Kay-Kay announced at lunch. "I have *got* to start exercising in the morning." She glanced at my tray. "And you've got to start eating better. What's with the gum and water for lunch?" she asked.

"Oh, I had something healthy earlier," I lied. "I'm just not much of a lunch person. So what were you saying about the mornings?" I asked, trying to get her back on safer subjects.

"Well, I was thinking that if I'm gonna have to look at Logan and Marta every day, I might as well have some endorphins running through my system to ease the pain a little. A morning workout might be just the thing."

"But I thought you needed to 'decompress' (Kay-Kay's word, not mine) after school?"

"Oh, I can always go to Harvey's Gym in the afternoons—*if* I don't have cheerleading, that is. I'd love for you to run with me,

Rosie." Kay-Kay and I had discussed this earlier in the week, but I insisted it wasn't a good idea. Reason one (which I told Kay-Kay): I can't run three miles (Kay-Kay says anything under three miles isn't worth the effort). Reason two (which I did *not* tell Kay-Kay): Sometimes, I fart when I run.

"It's not like we'd have to stay stuck together like conjoined twins or something. If you need to slow down, you can. Come on, Rosie, it's only three miles. It'll be fun," she pleaded.

"Fun?"

"Look, I'm gonna be waiting for you at Riverside Elementary tomorrow morning at quarter of six. If you come, great. If not, I reckon I'll go all by myself." Kay-Kay snapped a raw carrot in half with her perfect white teeth and smiled. We both knew she had me, since there was no way I'd stand her up.

At five-thirty my alarm went off. Even Mother wasn't up yet. "Oh, God." I groaned and stuffed my head under a pillow. There wasn't much choice, so I dragged myself out of bed, brushed my teeth, pulled my hair back in a ponytail, threw on sweats (I wasn't about to run in black shorts and a tube top), and headed toward my old elementary school. Kay-Kay was already there, of course. Sweat poured down the sides of her face and glistened on her small chest.

"You came!" she cheered, holding up her hand to slap me a high-five.

I tried to force a smile. "I sure did," I replied. I was dying to say something negative and sarcastic, but Kay-Kay was so earnest in her enthusiasm, I held back. "Did you already run or something?" I asked.

"Yeah, just a couple of miles," Kay-Kay confessed.

"So we only have to run one?"

"In your dreams! I'm just good and warmed up now! Come on, let's go!"

Thanks to my recent treadmill workouts, I managed to keep up with her that first mile or so (I also managed not to fart), but as we climbed the steep hill toward the center of town, I knew I had to slow down—or die. "I've got to stop," I managed to gasp.

"Don't *stop*," Kay-Kay warned. "You'll trash your heart rate. You at least have to keep walking." I nodded. "I'll meet you at the courthouse," said Kay-Kay. I watched as she tripled her speed and tackled the hill like a runaway gazelle. Her pace and grace were stunning. In regular school clothes, Kay-Kay just looks skinny and cute and harmless, but in her running shorts, she's all kick-ass, competitive jock girl.

In one way, I think Kay-Kay's good health habits (other than puking up wine coolers at the Sundown) might rub off on me. In another, I think trying to keep up with her might send me crashing through the glass of a snack machine.

Prying myself out of bed the second morning was even harder. For one thing, my legs felt like cinder blocks. Besides that, it was raining—one of those light, peaceful spring rains that makes you want to snuggle under the covers and drift off to sleep again. My window was cracked open just a little, and the drops sounded like a lullaby. It was also my birthday, which, appropriately enough, happens to fall on April Fools' Day. It was the birthday part that actually got me moving, though. I wanted to start the day feeling good about myself, and even though I'm miserable *while running*, I feel positively great about myself when it's over.

On the Spring Hill High School Morning News Feed—which is actually just a gimmicky way of making the morning announcements sound even remotely interesting—the senior class vice president reads a list of birthdays. Usually I think this is annoying, but not today, as my name was the only one on the list.

When I came out of homeroom, Kyle was waiting for me. "Hey," he said. "Happy birthday."

"Hey!" I replied. My voice came out too high-pitched, but Kyle didn't seem to notice. He handed me a piece of notebook paper folded to resemble a card.

"I doubt Hallmark'll be calling me with a job offer anytime soon, but it was the best I could do on such short notice." On the front he'd drawn a big smiley face. Inside, he'd chicken-scratched *Happy Birthday, Rosie.*

"It's the thought that counts. Thank you." I grinned up at him. His brown eyes were shining. His smile was aimed in my direction. I could smell his spicy, cheap shampoo, which I decided I'd have to start using myself just to keep his scent with me always. Suddenly, I felt the overwhelming need to pinch myself. *Was this really happening? Was I standing in the hallway on my sixteenth birthday talking to Enormous Strapping Jock Boy on the very same day I'd gone running with the beautiful, somewhat famous (at least in Spring Hill, Tennessee) Kay-Kay Reese?*

At lunch, Kay-Kay unwrapped a protein bar and stuck a candle in it. Since open flames result in automatic suspension, I blew out a pretend candle but made a real wish: *Please let my sixteenth birthday be my last fat birthday.* I took a bite of the gooey, tasteless protein stick and remembered the deliciously sinful cakes Mrs. McCutchin used to make for me every year. I tossed in two more wishes—one for Mother and the other for Mrs. McCutchin. I felt a little guilty I hadn't thought of them first.

I was all set to go into the shop, but Mother insisted I take the afternoon off, and said she'd pay me for my hours anyway as a little birthday bonus. The old Rosemary would've been delighted at her generous offer. I would've come home for a double feature: *Dr. Phil* and an entire can of Pringles; *Oprah* and a bag of peanut butter cups. The new Rosemary was different, or was at least trying to be.

To keep myself occupied and away from victuals, I climbed on the treadmill and blasted Sheryl Crow. Before I knew it, I'd worked out twice in one day—first with Kay-Kay at five forty-five, and once by myself. I peeled off my sweaty clothes and stepped on the scale—169 pounds—that's twenty-one pounds *gone* (thirty-four, if I count that brief but oh-so-frightening 203 hippo weight around Christmas). Looking backward felt incredible. I tried not to think about forward. I knew in no time I could be right back where I'd started if I wasn't careful.

Just as I was about to step in the shower, the doorbell rang. I threw on my bathrobe and tiptoed downstairs. Through the front window, I saw Kyle's Suburban. "Oh, my God!" I tore through the house and raced up the stairs. Frantically, I flung off my bathrobe. I started to put on my slimy workout clothes again. Ick. I threw open the closet door. Nothing but black. I glanced at my face in the mirror. Sweaty. Flushed. I sniffed my pits. Not bad, although a bit on the stubbly side. The doorbell rang a second and third time. I grabbed my bathrobe again and flew down the stairs. Just to be safe, I dashed into Mother's bathroom and spritzed some perfume. I took a deep breath, forced a smile, and opened the front door. No Kyle. No Suburban by the curb either, just a bouquet of pale pink lilacs and a note:

Happy 16th birthday!

Love,

Kyle

I sat on the cool porch step and sniffed the pale pink flowers. "Thank you," I whispered to the sky, inhaling their sweet smell. "Thank you," I said again, analyzing Kyle's use of the word *love*. Did he mean *love*, as in *I love you, Rosie*? Or, did he mean *love*, as in that's just what you write at the end of a birthday note?

I gave Kyle time to get home, then I dialed his number. "Thanks for the flowers," I said the minute he answered. I tried to keep my voice steady and calm. I didn't want to reveal the giddy, silly girl I had recently become. Truthfully, I was practically high on the whole Kyle Cox experience.

"Hey, Rosie," said Kyle. "Were the flowers okay? I was afraid they'd wilt before you got home," he said.

"Actually, I *was* home. I was in the shower," I replied. This was only a slight fabrication, as I wasn't about to tell Kyle I was running around the house naked when he rang the doorbell. "The flowers are perfect. My entire bedroom smells like spring," I went on.

"Good," said Kyle. "Would you like to do something tonight? I know . . . um . . . I should've asked you earlier. It's just with baseball and everything . . ."

"I'd love to," I said, completely ignoring the fact that Mother was taking me to the Lamplighter Inn for dinner.

"It's a school night," said Kyle. "I'll have to be home by ten."

"Oh, that's okay. I have to be home by ten on school nights, too," I lied (as if I ever actually go anywhere on a school night). The second I hung up, guilt overwhelmed me. *What was I thinking, telling Kyle I could go out with him?*

"Which do you want first?" asked Mother, stifling a cough. She was standing at the top of my bedroom stairs, home from work an hour early. In one hand, she had a small velvet box. In the other, she held a brochure on safe teen drivers.

"The box," I replied. Mother watched and smiled while I untied the curly pink ribbons and pried open the lid. "Oh, my God!" I gasped. "They're beautiful. Thank you! Oh, thank you!" I hugged Mother tightly. Too tightly, apparently. Her small, bony shoulders made a kind of crunching sound, and she wriggled out of my embrace. "Did I hurt you?" I asked.

"No," said Mother. "My allergies are just acting up."

"Allergies?" I asked.

"My lungs are a little tight today. Now put your earrings on. I want to see what they look like," she insisted. Obediently, I took out my silver hoops and inserted the small diamond studs. "Perfect," said Mother, standing back to admire them. "They look so pretty against your gorgeous dark hair." Mother tugged her cap down over her ears. "I'm proud of you," she said suddenly. "I know you're trying hard, Rosie. It's working, too."

I was just about to say thank you and nudge Mother out of my bedroom (so I could call Kyle to cancel our date) when Mother had a coughing fit. A *real* fit. The kind that goes on and on and on. By the time it was over, she could barely talk. I ran to the bathroom to get her a glass of water and watched while she sipped it slowly.

"Mother, that's not allergies," I said. "Something's wrong. Have you called your doctor?"

"Oh, Rosie. I just don't think I can go out tonight," said Mother when she was finally able to speak again. "I'm so sorry to do this, especially on your birthday."

"That's okay," I said. "Really. Actually, I . . . well, Kyle was hoping maybe I could go out with him tonight."

"But what about your Aunt Mary?"

"Aunt Mary?"

"She was supposed to come with us tonight. You can't cancel on her. She was looking forward to it."

"It's *my* birthday, not Aunt Mary's," I pointed out. "And I want to go with Kyle. You didn't say anything about Aunt Mary coming with us anyway. Why does she always have to come?"

"Because she's the only family we've got!" Mother snapped. Mother gave me her you're-the-world's-most-disappointing-ungrateful-daughter look and headed back downstairs. I felt guilty, but not guilty enough to spend my sixteenth birthday with my nosy, meddlesome, know-it-all aunt.

chapter twenty-five

The Story of My Life

Y

ou look great," Kyle said, smiling, when I climbed into his car. I was wearing a new black sweater and charcoal gray skirt sent all the way from Florida (courtesy of Grandma Georgia). The outfit was very flattering with my black boots. I had my new diamond studs in, too. "Is a burger okay with you?" asked Kyle.

"Sure," I lied. I'd had so little real food lately that the thought of a greasy hamburger made my already nervous insides churn. Kyle pushed in a Rolling Stones CD, and I tried to relax in the seat beside him. I didn't feel much like talking. The music was too loud, and I couldn't get Mother off my mind. I kept picturing her pale face, hearing her alarming cough.

"Are you all right?" Kyle asked. Already he was pulling into Frankie's Carhop, a retro drive-in restaurant that'd just opened downtown. The parking lot was packed.

"Oh, I'm fine," I lied again.

"It's crowded tonight," said Kyle. He pulled into a tight space and lowered the volume. Waitresses in colorful 1950s outfits zipped around on Rollerblades carrying trays overloaded with food and drink.

"This is Tina," the box just outside the car window squawked. "What'll it be?" Kyle hadn't even switched off the ignition yet.

"Do you know what you want?" he whispered. I shook my head and nudged him to order first. "I'll have a bacon-chili cheese-burger, extra-large fries, and a banana cream shake and a Coke," Kyle shouted toward the tiny microphone.

"Pepsi is all we got," Tina grumbled, "and you don't have to yell so loud. I ain't deaf."

"Pepsi's fine," said Kyle. "Sorry about the yelling."

I leaned across Kyle. "I'll have a salad with low-cal Italian dressing and a *Diet* Pepsi," I said.

"We ain't got nothing green tonight!" Tina snapped. "The truck didn't come," she added.

"Fine. I'll take a plain, *brown* hamburger," I shouted, "and a *brown* Diet Pepsi."

Kyle rolled up the window and burst out laughing. "Tina's gonna spit in your food for sure now," he teased.

"And I'll wring her neck like a Sunday chicken!" I snapped, sounding like Grandma Georgia. Kyle's eyes grew wide. "Sorry, I just hate poor service. There's no excuse for talking to us that way. If this were my business, I'd fire her on the spot!"

"Spoken like the Donald himself," Kyle grinned. I punched him lightly on the arm. "So did you have a good birthday?" he asked.

"My mother gave me these," I said, pulling my hair back to show off my new earrings.

"Nice," said Kyle. "How is your mother anyway?" His cheerful face clouded somewhat.

Fine was on the tip of my tongue, but I resisted. "I was supposed to go to dinner with her tonight, but she wasn't feeling well. She has this terrible cough. She had it when she first got sick, but then it went away for a while. Now it's back again. I'm not sure what it means. Could just be a cold. Chemo and cancer really lower a person's immune system."

We were silent for a while. Finally, Kyle said, "I've never been through anything like that. I bet it's tough." He placed his hand over my own. I nodded and stared at my lap. It *was* tough. And *scary*. And *very* lonely. And it was definitely anything, *anything*, but fine.

The food came, and the hamburger was a mixture of grease and gristle. With each bite, my stomach twisted into a tighter knot. Morbid thoughts tumbled through my head like gymnasts. *What if this wasn't my last fat birthday? What if it turned out to be my last birthday with Mother?* "I have to go to the girls' room," I announced suddenly, feeling as if I'd been struck with amoebic dysentery. "I'll be back in a minute."

"Okay." Kyle nodded and slurped his banana cream shake.

Quickly, I crossed the parking lot and tried not to look like someone from a you-never-know-where-you'll-be-when-diarrhea-strikes commercial. I banged into the foul-smelling restroom (clearly *I* wasn't the only one with intestinal issues) and let nature do its thing. Someone with chipped pink toenail polish and ragged Birkenstocks occupied the stall next to mine. I finished before Birkenstocks and hurried out to the sink to avoid embarrassing public-restroom eye contact.

But before I could escape, Birkenstocks was right beside me. "Don't I know you?" the woman asked suddenly. "Heavenly Hair," she said. "That's where I've seen you. Oh, these burgers just tear my stomach up. Spastic colon," she confessed. To my horror, I recognized her, too. Kyle Cox's mother! "Don't you dare tell Rose Warren you saw me," she went on. "I promised I'd get back for regular touch-ups and a trim. Another New Year's resolution down the toilet," said Mrs. Cox, laughing at her pun.

Her khaki trousers were baggy, and the white oxford button-down she wore looked like something she'd swiped from her husband's closet (or perhaps her large son's). She wasn't bad-looking. In spite of her wide, rumpled appearance, she was pleasantly efficient and sturdy in an earthy sort of way. "How is Rose Warren doing?" asked Mrs. Cox.

"She's doing well," I lied. Mrs. Cox had no idea I was Rose Warren's daughter (that day at the salon I'd avoided introductions). Obviously, she didn't realize I was her son's date either. I tossed a paper towel into the trash and inched toward the door. "Well, it was nice seeing you again," I said politely and bolted. We could meet each other officially another day, preferably when we hadn't just pooped side by side!

Just as I rounded the corner, I saw a thin, weathered-looking man leaning on the squawk box next to Kyle's Suburban. Mr. Cox, I guessed. "My mom and dad are here," said Kyle as I climbed back into the front seat. "Isn't that funny?" I could tell by the way he said it he did *not* think it was funny. "They didn't follow us here or anything weird like that. It's just a coincidence."

"I'm Fred Cox," said Mr. Cox. "Oh, here comes the wife now." Mr. Cox was rather small for a man, not at all the way I'd pictured, but he was handsome: dark eyes, strong smile. His hair was just like Kyle's, thick curls, except steely gray in color instead of brown. Kyle had obviously inherited his mother's bulky size.

"Nice to meet you," I said, reaching over Kyle to shake Mr. Cox's outstretched hand. "I'm Rosemary."

"Well, of all things!" Mrs. Cox laughed when she saw me in the front seat beside her son. "*You're* Rosemary?" I nodded. "You're Rose Warren's daughter?" I nodded again. "Well, I had no idea! We just met in the potty," Mrs. Cox explained. I searched the woman's face for a my-son-could-certainly-do-better-than-you look, but it never came. In fact, when Kyle wasn't watching, Mrs. Cox winked and thrust two Pepto-Bismol tablets into my hand.

"Your mom's nice," I said when they'd gone.

"I'm lucky," said Kyle. "I actually like my parents. Mama's pretty strict at times, but she's a great cook, so that makes up for it." He looked at me and grinned. "Are you and your mom close?" he asked.

"I honestly don't know," I said. The words came out of my mouth before I considered how weird they sounded. "We fight sometimes, mostly about my aunt."

"Why would you fight about your aunt?"

"I don't know that either," I said, and laughed. "Guess that's why I'm in therapy. You know, to figure it all out." *Why not tell Kyle about my flatulence troubles, too! Shut up! Shut up! Shut up!*

"You seem like the last girl who'd need therapy," said Kyle.

"Really?"

"Yeah. I mean you're a perfect student. You're nice. You're pretty. You're *not* a Bluebird. You seem totally normal to me."

"I do?"

Kyle nodded, and I could tell by the open expression on his face that he was interested in my story. Instinctively, I knew a person should seem as perfect as she possibly could be on a date. Otherwise, why go to all the trouble of looking your best if you're just going to ruin it by announcing your personality flaws? Somehow that thought hadn't worked its way down to my tongue yet, though.

"You've probably noticed I have . . . um . . . weight issues," I went on. "I mean, well . . . of course you've noticed." I laughed, but it wasn't funny. Heat crept into my face, and I felt strange, all of a sudden, as if I might burst into tears or have to run to the bathroom again. I swallowed hard and rolled down the window. I was sweating now, too. *Lovely,* I thought. *A fat, emotional girl with diarrhea and personal problems who also sweats profusely.* "Anyway, that's why I go."

"I guess we all have something to deal with." Kyle shrugged.

I figured Kyle would take me home right away, drive up to my house, and toss me onto the curb like a Sunday paper. Instead, he headed toward the park. The night was warm, too warm for boots and tights and skirts and sweaters (just when I had a cute outfit I could actually fit into for winter, it was already spring— the story of my life). Kyle switched off the engine but left the radio on and spread a ratty-looking blanket across the grass. We sat with our backs against a tree and listened to the Temptations turned down low.

I felt an overwhelming urge to ask Kyle what he *really* thought about my fatness, to pluck opinions out of his head like feathers, but instead I let it go and enjoyed the pleasure of his warm lips on mine.

Mother was asleep, of course, when I got home. There was a present on my bed, which I didn't bother opening. I knew it was from Aunt Mary. I thought back to Kyle's question earlier in the night: "Why would you fight about your aunt?"

The room felt cramped and hot. I pulled off my boots and tights, flung my skirt and sweater over the treadmill, and raised the window. A breeze ruffled the curtains and eased its way into my tight little room. I switched off all the lights except for the one on my bedside table and lay on top of the covers. I got up again and retrieved Mother's box of mementos. Closely, I examined the old prom picture—Mother's dazed expression, her pearls, Aunt Mary's pink dress and the way she leaned into Mother and squeezed her arm. The neighbor's porch light clicked on and cast a shadow across my wall. Her dog barked, and somehow the interruption provided clarity.

It was Mother and Aunt Mary's impenetrable closeness I so resented. The ever-present feeling of being on the outside looking in.

chapter twenty-six

Real Friends

All through study hall Kyle kept looking at me. I'd be working on something, feel his eyes on me, glance up, and he'd smile. This happened *four* times. I wish I could just enjoy his attention and not question it so much. He's brought me flowers, taken me out. He calls me, and considering his sports schedule, that's saying a lot. He even tells me I look pretty, *and* he laughs at my sarcasm. Most people don't even *get* my sarcasm (except for Richard, of course).

Mrs. Wallace said this would happen. She said, "You can change the exterior in a fairly short period of time, but the heart takes a whole lot longer." Still, I think if I could reach my goal weight of 120 pounds, I'd feel much better about our chances. At least then if some really cute, skinny girl decided to go after him, I'd have a fighting chance. I said this very thing to Kay-Kay during our run this morning, and she stopped right in her tracks—she didn't seem to care that she was trashing her heart rate.

"Rosemary!" she scolded. "That's the craziest thing I've ever heard. You can't lose weight for somebody else. You have to lose it for you! It sounds cliché and all, but it's true."

"I know," I said.

"Personally, I think you've been chewing way too much gum and not eating enough real food. I swear, it's affecting your brain. Kyle Cox is the least shallow person I've ever known, and he thinks you're perfect. I can promise you that whether you lose ten pounds or gain ten, he's not gonna care one bit! You're pretty, Rosie."

I rolled my eyes. "You are!" she insisted.

"Our heart rates are going down," I reminded her. Suddenly, I was sorry I'd brought it up.

"Do you know what Kyle said to me one day before he even *knew* you?" she went on. I shook my head. "Well, for starters his mama has always been all over him to get a social life. I kept trying to suggest different girls, but he said he had something specific in mind."

"Like what?" I asked.

"He said he wanted a girl who didn't think he was a weirdo because he liked to watch reruns of *Soul Train* and drive through the car wash, listening to oldies tunes. And he said his mama would kill him if she ever caught him at one of those keg parties out on Glen Mill Road, so she couldn't be the hard-core party-girl type either. He said he needed someone real; otherwise, he'd just as soon spend Saturday nights eating his mama's lasagna and homemade rolls." For a second my mind fixated on the home-made rolls. Kay-Kay looked at me bug-eyed. "He likes you for you, dork!" she teased and flicked me on the head. Before I could flick her back, she took off running again.

After we'd finished our three-mile run and half-mile cool down, Kay-Kay and I climbed the few steps to the courthouse square and stretched our quads and hamstrings in the damp grass. It was a hazy morning, but you could tell by the color of the sky it was going to be a pretty day. We must've been quite a contrast—Kay-Kay, lithe and fit and flexible, and me, big and clunky and stiff. The Spring Hill town clock clanged noisily above our heads, and I waited for it to stop. "So how long have you been doing this?" I asked when it finally did.

Kay-Kay was flat on her back with both legs stretched backward over the top of her head. "This is called the plow," she informed me. "You should try it. I've been running since I was eight."

"I don't think so," I replied about the plow. "You've been running since you were *eight*?"

Kay-Kay flipped her legs back over again and sat up in the grass. "Some teacher said I had attention deficit disorder. They did all these evaluations and tests and stuff and decided I needed to be medicated."

"I didn't know you had ADD," I said.

"Oh, I had ADD, all right," said Kay-Kay. "I renamed ADD to mean Always Doing Drills. It was no shocker that I couldn't pay attention. Mrs. Lunn was so damn boring. I swear, that's all we did in her class the entire year—drills. No wonder I couldn't sit still. Just to shut her up, Daddy promised to monitor my diet and increase my activity level. What that really meant was I had to give up Frosted Flakes, and he got me up at the crack of dawn to go running every morning before school."

"Did it work?" I asked.

"Yeah. I was too tired to cause any more trouble. The good part was it made me love running. Exercise is my one true addiction." Kay-Kay looked down at her neon pink nails self-consciously. A breeze rippled through the trees, and the leaves made a scratchy sound, like sandpaper. "I know you probably think I'm some lunatic after the Sundown episode. I never did apologize or thank you properly. I'll always be grateful to you for that night, Rosie."

"It's okay," I said.

"I was just having a bad time with all the Bluebird stuff."

I shrugged. "Does your dad still run with you?" I asked, somewhat concerned that Kay-Kay's father might just show up one morning.

"Naw. When Mama ran off with Sam Harris, that man who used to own the hardware store out on the Nashville Highway, Daddy quit running. He quit everything, really. Except his job; he's a builder. And ESPN and the Weather Channel. He'd never quit watching ESPN and the Weather Channel."

Since Kay-Kay hadn't included herself in this list, I wondered if Mr. Reese had quit her, too, but there was no time to get into it just then. We both had to head home and get ready for school.

Kay-Kay and I went in opposite directions, but on this particular morning, I was actually glad to be alone. I had the time and the quiet to think. Back before Christmas, I'd have been in bed still, probably dreaming about Krispy Kremes. Now I was getting up at the crack of dawn and running with Kay-Kay Reese, sharing the most intimate details of her life (which wasn't nearly as perfect as I'd envisioned). And we were becoming friends. *Real friends.*

At home, I peeled off my sweaty clothes and stood in front

of the mirror. I was a *real* girl, all right—a little too real, in fact. Shiny stretch marks streaked my sides and hips and thighs, almost as if they'd been cut there with a sharp knife (instead of with a dinner fork). Everything about me was plus-sized, but definitely *less* plus-sized than before.

My face was sweat-stained and gritty from the morning's run, but clear, not a pimple in sight. And my pores were exceptionally small, especially for a hormonal teenager. My eyes were shiny and wide with long lashes, even without mascara, and my teeth were naturally straight. I had never endured the medieval torture of braces or retainers. "You're pretty," I heard Kay-Kay say again. Kyle had said it, too, that night at Frankie's Carhop. It hadn't stood out so much since it was lumped in with *nice, not a Bluebird, smart,* and *normal,* but he had said it.

Standing there at the mirror, I could almost see what they were talking about. I could almost feel hope latching onto my heart and pulling it upward.

chapter twenty-seven

4 ROSIE

*M*other was supposed to have her third chemo treatment this morning, but Dr. Nelson, her cancer doc, said her lungs were infected, which explains the most recent coughing fits. Dr. Nelson was about to put her in the hospital, but Mother talked him out of it. According to Aunt Mary, Mother told him she's a single mom and has a child at home (I doubt she mentioned her *child* is sixteen). So Dr. Nelson gave her medicine and strict orders to slow down. Yeah, right. Mother's going to slow down the day Misty Winters turns nice.

The worst part is that now Mother has to *wait* to get her next treatment, a thought that terrifies me. In my head, those Hodgkin's cells look like tiny baseball players, and they have *H*'s sewn onto their caps. The Chemos have *C*'s. It's the third inning and the Chemos are down by a few points. *Why did this have to happen? Why did my mother have to get cancer?*

Even after her long day in Nashville with doctors and nurses and all kinds of tests, Mother insisted I keep my appointment with Mrs. Wallace. I didn't bother protesting. Mrs. Wallace greeted us, then led me down the hallway. Between the waiting area and her office, there were a few hundred square feet and two doors. Still, we could hear Mother coughing.

"I really don't think she should be sitting out there," said Mrs. Wallace.

"Oh, she's not contagious," I said. Truthfully, I wasn't so sure about this.

"It's not *that!*" said Mrs. Wallace. "I just don't think your mother should be sitting in a germy waiting room. She's very susceptible to infection right now."

Instead of keeping me the full half hour, Mrs. Wallace gave me my next homework assignment and sent me on my way. For next week, I'm to write a letter to Mother and tell her exactly how I feel about things. I don't have to send the letter; I simply have to write it. For Mrs. Edinburgh, I just finished a ten-page critical case study on William Faulkner. For Mother, I can't imagine writing even the most basic letter.

By the time we got home, Mother could barely drag herself inside. I tried not to panic. I tried not to let my mind wander to meds not working or cancer cells multiplying or the absence of chemo drugs. Instead, I made dinner for Mother. I opened a can of tomato soup, toasted a grilled cheese sandwich, and poured a glass of milk. It smelled delicious, but I had already sucked down my evening Pounds-Away.

Tray in hand, I stood in her doorway. The room was dark except for the glow of the television, and Mother wasn't even watching it. Her back was toward the television, and she was buried beneath pillows and eiderdown. Quietly, I took the tray back to the kitchen, then slipped inside Mother's room again and eased myself into the chair by the door. Keeping watch somehow, but for what I wasn't sure.

The bedroom was filled with the scent of her—freshly laundered sheets, a hint of lavender from a bureau drawer left slightly ajar, a vase of just-past-their-prime roses, Chanel No. 5. It struck me then how all the little distinctive fragrances blended together to create Mother's own signature perfume, a smell I'd always taken for granted. She wore it the way she wore her smooth skin or her eye color—it was simply a part of her. I breathed it in, savored it as if it were apple pie or the lilacs Kyle had brought.

Just as I was about to click off the television and head up to bed, Mother rolled over. "Come here," she whispered, and patted the place beside her. Up close, in the glare of the television, I could see she'd been crying, but I knew better than to point it out. I shoved some pillows off the bed and sat down beside her, taking her small, cool hand into my own warm one. Before long, Mother was snoring softly. I struggled to keep my eyes open, and when I couldn't any longer, I stretched out beside her. It wasn't until sunlight filtered through the curtains that I woke up again.

By Wednesday, Mother insisted on going back to work. She was pale and weak, but her cough was better, and the fever was gone. No one said a word. We all knew Mother wouldn't listen.

The rest of that week the Heavenly Hair climate felt odd. It's always a crazy place to work, but this was not the usual Richard-nearly-swallowing-bobby-pins crazy or Mrs.-Brunson's-hair-turning-green crazy or Mrs.-Tucker-ruining-her-color-by-adding-Tide-to-her-shampoo crazy. This kind of crazy was different—it was secretive, and it seemed directed toward me somehow.

Every time I hurried around a corner or banged through the front door or clomped up the basement steps, people stopped talking. Richard said it was my imagination. Miss Bertha claimed everyone was just admiring how good I looked. When I asked Drew, the new shampoo guy, about it, he said his spine was out of alignment and his ears had been ringing for days. With ringing ears, he couldn't possibly know a thing.

On Friday morning just after my run, Mother came up the stairs. "I don't know what you've got going on for the weekend, but don't plan a thing for tonight," she said. "And I'll be picking you up after school, so don't ride the bus."

"Okay," I said. Mother twisted her mouth sideways to keep from grinning and went back down to the kitchen again.

That afternoon, when the school day was finally over, I headed to the carpool line. Misty and Tara lurked by the flagpole, but for once they didn't crack any fat jokes. Truthfully, I don't think they saw me, since I normally ride the bus, and for once I wasn't wearing black. I'd ordered a new outfit off the Internet—a floral-print skirt and a lacy white blouse with a camisole underneath.

The first thing I noticed were my sneakers. They were on the front seat of Mother's car. "Why'd you bring those?" I asked.

Mother looked at me and smiled. "Because I nearly failed *my* driver's test in a pair of high heels."

"Are you serious?" I asked. "We're going right now?" Mother nodded.

Just as Mother pulled into a parking space at the Motor Vehicle Administration, the heavens opened up and hard rain pelted the Honda's hood like quarters. "Wanna run for it or wait a minute?" Mother asked.

"Do you *feel* like running for it?" I asked.

Mother groaned and rolled her eyes. Before I knew it, she was halfway across the parking lot, and I was trailing along after her.

A middle-aged woman with a very bad dye job looked up from behind the front desk. "Hidy," she said. "You here to get a license?" I nodded. "Well, we don't do driving tests in a deluge."

"I can't take the test?" I asked, alarmed.

The woman raised the dusty venetian blinds and peered out the rain-spattered window. "Oh, don't worry, this'll blow over in no time. You got to take the eye exam and the written part first anyways."

Mother grabbed a wad of stiff paper towels from the restroom, and we dried ourselves off while the woman arranged the testing station. Rain was still coming down in slanted gray sheets. *Please stop. Please, please, please stop*, I prayed.

I earned a perfect score on the written and vision tests. Even the bad-dye-job lady, whose name turned out to be Juanita, was impressed. "Hardly anybody's got eyes as good as yours," Juanita said. She grinned, fluffing up her already-too-pouffy hairdo. "You see like a frickin' hawk or something."

"Thank you," I replied.

"I told ya it'd slack off," she said, nodding toward the window. "I'll go get Finola. She's the one that does the drivin' part."

Wearing khaki shorts and black kneesocks, Finola strode out of the back room like a drill sergeant. "Rosemary *Goode!*" she snapped, examining her clipboard. There was no one else in the room (except for Mother and Juanita), but I raised my hand anyway. "So let me get this straight," Finola all but growled. "*You* want a *license* to *drive* in the *state* of *Tennessee?*"

"Yes, ma'am," I said, hesitating. "But . . . I'd also like to drive in other states, too. You know, for the future. I mean, I'm not planning on driving out-of-state today or anything." Juanita nearly fell off her chair laughing.

"That's the second one today, Finola!" Juanita cried. "You have *got* to rephrase that line! Sugar, this license is good most anyplace," Juanita explained.

Finola ignored Juanita. "Miss Goode, have you ever driven in precipitous conditions?"

"Yes, ma'am," I said, fairly certain *precipitous* was an adjective that described something steep instead of something wet. I didn't dare correct Finola, though.

Finola checked her watch. "Our ETA is sixteen hundred hours. Don't forget to clock it, Juanita. Move out, Miss Goode," Finola ordered. Juanita giggled. Mother gave me a look as if I were about to go in for triple bypass.

"Good luck," Mother mouthed.

"Thanks," I mouthed back.

I slid into the driver's seat of Mother's Honda, fastened my seat belt, and glanced at Finola. In the daylight, I could see her chin was covered with curly hairs, the most unsightly nest I'd ever seen. Heavenly Hair could make a fortune off Motor Vehicle Administration employees, I decided.

"Put your eyes on the road and keep them there," said Finola. I started the car, released the parking brake, and shifted the gear to *D*. "You're gonna head down to the town square, make a loop, and come all the way back here."

"Yes, ma'am," I replied, easing the car forward.

"I didn't say *go*!" Finola barked. I slammed on the brakes, and our heads jerked forward. Finola grimaced. "Are you trying to *kill me*?"

"No, ma'am!"

"Because if you're gonna try to kill me, we'll just go right back inside and send you to driver's ed all over again."

"But I really *am* a very good driver," I protested. Between two summers of driver's education and Miss Bertha's private lessons on our trips to and from Heavenly Hair, I really was very, *very* good.

"I'll be the judge of that," Finola snapped. "All right, *now* you can go," she said, nodding toward the road.

The rest of the test went smoothly. I stopped on red, slowed and proceeded with caution on yellow, looked both ways, *then* accelerated on green. I used turn signals for lane changes and kept both hands on the wheel. Even when Finola asked me a question, I remembered not to take my eyes off the road (Mr. Wigglesworth had tried that sneaky trick many times in driver's ed).

Finally, I pulled into the Motor Vehicle Administration park-

ing lot again and gave my most exquisite parallel parking dem-
onstration. The clouds had parted slightly, and sunshine slipped
through them like light under a door. I switched off the ignition
and waited while Finola made red marks on her clipboard. "Here,"
she said finally, shoving a slip of paper toward me. "Take this
inside to Juanita. She'll take your picture and get your license."

"Really?" I cried.

"You're an excellent driver," said Finola begrudgingly.

"Head to Bertha's," said Mother when we were on the road
again—this time *I* was driving.

"Why're we going to Miss Bertha's?" I asked. Mother didn't
look like she felt good enough to go anywhere except home.

"You'll see," said Mother. "Just drive."

Miss Bertha was in the yard righting tipped-over flowerpots
when we arrived. "Whose car is that?" I asked. A red Volkswagen
was parked by the toolshed.

"I don't know," said Mother.

"Did you pass?" Miss Bertha hollered across the yard. I held
up my driver's license and raced toward her. Miss Bertha hugged
me tightly. "Let me see it," she said. "Now that's just not fair. My
license picture looks like something from a police lineup. Yours
looks like *Seventeen* magazine."

"Yeah, right," I said, although it *was* a good picture. Still, I
would've preferred the weight section had said 120 instead of
165. "Whose car is that?" I asked, pointing toward the toolshed.
At that precise moment, I glanced toward the porch. A woman I

didn't recognize came out the front door. She smiled and waved at me. "Oh, my . . . Oh. My. *God!* Grandma Georgia!" I tore across the muddy yard and nearly knocked her over with my hug. "When did you get here? *How* did you get here? When did you get *red* hair?"

Grandma Georgia threw her head back and laughed. "Well, let's see—this morning—by plane—and two months ago. When did *you* get so skinny?" she asked. She held me at arm's length and looked me up and down. Actually, she just looked up and up. Grandma Georgia's barely five feet tall and claims she's shrinking all the time. "Oh, Rose Garden, you're beautiful! So beautiful!" she said.

"Hi, Mama," said Mother. "I like your hair."

"Oh, Rose Warren. It's so good to see you." Grandma Georgia gave Mother a hug and stepped back to look at her just the way she'd looked at me. Mother was wearing her pink hat today, a slim-fitting pair of jeans, and a loose cotton blouse. "You look tired," said Grandma Georgia finally. Her expression had changed from jovial to worried.

"Thanks a *lot!*" I knew Mother was trying to make a joke, but she came off stiff and defensive.

"Did we surprise you, Rosie?" Miss Bertha chimed in.

"Duh!" I laughed, watching as Aunt Mary slung her car into the driveway. "I got it!" she called, waving something in the air. "I got it!" she yelled again, stumbling slightly on a piece of broken sidewalk. Aunt Mary hugged Grandma Georgia and Miss Bertha and patted Mother's shoulder. Just as my aunt was about to latch on to me, she stopped herself. "Rose Warren, you've lost more weight just since a couple of days ago, haven't you?" It was more accusation than question.

"I'm *fine!*" Mother snapped. "And I wish everybody would stop commenting on my appearance! Do you know just how *many* times a day I hear how very shitty I look?" The whole family had been together less than five minutes, and already the air was thick with tension.

"I'm sorry," said Aunt Mary quickly. The moment should've been recorded in Spring Hill history books. Aunt Mary never apologizes for anything.

"Mary, go on and give it to her," Grandma Georgia interrupted.

"Before dinner?" Aunt Mary asked.

"Now is good," said Miss Bertha.

"Give who what?" I asked.

Dramatically, Aunt Mary cleared her throat. "Well, Rosie," she said, "we *all* wanted to do something special for your sweet sixteen, so Mama, Miss Bertha, Rose Warren, and I . . . we all chipped in . . ." She handed me a rectangle loosely wrapped in red tissue paper.

"What's this?" I asked. Miss Bertha broke into a full-face smile.

"Open it before I pop!" said Grandma Georgia. Quickly, I ripped open the package. Inside was a vanity plate, which read 4 ROSIE in raised black letters. Judging by the official-looking stickers, the car tag was authentic.

"Is that yours?" I asked Grandma Georgia, pointing toward the little red Volkswagen.

"Honey, I *flew*," Grandma reminded me.

"It's not mine," Miss Bertha added.

I couldn't speak. I *wanted* to speak. I *wanted* to put my lips together and get some words out. *Thank you* would've been a good start, but I couldn't. Instead, I took off across the soggy yard like a crazed *Price Is Right* showcase winner and examined MY NEW CAR! Grandma Georgia, Miss Bertha, Aunt Mary, and Mother all watched and laughed while I squealed and ran around the vehicle and squealed some more.

"We all chipped in on it," Aunt Mary explained. "It's not new. Actually, it's five years old, but the mileage is low. I'm the one who found it," she said proudly.

"And I came up with the vanity plate idea," said Grandma Georgia. "See, there are *four* of us," she explained, counting off Mother, Aunt Mary, Miss Bertha, and herself, "and the car is *for* you, Rosie. Get it? *4 Rosie*."

"Thank you all," I said, passing out hugs. "Oh, thank you!"

Over dinner, fettuccine Alfredo, spinach salad with homemade dressing, big fat buttery rolls, and chocolate birthday cake, all of which I actually ate (in moderation), Grandma Georgia described her future plans, my third wonderful surprise of the evening.

"I knew the day I got down to Naples and started sweating my nipples off I'd made a huge mistake," she said, plunking two ice cubes in her white zinfandel. "Keith loved it, mind you. Golf every morning. Early-bird specials every afternoon. Bingo on Saturday nights. For years I've stuck it out, then . . . well . . .

when I first got Rose Warren's news, something grabbed ahold of me and said, *Woman, you got girls in Tennessee."*

"So what are you saying, Mama? You and Keith are getting a divorce?" asked Aunt Mary.

"You always were so dramatic, Mary. Heavens no! We're gonna split our *time*, not our holy union. We'll rent some little rinky-dink place in Spring Hill and scale back our Florida living. We'll stick around here till after Thanksgiving. If y'all want to see us Christmas, you'll have to come down there. I just think family should be together," said Grandma Georgia. "Don't you, Rosie?"

"I would love to come down to Florida next Christmas!" I said.

"But that's enough about me and my dumb old-lady plans," said Grandma Georgia. "I wanna talk about Rosie here. Rosie, I've decided you need to be a debutante!"

"A *debutante*?" I laughed.

"Just so you can show off your *dergreykh*." The word came shooting out of Grandma Georgia's mouth like something she'd cleared from her throat.

"I don't think I'll be showing *that* in public," I replied.

Grandma Georgia laughed. "*Dergreykh* means your accomplishment. I'm learning Yiddish," she said proudly. "Anyway, Rosie, honey, you look so pretty I can hardly take my eyes off you. And how much weight have you lost exactly, if you don't mind tellin' it?"

"As of this morning, I've lost a total of thirty-eight pounds," I said (I counted my 203 weight just to make the accomplishment even more impressive).

"That's *wonderful*, sugar," said Miss Bertha, squeezing my hand. I glanced at Aunt Mary. Her mouth was hanging open.

"You've lost thirty-eight pounds?" Aunt Mary asked. Judging by the incredulous look on her face, I thought she might cart me off to Miss Bertha's bathroom and weigh me.

"Can't you *tell?*" I snapped. Mother kicked my leg under the table. I took a deep breath. "Yes, that's right," I said nicely (irritating or not, the woman *had* just chipped in on my car).

After the congratulations and the we're-proud-of-yous were over, the table grew quiet. Aunt Mary picked at her napkin. Mother leaned on both elbows and tugged at her cap. Miss Bertha scraped leftovers into a scrap heap. Grandma Georgia was the only one still enjoying herself. She'd topped off her wine and settled back in her chair. My stomach was rumbling and gurgling something awful (real food was throwing off my digestive tract). Just to cover up the embarrassing noises, I said the first thing that came to mind: "I've got a boyfriend!"

Mother and Aunt Mary looked up at the same time. Aunt Mary's eyes were wide with *Are you kidding me?* Mother's were wide with *Please don't talk about this now!* I realized then that Mother hadn't told Aunt Mary about Kyle.

"Well, slap the dog and spit in the fire!" said Grandma Georgia. She slammed her fists so hard on the table that two forks clattered to the floor, and an empty wineglass tipped over—its stem snapped right in two. "What's he look like? Tell me every detail! I'll bet he's just crazy about you!"

"Personally, I think it's time to get Rose Warren home," Aunt Mary interrupted.

chapter twenty-eight

The Letter

Dear Mother,

I know you've succeeded in your life by being tough, by not showing your feelings, by never stopping or slowing down or giving up.
I admire all those tough qualities about you, really I do. But, I just
want you to know that I'm not a little girl anymore. I see what's
really going on even when you try to hide it. I wish you'd let me
comfort you just a little. I wish you'd talk to me about how you feel—
your fears, your worries, your hopes for your future. I think if you
actually talked about these things, we'd both feel better. When you
try to protect me by always saying everything's "fine," it only makes
me worry more, because I KNOW things are not fine right now.

I also know that things are complicated with Aunt Mary. You
two were sisters long before I came along. Since I don't have a
sister, I don't know what that's like, but I wish you'd try to see my
side of things once in a while instead of always defending her.

Love,
Rosie

After I finished Mother's letter, I sat gazing out my bedroom window. The trees were covered with fresh leaves; the grass was newly green. Flowers were blooming and the sun had that strong, vigorous feel to it. I read the letter over and over again, but I knew I'd never send it. If cancer couldn't open Mother up, *I* certainly wasn't going to, not with my one boring letter. Mrs. Wallace was right, though. It felt good just to get my feelings on paper. Liberating, somehow.

chapter twenty-nine

Trust in Me

Rosie, you can't keep drinking that nasty Pounds-Away!" said Kay-Kay. We were climbing the huge hill toward the courthouse, and Kay-Kay was chattering like a songbird. "You have got to readjust your body to real food. I don't know how you've stood drinking that stuff this long, Rosie! And that's why you had chewing gum and water for lunch every day?" I nodded. It felt good to finally tell someone the truth. Ever since the delicious birthday dinner, the old food fantasies were haunting me again, and I feared a relapse was imminent if I didn't do something. Still, I was sick of Pounds-Away. There had to be another solution, and if anybody could figure it out, Kay-Kay could.

"So did you overeat at the birthday dinner?" she asked.

"No! That's just it," I panted. "I did great with everyone watching. I had small portions of everything. It was when I got home that it started hitting me again. Maybe one Snickers bar wouldn't hurt. Maybe just one bag of cheese curls. Dear Lord, it's hard to talk and run at the same time!"

"Well, one snack every now and then probably wouldn't hurt you, as long as you didn't eat too much," said Kay-Kay, not even winded.

"No, you don't understand. We're talking Hollywood teen star fresh from rehab here, where the world is just one big nightclub, except in my case, it's a grocery store." Kay-Kay laughed, but I shot her a look. I was serious.

Kay-Kay stopped suddenly, and I nearly did a face-plant on the sidewalk. "Look at me!" she ordered.

I stopped and gasped for air. Every single part of me hurt—my legs, my sides, my feet, my lungs. "What?" I managed.

"Look in my eyes right this minute." I looked into Kay-Kay's eyes and wondered what Logan Clark must've been smoking to trade Kay-Kay for Marta. For starters he probably never bothered to look above Kay-Kay's chest. Her eyes were so blue they appeared almost hollow, as if a person could look into them and see all the way to China, or Hawaii at least. "*I* have confidence in you," said Kay-Kay softly. "But what you really need is confidence in here," she said, pounding her bony chest. "Please don't waste your money on any more of that stuff. It's not healthy, and you don't need it. You can do this!"

"But what if I go off the deep end again?"

"If you get into trouble, you'll call me!" said Kay-Kay.

"Great," I joked, "and you'll make me run ten miles instead of three." Kay-Kay gave me a sadistic grin and sped up.

We finished the climb toward the courthouse, did a loop

around the square, and passed by Reynold's Drugstore, which was dark. I knew Charmaine wouldn't show up until eight or so. All the way to the Episcopal church, I thought about what Kay-Kay had said. Maybe she was right. Maybe I just needed to trust in *me*.

After a shower and my very last Pounds-Away (ever, supposedly), I hopped in my car and headed toward Spring Hill High School. With tunes blasting, windows rolled down, and the sunroof popped open, I zipped into the school parking lot and took the last space in the back row. I shut off the engine, but left the radio playing. My all-time-forever-until-I'm-dead favorite song was on, "Ain't No Mountain High Enough," the Diana Ross version. I sang along softly to the *ahahahah, ahahahah* part and checked my makeup in the rearview mirror.

Just as I was smearing on fresh lip gloss, I felt prying eyes. Casually, I glanced over, and sitting in the car right next to me, smoking cigarettes and gawking like pigeons, were Misty Winters and Tara Waters. For once, my whole body didn't tense up into tiny nervous knots the way it always does when Bluebirds are around. Instead, I looked straight at the chain-smoking, future lung-cancer victims of America and felt an eerie sort of calm.

I took a deep breath, shut off the radio, gathered up my books, and headed toward the school building. I wasn't even thinking about how big my butt looked from behind. When I was nearly to the sidewalk, I heard, "Hey Artichoke!" (it was Misty's nails-on-chalkboard screech). I kept walking. "Hey, Artichoke!" she tried again. Still I didn't turn around. "Hey, fat-*ass*, the bakery's the other way!" she yelled loud enough for everyone in the whole entire parking lot to hear.

I kept walking.

I saw Kyle first thing in the hallway. I couldn't tell for sure, but he seemed to be waiting for me. "Hi," I said, looking up at him.

"Hey." He grinned and grabbed my hand. He slipped a note into my palm and winked. "I've got a test first period, so I have to go," he said reluctantly. The note was warm in my hand, and my heart twittered slightly as I watched him walk away. I glanced at the wad of paper:

Rosemary,
Will you go out with me Saturday night? Circle yes or no.
Kyle

The unpleasant parking lot scene melted quicker than a Hershey bar on the dashboard in August. Later on in study hall, I handed the note back to Kyle, then went to sit across from Ronnie Derryberry. Even though it was still April, Ronnie already had his summer buzz cut. He's been getting the same buzz cut every year since second grade when he came down with head lice. Mrs. Fowler, our teacher that year, sent home one of those bright pink notices to all the parents: *One of our classmates has experienced a case of head lice. . . .* When Ronnie showed up two days later with no hair, we all knew it was him. I felt a sudden surge of sympathy and tried to remember if I had laughed along with the other children. I was pretty sure I had.

I glanced over at Kyle, and he smiled and gave me the thumbs-up sign. "Seven o'clock," he mouthed.

"What?" I mouthed back.

"Saturday. I'll pick you up at seven," he tried again.

I nodded and smiled at him, then took out my biology book. My stomach made an awful groaning sound. I glanced around quickly, but Ronnie was already snoring, and judging by the bored expressions on the faces all around me, no one had heard. Somehow I would have to transition from liquids to solids before Saturday night.

chapter thirty

Just Right

Kay-Kay's pace was even faster than usual, if that's possible, and I thought I was going to drop dead right smack in the middle of Spring Hill. She's all worked up over Logan and Marta. She heard through Irene, the assistant manager over at Landis Lane, that Marta and her pendulous breasts are going to the prom with Logan. According to Irene, Marta's dress is more MTV Awards than Spring Hill High School prom. Kay-Kay had been holding out hope that she and Logan would make up and go together, but it seems that's out of the question now.

Kay-Kay hardly said a word while we ran. I could tell she was dying to take off and leave me. "Go on," I said finally. "You're not gonna hurt my feelings if you take off." In truth I knew if Kay-Kay went on ahead, I could slog out the remainder of the run without embarrassing myself.

"Are you sure?" she asked. I nodded, and Kay-Kay shot off

like a rocket. She made it to the Episcopal church in record time and was headed toward the courthouse again. For the rest of the run I tried not to think about my own prom situation. Kyle hadn't mentioned anything about it, and I wondered if maybe he already had a prom commitment. Kids are known to do that—make prom dates in January just to make sure they have somebody to go with when the time comes.

When I finally reached the courthouse again (also in record time, the *slowest* record, that is), Kay-Kay had finished her stretches. She was sitting cross-legged on the lawn and pulling up plugs of grass. In front of her was a small pile, and right next to it a bald spot. "Uh, I wouldn't do that if I were you," I said, huffing and puffing like the Big Bad Wolf.

"What? Are they gonna arrest me for pulling up grass? Well, I hope they do!" she said. "Let them just try!" I did not inform Kay-Kay about the difficulties of maintaining a good lawn, but it was killing me to watch her do that.

"I think I'm stuck," I said, trying to get her mind focused on something other than Marta and Logan. "Since my surprise birthday party I've only lost three more pounds."

"That's because you need a weight-lifting program. You've hit what's known as a plateau. Unless you change something, you'll stay stuck." I nodded and thought this over.

"Do you think they're doing it?" A wrinkle creased Kay-Kay's normally unlined forehead, and her blue eyes were cloudy today. I shrugged. "I *want* your opinion, Rosie," said Kay-Kay sharply.

"Yes, I think they probably are," I muttered, and plopped down in the grass beside her.

"I do, too. I also have a feeling about them. I think they're it."

"It?"

"I think she's the girl Logan's gonna marry."

"Oh, Kay-Kay, they're seventeen! They're not gonna get *married*!" Even as I said it, it occurred to me that Logan was already doing an apprenticeship with a local plumber, and Marta didn't exactly seem like the college-bound type. Maybe they would get married just because there was nothing else left to do.

"I knew before Mama left she was gonna go. I predicted it long before Daddy suspected a thing. I'm not, like, psychic or anything, but I get this sense about a situation, and I know how it'll play out based on my gut feeling." I was dying to ask Kay-Kay what her *sense* was of me, but I figured we'd already spent too much time focused on my problems. If I was going to be a true friend, we'd have to stick to Kay-Kay's issues for a while.

"When I'm really obsessed about something, I dive into schoolwork," I offered. "Until recently, I dived into carbs, too." Kay-Kay didn't laugh. She just plucked up another plug of government grass and added it to her pile. "Kay-Kay, stop!" I said, pressing my hand over hers. "This is sod. It's expensive."

"I just don't know how I'm gonna get over this."

"Maybe you should try going out with someone else. At least you'll make Logan think you've moved on. Maybe that'll shake him up a little."

"Billy Gardner's been asking me out forever. I reckon I could make a date with him."

"Billy Gardner, as in, rich-lawyer-daddy, fancy-car, so-over-the-top *Billy Gardner*?"

"That's the one," said Kay-Kay glumly. "Are you and Kyle going to the Sundown Saturday night?"

"We've got a date, but Kyle didn't say where we're going."

"You're going to the Sundown. This time of year that's about all anybody does. Maybe me and Billy can park beside you." Kay-Kay's voice was flat, not a hint of the usual rah-rah in it. I knew the minute we took off in opposite directions, I'd given her the wrong advice.

Kyle picked me up at seven. He looked delicious in a pair of jeans, a pink polo shirt (without the horse) and flip-flops—he even has nice *feet*. I wore brown slacks, a white T-shirt, and new sandals, which killed my feet but looked great with the new pedicure Mildred had given me. We stopped at the Swan on Riverside Drive for some Chinese takeout, which we *took* to the Sundown Drive-in. I had the small-sized low-fat lo mein, and Kyle ordered so much food I couldn't really tell what he was having. We were just getting started on what promised to be a perfect date (my intestines were fully cooperating) when I saw Logan and Marta cross the parking lot. The two of them appeared to share epidermis.

"It's a shame," I said, just making conversation.

"What?" Kyle mumbled through bites of an egg roll.

"That Logan and Kay-Kay broke up."

"Oh. Yeah." Kyle seemed far more interested in his egg roll than Spring Hill High School couple gossip.

"Well, it's just a matter of time before Kay-Kay is officially with someone else anyway. She's got a date tonight with Billy Gardner," I announced.

"The show-off with the car Billy Gardner?" I nodded and tried to smile like this was a good thing. "Aw, man! What was she thinking? Why, he'll be stuck to her like that shiny stuff he puts in his hair all the time. What's it called?"

"Gel," I replied, glancing up at Kyle's soft, product-free curls.

"*Oooh*. Yeah. *Gel*." He said the word as if it were a sign of infection.

Just then, a shiny black Escalade pulled up beside Kyle's Suburban and honked. Kyle groaned and rolled down the window.

"Hey!" Kay-Kay called.

"Hey," Kyle and I replied in unison. Billy gave a salute and winked, and Kyle mumbled something under his breath.

"Hey, Rosie! I have to go to the little girls' room! Come with me!" Kay-Kay shouted loud enough for the whole entire parking lot to hear. I'd practically induced dehydration just to avoid the Sundown restroom, but judging by the silly grin on Kay-Kay's face, she'd been into the wine coolers again, and with Marta and Logan and Bluebirds lurking all around, I couldn't let her go alone.

Kay-Kay stumbled out of the car and hugged me. "Hey, Rosie. What-cha doin'?" I expected the sickeningly sweet scent of alcohol, but instead, Kay-Kay reeked of Polo cologne.

"What'd you do? Use the wrong tester over at Belk's?"

"He hasn't even touched me, and I smell like his stinky old perfume, and this shirt has to be dry-cleaned!" she complained loudly. "What boy wears this much perfume, is what I want to know. His smell alone is enough to drive a girl away."

"*Shhh*," he'll hear you, I warned, glancing back toward Billy's car. Thankfully, the windows were up, and he had the motor running. "Kay-Kay, how much did you drink?"

"Just two wine coolers," said Kay-Kay, holding up three fingers.

"Is Billy drinking and driving?"

Kay-Kay shook her head. "He stole the liquor from his parents. I knew I'd need something to get me through this date. I swear, he'd rob a convenience store if I asked him to. God, I miss Logan." Kay-Kay swayed, and I glanced up to see the happy couple pass by. Unfortunately, Kay-Kay saw them, too.

"I'm gonna go tell that big-booby girl what I think of her!"

"No, you're not!" I said, grabbing her arm tightly. A gaggle of Bluebirds drifted by. Luckily, they didn't see us in the darkness. "*You* are going back to the car, and you're not drinking anything else. Do you hear me?" Kay-Kay pursed her lips together and gave me the look she'd probably given her father back when he took her Frosted Flakes away. "I mean it," I warned.

"Then *you* can't have any more Pounds-Away!"

"I quit Pounds-Away. I told you that already," I replied.

"Okay, then you have to start lifting weights!" Kay-Kay extended her little finger. "Pinkie swear. And you can't take it back."

Reluctantly, I hooked my finger around Kay-Kay's. "Do you really have to pee?" Kay-Kay shook her head. "Okay, I'm going to the concession stand to get you a Coke and a hotdog. You go back and wait in the car."

"Nuh-uh, I'm coming with you!"

"No, you're not!"

Kay-Kay latched onto my arm. "Yes, I am," she said, giggling.

Slowly, we made our way through the parking lot. Kay-Kay smiled and waved to each and every car we passed as if she were the Rose Bowl queen on New Year's Day.

A Volvo station wagon was parked just in front of the concession stand, and clustered around it were a dozen or so Bluebirds. They practically glowed in the dark with their brightly colored sundresses and matching handbags. "Keep walking and *don't* say anything," I told her. Kay-Kay let go of my arm suddenly.

"There must be an open bar and a buffet!" Misty shouted.

"Ignore her," I whispered, but Kay-Kay didn't listen. Before I could stop her, she took off in Misty's direction. It was one of those slow-motion moments, and I just stood there, helpless, wondering what my small-but-very-kick-ass friend might do. Unfortunately, I never found out. Kay-Kay was down before she got there, splayed out on the gravel like a face-first snow angel.

After a trip to the restroom (to pick pebbles out of Kay-Kay's bloody knees) and the concession stand (for that sobering hot dog and Coke), I got Kay-Kay back to Billy's SUV. She climbed in and leaned her head against the sleek leather seat. Within seconds, her eyes were closed.

"If you give her another wine cooler, I will personally sue you," I whispered. Since Billy's daddy was a hotshot Nashville lawyer, I figured he'd understand legal threats better than physical ones. "It would be really bad, especially considering the liquor came from your dad's house." Billy nodded meekly.

"You're right. It would be bad. I'm sorry." Billy's silky shirt still had the *Size M* sticker on the breast, and on the floor next to Kay-Kay's feet was a huge bouquet of now-wilted hothouse roses. Clearly, he had gone to a lot of trouble for their first date. "I just wanted her to have a good time," he explained.

"Then next time take her to Harvey's Gym, and y'all can work out together," I said, handing him the hot dog and Coke. "I don't think she's gonna eat this. You can have it if you want. And you might wanna get some paper towels out of the men's room. You know, in case she gets sick." Billy smiled at me and nodded enthusiastically.

"You look different," he said just as I was about to close the car door.

"Really?"

"Yeah, you've lost weight."

"Thanks." I hesitated, wondering whether or not I should give Billy the advice that was ready to dive off the end of my tongue. Kay-Kay snored softly now, and her mouth hung open a little. "Um . . . Billy, you should know that Kay-Kay's allergic to Polo," I whispered.

"You mean my cologne?"

"No, the sport with horses and sticks. Yes, your cologne."

"Oh, no! Really? I knew I should've worn Euphoria instead."

"Um . . . she's allergic to *all* men's cologne," I added (I was fairly certain Billy would never be able to restrict himself to one conservative spritz, no matter what the brand).

"Got it," he said, and saluted me again.

"I thought you'd left me!" said Kyle when I returned to the car. "What's going on next door? Did Billy name their first child yet?"

"Sorry, there was another wine cooler crisis. I think it's okay now, though. Billy seems nice, and I told him we'd sue him if anything happened to Kay-Kay."

Kyle smiled at me. "You're the one who's nice. Mama always said Kay-Kay was a little lost, you know, since her mother left. I'm glad she's got you lookin' after her instead of those buzzards."

"Oh, it's not all one-sided. Kay-Kay looks out for me, too."

"You mean with your mom?"

"Not exactly . . ." I hesitated. "We . . . um, run together every morning before school. Kay-Kay helps keep me disciplined with my weight-loss plan."

"I didn't know you were a runner. We should go together sometime."

I thought of my flatulence issues, which had hopefully disappeared for good. "Uh, we'll see," I replied.

"You're not gonna get *too skinny*?"

"One can only hope," I joked.

"But you don't wanna end up looking like those girls in the tabloids! They look plumb awful, if you ask me. I bet if they were in a third-world country, folks'd be sending them UNICEF donations." I burst out laughing, and Kyle took my hand and squeezed it slightly. "I think you're just right. Not that I'm trying to tell you what to do or anything," he added.

I leaned in closer to Kyle, and he wrapped his Enormous Strapping Jock Boy arms around me. When he kissed me, my whole body tingled. Right then and there, in Kyle's arms, with my eyes closed, I felt just right to me, too.

We were startled when someone tapped on the glass. I opened

my eyes and was surprised to see the windows fogged up. Kyle rolled down the window, and Logan peered into the car. Marta was super-glued to his side, of course.

"My truck's dead. I hate to bother you, but I tried jumper cables. It's not the battery," said Logan. "Could you give me a ride home so I can get my dad out here?" Logan's dad was a mechanic, I knew. He'd repaired Aunt Mary's car on numerous occasions. "Man, there's no way I'm leaving my truck here over-night. Not with the new wheels, you know?"

My lips were practically numb from all the kissing, and Marta was blinking at me, sizing me up as Kay-Kay's friend, I guessed. I glanced over toward Billy's SUV, but it was gone. Something resembling panic shot through my chest. I wondered if Kay-Kay was sober enough to handle a boy who was obviously so crazy about her.

The next thing I knew, Logan and Marta were in the back seat, and Kyle was driving Marta home. "What the hell?" she kept say-ing over and over. "What the hell?" It was a sentiment I shared, but I had enough sense to keep my what-the-hells to myself. I was all set for more kissing at the Maury County Park, and I knew we wouldn't have time for that now.

"Marta, I don't know how long it'll take to fix the truck," Logan explained. "I cain't leave it at the Sundown all night. I just cain't."

"First off, you are way too in love with that dumb old truck!" Marta snapped. "And I don't like being stood up, Logan Wesley Clark."

"I didn't stand you up, Marta," Logan pleaded. "I just have to go is all. That truck is my responsibility."

Marta's house was a rancher over in Shawnee Acres, a boxy little structure with fake rabbits and deer and a statue of an old lady bending over in the patchy front yard. "I'll get you for this, Logan Clark," Marta threatened. "You'll be sorry you missed out on a night with *me*. And where is *she* going?" asked Marta, glaring at yours truly. "How come *she* gets to go, and I don't, huh?"

"Oh, they're taking me home, too," I said.

"Well, they're taking you home *last*," Marta pointed out. "How come you're not taking *me* home last—?"

"I have a curfew, Marta," Kyle interrupted. Marta got out of the car. "See you later," he said and pulled away.

"I see Kay-Kay had a date tonight," said Logan the minute we left Marta. "So Billy Gardner finally got her to go out with him. Man, he's such a puss—uh, *girl*!"

Kyle didn't say anything. I just shrugged and turned back around in my seat. We dropped Logan off at his house, which was a pretty place across town, nothing like Marta's neighborhood. "Thanks for the ride," said Logan, hopping out. "Tell Kay-Kay . . . Oh, never mind," he said to no one in particular.

"Do you think we could drive by Kay-Kay's house real quick?" I asked the minute we pulled out of Logan's driveway. "I just wanna make sure Billy took her home."

Kyle glanced at the dashboard clock. "No problem," he said. "Kay-Kay's not far from you."

The house was a small, unkempt structure. Piles of lumber on the front porch, a still-in-progress roof covered with blue tarp, a Reese Construction van in the driveway. The house was dark except for a television glow through the front window—her dad's

ESPN or Weather Channel, I guessed. It was a mismatch somehow; a girl as pretty as Kay-Kay belonged someplace better. Our
house was no mansion, not by any means, but Mother had worked
hard to give it curb appeal (her words, not mine). I felt grateful for
her efforts once again.

Kyle put the car in Park and switched off the headlights. "I'll call
just to make sure she's home," I said, pulling out my new phone (a
gift Grandma Georgia insisted on now that I had a car).

"Hello," said Kay-Kay groggily.

"I'm just making sure you're okay. Billy brought you home?"

"Where are you? What time is it?" asked Kay-Kay.

"It's nearly midnight, and I'm sitting in front of your house
with Kyle." A light switched on, in Kay-Kay's bedroom, I guessed.
She pulled back the curtain and waved, but she had lost her Rose
Bowl queen enthusiasm.

"Thanks for looking out for me, Rosie. Billy's pretty nice,"
said Kay-Kay. "I got sick in his car, and he held my hair back. On
the way home he bought me ginger ale and saltines."

"You threw up in his *Cadillac*?" I said, glancing at Kyle.

"Good grief," Kyle mumbled, and rolled his eyes.

"Yeah, but he had paper towels, so it was okay. The new-car
smell's probably ruined, though."

"Logan asked about you," I said, watching Kyle sort through
his CD collection. I could tell he'd already given up on making
his curfew.

"Good for Logan," said Kay-Kay flatly. "I'm done with him.
I'm done with wine coolers, too," she vowed.

"We'll talk tomorrow, okay?"

"Definitely," said Kay-Kay. "You go enjoy your good-night kiss. And don't think I was too drunk to notice the fogged-up windows!" she teased.

Kyle popped in a James Taylor CD, and we headed back down Riverside Drive again. The windows were down, and we were both singing along. In no time we were sitting in front of my house. All the lights were on. Grandma Georgia, I thought, and smiled.

Kyle lowered the volume and leaned over to kiss me. "I'm late now for sure," he said, lingering. "If I'm not grounded, I'll call you tomorrow."

I climbed out of the Suburban and stood barefoot in the prickly, damp grass (I'd given up my uncomfortable new sandals hours ago). "Bye. Thanks," I said. Kyle gave me a Billy Gardner salute and winked, and we both laughed.

chapter thirty-one

The Gravy Train of Self-confidence

The salon was so packed and noisy Miss Bertha had to prop open the front door just to let the air circulate a little (Mother refuses to turn on the air conditioner before Memorial Day). Everywhere I turned there was a pretty, skinny, perfect girl: Margaret Abernathy and Rolanda Davidson waited on the bench by the front window; Peggy Wells had already parked her size-zero butt in Richard's chair; Annelise Marley, a new but already screamingly popular junior, was talking with Mother. The Bluebirds were sure to show up, although I didn't look at the schedule to find out exactly when they were due.

It was the annual Heavenly Hair Pre-prom Up-do Dry-run, which is basically just what the title says: a chance for girls to do a practice hair style a couple of weeks before prom night. As usual, Mother had gone to a great deal of trouble for the event. She'd hung an enormous plastic banner off the front of the building.

She'd ordered cookies from Town Square Bakery and bought a whole stack of age-appropriate magazines. In the waiting area was a giant metal tub filled with ice-cold Diet Cokes and bottled water, and Miss Bertha had even switched the radio station from oldies to alternative rock. Mildred was in Gatlinburg for the weekend, so Grandma Georgia agreed to fill in as manicurist. Her cosmetologist license is still good, and besides that, she's trying to get Mother to let her take over some clients (just temporarily, so Mother can get that rest her doctor keeps ordering).

My stomach was clutched up with nerves, and I longed to escape to the basement, but the snack machine was freshly restocked—too dangerous. Instead, I grabbed a broom and started sweeping.

"Now, Peggy, you have just the sort of face for an up-do, a down-do, whatever you want, honey," Richard cooed. I shot him a dirty look and ran the bristles of my broom over his sandal-clad toes.

"Whoops, sorry," I said, then did it a second time. Peggy glanced up at me with that vague don't-I-know-you-from-somewhere expression, then focused on Richard again. Richard is completely, openly gay, and yet half the girls at Spring Hill High School would run away with him if he asked. He's beautiful, for one thing. For another, he dresses like someone off the streets of New York City, which has quite an alluring effect in a place like Spring Hill, Tennessee, among the adolescent female population anyway. And, finally, Richard knows how to concoct just the right mix of friendly and bitchy.

"Well, what I'd like to do, Richard, is figure out a hair style for the prom *and* for the Miss Fireworks Pageant. I'm a contestant this year," Peggy announced, batting her green eyes with the mile-long lashes.

"Well, congratulations!" said Richard, glancing at me nervously. I could tell he wanted to gush all over Peggy, so I swept my way over toward Mother's station, where the dark-haired, blue-eyed, perfect-smiled Annelise was discussing how difficult it is to manage such thick hair. "Oh, you're right," Mother agreed. "Damaged, thin hair is much easier to style, especially with an up-do. Your hair is so glorious, I actually think you should leave it down. Maybe do it slightly off to the side with a clip of some sort. Rhinestones, maybe." Mother's voice sounded wistful. She scratched her head, and the wig she wore shifted to the left slightly.

Rolanda, with her chocolate skin, regal carriage, and perfect smile, was delicately nibbling a cookie that I could've easily consumed in one bite, and next to her Margaret Abernathy flipped through the latest issue of *Seventeen*. Margaret's face wasn't quite as pretty as the other girls', but her killer body made up for it—long, shapely legs, large bosom, lightly tanned skin, wide shoulders, narrow hips (Barbie come to life). And my guess was Margaret wasn't grunting and farting her way up North Main Street every morning to get that perfect body either.

Suddenly, I was back inside my 203-pound frame. I wasn't Rosie with the cute boyfriend, Rosie with the beautiful best friend, Rosie who had run every morning for the past several weeks, Rosie who had struggled and suffered and clawed her way to 161 pounds and holding. I was the old, fat, miserable Rosemary Goode. I stood there in the middle of Heavenly Hair, and for a second it was the day after Christmas all over again. I glanced at the corner where the dried-out little tree had stood. I looked out the window and half expected Mrs. McCutchin to rap on the glass.

"Rosie. *Rosie*." Miss Bertha was calling me from across the room. Margaret and Rolanda were staring at me with their matching like-what-is-your-problem expressions. It was the Quilters and Hilda May Brunson and Mrs. McCutchin's Christmas cookie episode all over again.

"Yes," I said.

"Rosie, can you mail these bills for me, sugar? The postman's coming any second, and Reda's supposed to call from Memphis. I don't wanna leave the phone." Reda is Miss Bertha's youngest daughter.

"Sure," I said. I took off my smock, grabbed my purse, and flew out the door. I hurried toward the mailbox at the end of the street, opened the metal mouth, stuffed in Miss Bertha's mail, and headed toward the salon again, but stopped when I caught a glimpse of myself in Milly's Luncheonette plate glass window. I half expected to see the girl from nearly five months ago; instead, I saw a thinner, not skinny or perfect like those other girls, but much-improved me. She was staring back at me—blinking and breathing, yet I didn't know her. A horrible thought ran through my mind. Maybe I could weigh 110, look like whatever Brad Pitt and Angelina Jolie's daughter is gonna look like one day, but I'd still feel this way. Maybe, no matter how hard I tried, I'd always be fat on the inside.

Two young moms strolled their babies past me. An old man with a ringing hearing aid ambled by. I watched Mr. Tankersley, the mail carrier, empty the contents of the stocky blue box into his pouch. He had a large potbelly, gray-blue Bermuda shorts, black socks, and orthopedic shoes. He was whistling something. "Chattanooga Choo Choo."

I pictured it then, a large, steaming engine with an endless line of freight cars. It spitted and hissed and squeaked its way up the street, stalled slightly, then roared on by. It was the gravy train of self-confidence, and I had missed it.

I didn't go back to the salon. Instead, I got in my car and went home.

The afternoon was the very *definition* of spring—lawn mowers purring like kittens, the smell of warm boxwoods, cut grass, roses. Swing sets squeaked in backyards, and the little kids across the street ran naked under a hose. All at once I ached for my childhood. I missed the way Mother would tuck me in bed at night or how Aunt Mary would occasionally pick me up from school and take me to get an ice-cream cone at the Dairy Queen. I missed the way Grandma Georgia would play round after round of putt-putt golf with me (*before* she ran off to Florida with Mr. Keith).

In the garage, I found my old plastic wading pool. It was dirty and covered in cobwebs, so I scrubbed it out with dishwashing liquid and filled it with water. I cinched in last year's too-big bathing suit (which I never actually wore) with a safety pin and switched on the kitchen radio. It played faintly through the open window and filled the backyard with the sound of Lynyrd Skynyrd's "Sweet Home Alabama." I rubbed my pale skin with Coppertone sunscreen and sang along softly.

The water was shockingly cold. I lay down in it, closed my

eyes, tilted my face toward the sun, and pictured my worries flut-
tering off like butterflies. I was submerged in a fairly sufficient
Calgon moment when someone tapped me on the shoulder.

"Are you okay? Hey, Rosie? Are you okay?" I did not want
to open my eyes. Right at that very moment, I wanted to float off
with the butterflies. FAT GIRL DROWNS IN KIDDIE POOL. The
sun hung high above him. I squinted against it and reluctantly sat
up, curling my legs tightly against my chest.

"What are you doing here?" I asked.

"Oh, well . . . um . . . I'm sorry. I tried to call first, but I guess
you didn't hear the phone ring." Kyle was staring at me. *Oh, God.
Old bathing suit with a safety pin! Stretch marks exposed! Fat rolls
everywhere!* Music wafted across the yard. It was an oddly nasal
voice I couldn't place. "I wasn't sure if you were home, so I left
the car running," Kyle explained.

"Could you hand me that towel over there, please?" I pointed
to the porch railing clear across the yard.

"Sure," said Kyle, but he didn't move. Before I could jiggle
across the yard and retrieve the towel myself, he squatted down
beside me. A current ran through my body. It started at the top
of my head and radiated out to my extremities. I could feel it pulsing somewhere just beyond my sea-foam green toenails. Kyle's
face was flushed, and he was sweating a little. "Um, there's something I've been meaning to ask you, Rosie. Will you be my date
to the prom?"

My heart pounded out a drum solo. "Go get that towel while
I think it over," I replied coyly. Kyle hurried across the yard and
grabbed my towel.

I.

Stood.

Up.

In my too-big, safety-pinned bathing suit, half expecting the world to come to an abrupt and violent end, I stood up. The world did not end. Instead, Kyle grinned and wrapped the sun-warmed towel around me the way Mother used to when I'd just come out of the tub. "Okay, I'll go," I said, smiling up at him.

Kyle laughed and put his giant football arms around me. "I'm so relieved you said yes."

"I'm so relieved you asked. Is that Wayne Newton on the radio?"

Kyle held me at arm's length. "You seriously *know* who that is?" he asked, wide-eyed. I nodded. "I can't believe you know who that is!"

"Well, he's singing 'Danke Schoen,'" I pointed out.

"I bet there's not another girl at school who would know that besides you!" Kyle beamed with pride at my oldies prowess. He grabbed me and pulled me close again. "'I can see hearts carved on a tree,'" he sang off-key in my ear, "'letters intertwined, for all time, yours and mine . . .'"

chapter thirty-two

Lucky

I had just finished my treadmill workout, and was glancing over a nutrition book Kay-Kay picked up for me at the library, when I heard Aunt Mary's car pull up. I could tell by the way she slung it into the driveway she was angry about something. She and Mother had gone to Nashville for an appointment with Dr. Nelson, and I'd heard through Grandma Georgia that Aunt Mary intended to tell him about Mother's not following his orders. I glanced out the window and watched Mother press up the sidewalk, Aunt Mary close on her heels. The minute they burst through the door, the shouting started. "You need to mind your own business!" Mother exploded.

"And if I mind my own business, you'll be dead in a year!" Aunt Mary shouted back. "Is that what you want?"

"If I don't have the right doctors taking care of me, I'll be dead in six months," Mother retaliated. I put my book down and crept to the bottom of the stairs where I could hear better. "You are always in our business, Mary. You don't know when to stop butting in. Rosie's right, you know. She gets tired of it, too. And in case you haven't noticed, your social calendar isn't exactly brimming with invitations! Maybe other people feel the way we do, except they're not *stuck* with you! You're nothing but a big know-it-all who doesn't know a damn thing!" I couldn't believe Mother was saying these things. They were true, but still . . .

"Now you're just being mean, Rose Warren. Well, just so you know, I am not afraid of your anger!"

"God, I wish you'd stop with the armchair psychology bullshit! It's enough to *make* me crazy!"

"I swear to the good Lord in heaven, I will call Dr. Nelson's office every single time you defy his orders. If you go to work, I'm calling. If you clean the house, I'm calling. Mama has already agreed to work for you. And Rosie can help out around here. It's not like she couldn't use the exercise."

I bristled at the insult. "You hush up about Rosie! She does plenty to help me out. And she's up at the crack of dawn running every morning. See, this is exactly what I'm talking about! You judging our lives every five seconds! Maybe you should take a good hard look at your own life, Mary. It's not so hot, in case you haven't noticed."

"I am your official spy. I will tell Dr. Nelson, and if he drops you from that practice, it's your own doing," said Aunt Mary. She was using her quietly condescending voice now.

"You are no longer welcome in this house! You can just spend Saturday nights with that pissing, hissing fur ball of yours!"

Mother was treading on shaky ground now for sure. I waited. I listened. I held my breath. It was the calm before the storm. Suddenly, the front door slammed so loudly the whole entire house shook. "And don't come back!" Mother yelled. She was cursing under her breath and slamming things around.

I crept back up the stairs again. The last thing Mother needed was somebody else spying on her. Normally, I would take Mother's side in a heartbeat over Aunt Mary's, but I knew my aunt was partly right about this particular issue. Mother hadn't slowed down a bit. All along I'd wanted to say something, but it was a little like Aunt Mary's comments about my weight. They never made me lose weight; they just made me mad. Besides that, I remembered Mrs. Wallace's words about how Mother would have to handle her illness her own way.

Later, I got the full story from Grandma Georgia. Apparently, while Mother was in the examining room with Dr. Nelson, Aunt Mary confided in his nurse. Aunt Mary told her how Mother was still working full-time and doing too much around the house and attending downtown merchants' meetings and having special events at the salon. Mother was with the receptionist making her next appointment when Dr. Nelson called her *and* Aunt Mary back to his consult office. The last thing he said to Mother was, "Lady, this is your life you're playing with here. No chemo, no remission. No remission and your cancer gets worse. Continued noncompliance and you can find yourself a new doctor."

Maybe Mother was so angry with Aunt Mary this time because deep down she knew she was right.

Our Mother's Day brunch included Mother, Grandma Georgia, Aunt Mary (so much for not being allowed in our house), Miss Bertha, and me. It wasn't much of a celebration, however. Miss Bertha was missing her own children and grandchildren something fierce. Grandma Georgia was irritated because Mother and Aunt Mary still weren't speaking to one another (Mother wasn't really talking to anyone). I was trying to navigate my way around the fattening lunch—fried chicken, mashed potatoes, corn bread with butter, macaroni and cheese, and string beans. I considered avoiding the whole menu and having a salad instead, but that seemed rude after Grandma Georgia had spent the entire morning cooking. Instead of helping her, which I should have done, especially since it was Mother's Day and all, I spent the morning with Mother.

After my run and before my shower, I hid the gift bag behind my back and slipped into her bedroom. I had a present for Grandma Georgia, too, but I wanted a little time with Mother, just the two of us. She was lying in bed staring at the ceiling when I went in. "I'm tired of this," she said to the ceiling.

"What?" I asked, shutting the door behind me.

"I can't take staying home and doing nothing. I'm sicker here than if I work all the time. And what if I'm dying?" she asked, suddenly angry and sitting up in bed. "Does your goddamned, nosy-assed aunt want me to spend my last days wallowing in bed sheets?"

I was too stunned by Mother's remark to say anything. I had never heard her speak that way about Aunt Mary. In fact, I'd never really heard her speak that way about anybody. I waited for Mother to backtrack or apologize, but she didn't. A few minutes passed. Maybe it was only a few seconds, but it felt like an eternity standing there in the middle of the floor—*waiting.*

"Happy Mother's Day," I said finally, tiptoeing toward the bed. "I brought you something." I took the gift from behind my back and put it on the bed.

"Oh, Rosie, I'm so sorry. Here you came to give me a present and I—"

"It's okay. Just look inside." Mother peered into the bag and pulled out the various bottles and tubes.

"Thank you," she whispered. "Oh, but it's too extravagant, Rosie."

"Don't worry. I didn't pay retail," I explained. "I used your vendor number and found a discount place online." I'd dipped into my savings account and purchased the finest moisturizing products available. They were guaranteed to help Mother's chemo-ravaged skin. If nothing else, the products had certainly ravaged my bank account.

Mother patted my hand. "Even at a discount, this was extravagant." Her eyes welled up, and she grabbed a tissue off the nightstand. "You're a good daughter," she whispered.

"You're a good mother," I replied.

Mother dabbed at her eyes and blew her already red nose. "You know, before this happened, I had no idea how lucky I was. I mean, I worked hard, I know that. Luck didn't get me the salon or this house. Luck didn't turn you into the fine girl you are. I've worked hard for everything in this life, but I was also lucky. I was so lucky to have the *energy* to work that hard. Oh, God, I miss pulling fifteen-hour days at the salon! I miss tearing out a wall and tiling a floor and hanging bead board!" She glanced around the room. "What I wouldn't give to paint these walls."

"You just repainted last year," I reminded her. The pale butter-yellow color was perfect for Mother's bedroom, and there wasn't a scratch or scuff mark anywhere.

"That's not the point," Mother explained. "I'd like to *be able* to paint them." She flopped back against the pillows and sighed. I thought she might cry again, but she didn't. "Promise me, Rosie," she said, taking my hand.

"What?" I asked.

"That you'll be okay. That no matter what happens to me, you'll be okay."

"I *am* okay," I replied, pretending I had no idea what Mother really meant.

"You wanted this, Rosie." Mother drew in a ragged breath and sighed it back out again.

"Wanted what?" I asked.

"I read your letter. I know I shouldn't have, but it was hanging out of your purse, and it had my name on it, so I read it." My heart sped up; my cheeks burned.

"That letter was an assignment from Mrs. Wallace. I didn't give it to you," I said, trying not to let anger seep into my voice.

"I know, but I need you to promise me that if I die, you'll go on with your dreams . . . with your life."

"Wha—?"

"I have life insurance. If Mr. Decker down at the bank invests it well, there'll be enough for Vanderbilt," she said. "Isn't it sad that I'm worth more dead?" She laughed ruefully.

"Mother, don't—"

"No, let me finish. Now you'd still probably have to get a scholarship or some sort of financial aid, but the insurance money would certainly help. Even with good investments, there probably wouldn't be anything left for you after college. You might want to consider studying something practical, you know, like business. Something that would provide a nice living when you graduate."

Between the bold words and the bald head, I barely recognized the woman beside me. For months, I'd wanted to support her, to be included in her struggle, to be one of the adults. Hadn't I said all along I wanted my mother to talk to me? Now I wasn't so sure. A shadow box hung on the wall just above Mother's head. Inside it was a picture of a little girl holding a bird. The creature looked as if it were poised to fly away at any moment. "I promise," I said. "I promise," I said again, and hugged Mother.

Later, in the shower, I thought about things. *Did it mean something that Mother and I had openly acknowledged death's unwelcome presence? Was it some sort of omen?* A shower is the perfect place for crying. No one can hear you if you do it quietly, into a washcloth, with the water running.

At lunch, Aunt Mary went on and on about how much weight I'd lost. "Well, we're finally getting you there, aren't we, Rosie!" she said loud enough for everyone to hear. "All those books, the treadmill. My efforts are finally starting to work!" *Your efforts, my ass!* I felt like saying, but I didn't. I could tell Aunt Mary was just trying to get on Mother's good side again, and no one was paying her any attention.

Mother was sorting through a new batch of get-well cards, and Miss Bertha and Grandma Georgia were debating how much longer to bake the apple crisp. I was looking over my notes for a unit test in Mrs. Edinburgh's class.

By the time we were gathered around the table, Aunt Mary had downed three mimosas. She's never been much of a drinker, and I wondered if a Kay-Kay scene might soon follow. She raised her champagne flute so high it was just millimeters from crashing into our low-hanging chandelier.

"Watch what you're doing, Mary!" Grandma Georgia scolded, and tugged her arm down a notch. "And make it quick. I didn't bust my *tokhes* all morning to eat cold food!"

Aunt Mary giggled, but I could tell the scolding had hurt her feelings. The showiness went out of her voice. "I just wanted to toast Rosemary's success," said Aunt Mary, swaying ever so slightly. "How much weight have you lost now?" she asked.

"Forty-five pounds," I lied. Really, it was only forty-two still.

"Here's to . . ." Aunt Mary stalled. "How much?"

"Forty-five pounds," I said again as if my aunt were deaf instead of drunk.

"Well, here's to fifty-three pounds!" said Aunt Mary. Mother reached for my hand and squeezed it tightly, but she didn't raise her glass. She just narrowed her eyes and glared at my aunt.

Lunch ended abruptly. Miss Bertha and Grandma Georgia made arrangements to drive Aunt Mary home. Mother went back to bed, and I headed for the kitchen. Someone had to tackle the mess.

I switched on the radio, donned rubber gloves, and filled the sink with hot soapy water. Mick Jagger wailed on the radio. I turned the volume up and tried not to think about Mother's words that morning. I tried to distract myself with prom dress worries. When that didn't work, I switched my brain over to the English test, but I'd studied too much to obsess over it. I knew I'd get an A. Finally, I settled on the Bluebirds, always a good source of tension. But no matter what I tried to torture myself with, I kept coming back to Mother again. *Did she think she was going to die? Was there some piece of information she was keeping from me? Maybe Dr. Nelson hadn't taken her off chemo. Maybe they were secretly giving up.* Panic rose in my chest.

I heard Grandma Georgia come through the front door. "Hi, there, Rose Garden. Now *that* was what I call a Mother's Day lunch. The perfect reminder of how much trouble it is to have children!" She laughed and kissed me on the forehead. "If I'd known how much nicer grandchildren are, I'd have had you first," she whispered.

I smiled, and the panic died down a little. Grandma Georgia tugged a fresh dish towel from the linen drawer and began drying. In no time we had the entire kitchen cleaned up. It was good to work side by side without talking. Just having my grandma there made things seem better somehow. I pulled off my rubber gloves and hugged her. "I'm so glad you're here."

"Oh, my little Rosie, I love you, sugar," she said.

That night Grandma Georgia and Miss Bertha went out to the movies. Mother was in bed, glued to an episode of *Divine Design* (apparently, if she couldn't rip out a wall herself, watching Candice Olson do it was the next best thing). I imagined Aunt Mary was curled up with Tom Cruise and sleeping off those mimosas.

It was long past dinnertime, and my stomach rumbled. Determined to succeed, I measured out a bowl of Cheerios with one cup of skim milk and sliced up half a banana. I ate slowly. I tried to "savor the taste, the smell, the sensual pleasure of eating . . . ," something I'd read in the book Kay-Kay had checked out for me. Finally, I gave that up, wolfed down the rest of the Cheerios in two efficient bites, and trudged upstairs to call Aunt Mary.

"Hello," she said on the first ring. I knew she was probably hoping it was Mother calling to make up.

"It's just me, Aunt Mary," I said. I still had no idea what I planned to say.

"What's wrong!" she said, panicked.

"Nothing's wrong. Mother's resting. Grandma Georgia went to a movie with Miss Bertha."

"Oh," she said. "Well, that's good, I reckon." A long silence passed, and I could hear Tom Cruise purring.

"Did you ever get him declawed?" I asked.

"No, I decided it might make him feel like less of a man. I mean, I already had him neutered."

"I'll be glad to pay for it if you want. I could take the money out of my savings."

"Why, Rosie. That's so sweet. But no. No, thanks."

"Okay," I said. More silence.

"I was a little tipsy at lunch, but how much weight did you say you'd lost again?"

"Well, I said forty-five, but it's really only forty-two."

Aunt Mary laughed. "It says I'm five feet seven inches on my driver's license, so don't feel bad."

"Well, I guess I better go. I just wanted to say . . . well, things will get better with Mother. She's more mad at the cancer than she is at you."

"You think so?" my aunt asked hopefully. "I've never seen her like this."

"She's never been sick before," I pointed out.

"That's true. I'm really glad you called, Rosie."

"Me too," I said and hung up.

On Monday afternoon, I drove over to see Mrs. Wallace. I barely sat down before I started spilling my guts. I told her about Mother and Aunt Mary's big fight. I told her about Aunt Mary's drunken toast. I described in great detail my conversation with Mother about death and going on with my dreams and my phone call to my aunt.

"You've wanted your mother to really talk to you for a long time. Do you think she finally did so because of your letter?" Mrs. Wallace asked. I shrugged. "Well, whatever prompted it was good. In this profession we call it a breakthrough."

"I think I screwed up." Mrs. Wallace gave me her do-go-on expression. "I promised Mother I would . . . that I'd go on with my dreams, even without her."

"That's screwing up?" asked Mrs. Wallace.

"It was morbid. I should've consoled her more, told her every-thing would be *fine*." The second the word *fine* came out of my mouth I had an ah-ha moment, the kind with the lightbulb and the game show *ding-ding-ding!* Mrs. Wallace looked at me, and I could tell she was trying not to smile. "But didn't my promise just give Mother permission to die?" I asked.

"Does your mother *want* to die?" asked Mrs. Wallace.

"No!" I replied.

"Listen," she said, leaning in close to me, "any mother who thinks there is even the slightest possibility she could die wants to know her child will be okay. That's a mother's job. It's nature at its finest, survival of the species and all that. Maybe you consoled your mother in the very best way possible. Maybe your promise gave her permission to focus on herself for a while."

chapter thirty-three

Twists and Turns

I had just returned from a solo three-mile run (Kay-Kay's in Destin with her daddy for a long weekend) when the phone rang. "Does Rose Warren want me to drive her to her appointment?" Aunt Mary asked. "I took today off, so tell her it's no trouble," she added. I relayed the message to Mother, who was still in the shower.

"I'm perfectly capable of driving a car!" Mother shouted loud enough for Aunt Mary to hear (unfortunately, I didn't have my hand over the mouthpiece). I didn't even have to *try* to put Mother's harsh words into kinder, gentler terms. When I put the phone back to my ear, Aunt Mary had already hung up.

There was a teachers' in-service at Spring Hill High School, and I intended to spend my day off prom-dress shopping at Cool Springs Mall. Mother padded through the kitchen, appearing slightly less doom and gloom than usual. I could tell she was looking forward to getting out of the house, even if it was to drive to Nashville for a chest scan. "I could come with you," I offered. "We could shop for a dress together when you're done." I took a sip of my strawberry-banana smoothie and watched Mother pour hot water into her favorite mug. She sat down at the kitchen table across from me.

"I would love to come with you, Rosie. Really I would, but who knows how long this appointment will take. You think you're going in for something simple, and it eats up the whole day. You'd better go on your own if you want to get anything accomplished."

"So what's your gut feeling?"

"About the scan?" I nodded and watched Mother swirl a black-mango teabag around in her cup. "I've stopped trusting my gut feelings, Rosie. I feel a little better, but who knows if that means anything. Cancer isn't an illness you can trust. It takes all sorts of unexpected twists and turns. At the very least, I won't have your aunt blasting her mouth off to Dr. Nelson." I could tell by the look on Mother's face she was still really mad.

"Mother, I . . . well, she was right about your needing to rest," I pointed out. I'd waited my whole entire life for a schism between my mother and my aunt, and now I was trying to patch things up. It didn't make sense.

"It's not that, Rosie. I know she was right about that. But it's the way she goes about things." Mother sighed and took a sip of tea. "Like Mother's Day. Did you hear her completely take credit for your losing weight?"

"Oh, yeah."

"You'd think with all her self-help books she'd have a little more insight into how ridiculous she sounds. Of course, she's too busy doling out those books to everyone else to actually read them herself. I know I'm not perfect by any—" The guest bedroom door clicked open, and Mother stopped talking.

"Well, I'm off!" said Grandma Georgia, bursting through the kitchen like a misfired pistol. Briskly, she kissed the top of Mother's head, leaving pink lip prints behind. "You have a full schedule today, Rose Warren. Not a single cancellation!" Grandma Georgia's new mission in life is to keep Mother *and* Heavenly Hair alive and well. "Rose Garden, here's a little something for you, sugar," she added, shoving a wad of bills into my hand.

"What's *this* for?" I asked.

"Prom," said Grandma Georgia. "You'll be the prettiest girl there. As long as you don't wear *black*!"

"You don't have to give me money. I already took some out of my savings account."

"Well, put it back! Oh, and make sure you look nice today when you go shopping. Put on a little makeup. Curl your hair."

"I'm just going to the mall," I pointed out.

"Salespeople treat you better when you look good. You'll get a better idea of how you'll be on prom night, too."

"She's right," said Mother. "It's the same thing with hairdressers. The prettier you look when you get there, the prettier you look when you leave."

"That's as bad as the it-takes-money-to-make-money rule! Who comes up with this stuff?" Mother and Grandma Georgia laughed. Miss Bertha honked out front.

"There's my ride. I'm off to the races! Good luck to both my girls today," said Grandma Georgia. She winked at Mother and blew me a kiss.

As much as I hated the idea of going to Cool Springs Mall by myself, I knew shopping alone wouldn't be all bad. At least I wouldn't have to tolerate unwanted opinions, and there'd be no one in the dressing room making me feel self-conscious or mentioning the dreaded words *size two*.

The phone rang just as I was slathering on an oatmeal-and-banana facial (I'd decided Mother and Grandma Georgia were probably right about looking good). "Hey!" said Kyle when I picked up. His voice was warm and friendly (and sexy) on the other end of the line.

"Hey!" I replied, trying not to get goo all over the phone.

"Okay, you'll probably question my masculinity after I say what I'm about to say, but . . . *well* . . . Mama thinks we should color-coordinate." The words came out as if he were spitting a stray hair off his tongue. "You know, like my cummerbund should match your dress. I keep tellin' her I don't *know* the color of your dress because you haven't bought it yet, but she doesn't believe me. I think if Pigg and Parsons runs out of pastel cummerbunds, she may have to be medicated."

"I promise to notify the Associated Press the minute I find a dress," I said, laughing, "but don't expect any miracles. Prom-dress shopping sounds much easier than it is. I may end up at the Farmers Co-op in search of a feed sack. I could always dye it pink, I guess."

"Well, it wouldn't matter. You'd look good in anything," said Kyle.

Downstairs, the hall closet door squeaked open and snapped shut again. Mother's car keys jangled against the glass bowl by the door. "I have to go, Kyle. Mother's about to leave for her appointment. I'll call you later," I said, and hung up.

Quickly, I rinsed the crusty oatmeal concoction off my face and tugged on a black skirt and white T-shirt. The thought of Mother's scan made my stomach clutch up with fear. I bounded down the stairs and found her staring out the window. "Sit on the porch with me a minute," she said.

"The porch?"

Without a reply, Mother swung open the front door—light spilled across the honey-colored floors, and dust particles danced wildly. Outside, she settled herself on the warm concrete step, and I sat down beside her. This seemed an odd thing to do when we both had places to go, and I was praying Mother wouldn't start talking about dying again. "The sun's pretty hot and with your chemo—"

"I'm well aware of the sun risks associated with chemotherapy," Mother replied, cutting me off. As if shaking off the cold, she hugged herself and rubbed her small hands up and down her thin arms. The smell of geraniums and boxwoods permeated the air, and already, even before nine o'clock, the sun felt like July instead of May. The lawn was green and lush, and the white picket fence, which Mother had repainted just last summer, gleamed in the light.

Neither of us said a word. No talk of dying, no complaining about Aunt Mary. We just sat there, side by side, on the rough cement with our knees touching. Mother picked a dead bloom off the geranium, and I watched the frail wisps of chemo hair lift slightly and catch the faint breeze. At home, Mother had stopped wearing head coverings of any sort. Even the summer hats were too hot, and the wigs itched her dried-out scalp something terrible.

She dead-headed another bloom and tossed it under the large boxwood next to the porch. Now that the dried-out blossoms were gone, the tight-fisted, verdant ones were visible. Already you could see hints of pink beneath the green.

Cancer isn't an illness you can trust. It takes all sorts of unexpected twists and turns. I thought about Mother's words. Today was another turn, I knew. I closed my eyes and let the sunshine solder Mother's image onto my memory. Just in case, I wanted every detail of her engraved there.

chapter thirty-four

Over

The whole drive to Cool Springs Mall I couldn't get Mother and our front-porch moment out of my head, and I was being selfish, I knew, because instead of dwelling on my mother and what might happen to *her* if the chest scan wasn't good, I kept thinking about myself and what would happen to me. What would *I do* without her? Live with Grandma Georgia and Mr. Keith in some bingo-playing, Depends-wearing retirement home for half the year? Stay with Aunt Mary and spend my life in the Petco searching for quirky cat toys? And what about Heavenly Hair and all Mother's clients? And my house? What about my charming, well-decorated, comfortable, I-have-my-own-bathroom house?

The mall was overstuffed with gaggles of girls, some of whom I recognized from Spring Hill High School. Luckily, I knew for certain Misty Winters and Tara Waters weren't among them. The Bluebirds had a car wash at the Middle Tennessee Bank today.

They were raising money for their end-of-year presentation.

The food court threatened to lure me in, so I hopped on the escalator and rode up to the third floor. Window after window offered nothing better than one size-two cupcake dress after another. I didn't even bother going inside the stores. No matter how much money Grandma Georgia handed out, I would *never* wear a cupcake dress. After an hour or so, I gave up and headed for my car.

Just before I reached Spring Hill, I pulled over at a rest stop and called Heavenly Hair from my cell. Richard was the only person who might provide some insight on where to find a fat-girl prom dress, but he couldn't come to the phone. He was having highlights put in his hair. His latest craze (other than newly hired Shampoo Drew) was pursuing a modeling career, and there was some casting call for country-music-video extras up in Nashville.

"Can you believe it's just me and Bertha handling this whole salon on a Saturday?" Grandma Georgia yelled into the phone. "Hell, I didn't even lose my temper when I found out Richard took the day off and booked hisself for highlights. Why, I'm busier than a one-legged woman in a ass-kickin' contest, and I am loving every minute of it. Any luck with a dress?" she asked.

"Not yet," I said, trying to sound hopeful, as if the perfect gown were wrapped up in a box and lying on the side of the road somewhere. "I could always shop another day and come help you instead, Grandma." Secretly, I hoped she would take me up on the offer.

"Hell, no, Rose Garden! I was born for this. Now you have a good time shopping, and don't come home with *schmatte*, hear?" said Grandma Georgia.

"Oh, I won't," I promised (even though I had no idea what *schmatte* meant).

I passed the Spring Hill exit and headed toward nearby Columbia. There was a place called Renee's, a high-end shop, but I figured with Grandma Georgia's cash and my own money from savings I could maybe afford something—*on sale*. Among the BMWs and Mercedes in the parking lot, my Bug stuck out like a fat girl in *Vogue*. I parked and went inside.

An X-ray thin blonde stood just inside the front door (as if waiting especially for me). Her expensive suit was neatly tailored, her hair cropped daringly short. She smiled tightly and said, "You must be Lori's girl. Right this way." I had no idea what she was talking about, and I hardly felt brave enough to contradict, so I followed her to the back of the store and into the stockroom. "This is what I'm talking about," she said, gesturing all around. "I pay your cleaning crew good money, and yet they hardly touch a thing!"

"Excuse me?" I said.

"Look! They hardly vacuumed! The bathroom's a mess!" she snapped, flinging open the door to what looked to be a spotless lavatory.

As I bolted toward the parking lot, my heart made a *swish-swish-pfsssh* sound in my ears. I'd been mistaken for a cleaning girl instead of a customer! "I guess fat girls don't shop at Renee's!" I shouted out my car window. Two women getting out of a Lexus gawked.

———

The Dairy Queen was a much friendlier place with its clean, cheerful landscaping, meat locker air-conditioning, colorful posters of hamburgers and fries, and its well-stocked freezer of assorted ice-cream bars and cakes. According to the diet book I'd been reading, it's important to indulge yourself once in a while. I hadn't eaten since the early-morning smoothie, and my stomach rumbled, so I figured now was as good a time as any to "indulge." The first two bites of the chocolate-dipped vanilla cone tasted like love on my tongue; the third and fourth were more like sweet guilt; the last one was Bluebird mean.

Back in my car again, I turned up the radio and tried not to think about chemo and cancer and skinny, chichi bitch stores. I drove through town and thought about Julia Roberts in *Pretty Woman*, that scene when she goes shopping on Rodeo Drive, *after* Richard Gere (and his money) intervene. I popped open the sunroof and tried to think about Kyle's kind words, *You'd look good in anything. . . .* The gas gauge gave me its friendly *get-gas* ding, so I pulled over at the Jim Dandy Market.

While the tank filled, I went inside to pay. I glanced furtively at the pastry rack—donuts and Ring Dings and Twinkies smiled up at me. I grabbed three packages and placed them on the counter along with a twenty-dollar bill. The greasy clerk didn't even look at me. He kept his combed-over head down as if I were buying some kinky brand of condoms or Tampax.

"That'll be another $4.56," he grunted. I handed him a five, and glanced up at the security mirror above his head, but it wasn't my own distorted image I saw. It was Mrs. McCutchin's. She wore the familiar navy pup-tent blouse, the one with the purple sweat stains under the arms. From behind the tube in her throat, she rattled *"Don't"* and disappeared. My hands shook as I placed the Twinkies and Ring Dings and donuts back on the rack. "But you already paid for them," the clerk said. I took the snacks back again and slid them across the counter.

"Then these are for you," I said and left.

Anger was so built up in me I thought I might explode, little bits of ice cream and chocolate spattering all over the windshield. I sped past Taco Bell; I was angry at cancer. I shot through a yellow light in front of the Sonic; I was angry at fat. I turned at a NO TURN ON RED sign right by McDonald's; I was angry at judgmental, snotty store clerks and Bluebirds and NBs and basically anybody who had ever, in any way, shape, or form, done me wrong. It hit me then—I needed my car washed. I made a left onto Carmack Boulevard and drove toward the bank parking lot.

Clad in bathing suit tops and too-short shorts, the Bluebirds lathered, rinsed, and dried. They must've been raking in the money. A whole string of cars, mostly trucks with gawking boys inside (and a few old-fart creepy types), waited in a very long line. I debated on whether or not I really wanted to do this. It would eat up a good chunk of the afternoon, and I was inviting trouble, certainly.

An SUV honked behind me. "Go!" some woman shouted out the window. Right at that moment, as if it were a sign, Roy Orbison's golden voice drifted out of the speakers. *Pretty woman,* he sang, *walking down the street* . . . I smiled and pictured Roy and Julia crammed in the back seat, the two of them egging me on.

Misty spotted me first (a bright red Bug *is* hard to miss). Ever so slightly her mouth dropped open. I took a deep breath and pulled forward a little. The SUV squeezed in tight behind me. *No escaping now,* I thought. My heart pounded, and I dialed Kay-Kay's cell phone.

"Hey," she said, her voice friendly and light (and tan) on the second ring.

"How's Florida?" I asked.

"It's great! Listen!" She held the phone out, and I could hear beach sounds—crashing waves, squealing children, a dog barking. "Guess what me and Daddy did this morning? We ran on the beach! Can you believe it? It was fun," she said, "although I think I nearly killed him. He's so out of shape."

"I'm sitting in the Bluebird car wash line."

"What!" Kay-Kay cried. The car in front of me pulled forward, and I spotted a couple of the Bluebird sponsors standing off to the side. They looked like Renee's customers, or grown-up Bluebirds, or both. "Rosie! What are you doing there?" There was no way I could explain about Twinkies and the Dairy Queen and Renee's and *Pretty Woman.* Jumbled all together, it didn't make any sense.

"Rosie? I said, 'What are you—?'"

"I don't know exactly. I don't *know* what I'm doing. Just stay on the line, okay?"

"Okay," said Kay-Kay. "Take a deep cleansing breath and try to slow your heart rate a little."

My heart *was* pounding, and my sweaty thighs were stuck to the leatherette seat, and the chocolate-coated cone churned in my stomach, and there was a marching band inside my head, and they were tuning up. Suddenly, it was my turn. "I'm up. Stay on the line, okay?"

"I'm not going anywhere," Kay-Kay replied.

I closed the sunroof, left the key in the ignition, grabbed my purse, and pried myself off the seat. Misty made a beeline in my direction, and judging by her swagger, it wasn't to ask what kind of air-freshener I preferred.

"What are *you* doing here?" she hissed. Tara came up beside her.

"I'm here to get my car washed," I replied coolly, clutching the phone tighter.

"I'm not washing your damn car," Misty snapped.

"Me neither," Tara chimed in.

"Girls, is there a problem?" one of the sponsors called out.

"No, ma'am," Tara replied sweetly. I waited. They looked at one another, and it occurred to me how small Misty and Tara were. Not just small in the philosophical way, although they were certainly that, too. But *small* small, as in, I towered over them. Their size was a disappointment somehow.

"Then hurry up and wash that cute little Bug. It shouldn't take y'all more than five minutes. That's a cute car!" the lady called out to me, and waved. Misty and Tara went to work soaping and scrubbing. I could tell by their herky-jerky movements and dagger glances that they were beyond angry.

"I have to go, Kay-Kay," I whispered.

"Are they washing your car?!" she squealed.

"Yeah, and I wanna get a picture with my phone before they're finished. I'll send it to you."

Surreptitiously, I snapped a couple of shots—Misty crouching down scrubbing tires; Tara accidentally spraying Misty with the hose. It was like watching two wet cats. When they'd finished I paid them the exact amount (no tip, mind you).

"Monday's gonna be fun for you," Misty whispered.

I searched my mind for something smart-ass to say, but my tongue was worn out, all the energy gone out of it. Instead, I said the only thing I could think of. "It's over."

"What's *over*?" Misty snarled. "What are you *talking* about?" She had her hands on her skinny, wet hips, and she was glaring, her face contorted into a big, unpleasant grimace.

I ignored her and got into my soap-streaked, half-ass-clean Bug and drove off. Just up Carmack was Zippy's Self-serve Car Wash. I pulled into an empty stall and stuffed eight quarters in the machine. As I stood there holding the nozzle, watching the water bead up on top of the wax, I realized what I'd meant. It really was over. Maybe Misty and Tara would still harass me. In fact, I knew they would still harass me. On Monday, they'd give it their best effort, no doubt. But their fun wasn't in the harassment itself; their fun was in my reaction to the harassment. And if I refused to react, at the very least I'd kill their fun. My best defense was no defense.

Ah-ha! Oh, Mrs. Wallace would be proud!

Mother was dozing under the awning on the back deck when I got home. "You get a dress?" she asked, jerking awake. The sound of her voice made me feel safe.

"No luck," I replied, plopping down in the chair beside her. "I'll look through some magazines tonight. Get some ideas. Maybe you could help?" I asked.

"Sure," said Mother, yawning.

We sat for a while longer, neither of us saying anything. We were avoiding the cancer elephant in our backyard. It was standing on its hind legs. Its trunk was raised. It was making that explosive sound elephants make, and we were both ignoring it. Mother didn't give me her news, and I didn't ask.

After a few minutes, she was asleep again. Her breath came in a peaceful, even rhythm. "I love you," I whispered, thinking how awkward the words felt on my tongue, a bit like trying out one of Kay-Kay's contortionist-type stretches.

I love you wasn't something Mother and I said much. I suppose we'd just never gotten in the habit of it.

chapter thirty-five

Prom Day!

I've eaten nothing but carrot sticks and celery and rice cakes and lettuce and plain tuna for a solid week. I've counted every single calorie within a forty-mile radius. I even joined Harvey's Gym (Kay-Kay swears by Harvey), *and* I started a spinning class (no, that does not mean turning around and around in circles). Even though this healthful food is boring, it's better than being on Pounds-Away and having a stomachache all the time.

As of five minutes ago, I weighed 158, which is far from svelte, but at least it's better than last week's sudden premenstrual jump to 162 again. I swear I can plump up faster than a Ball Park Frank.

On the Tuesday following my disastrous shopping trip and near Twinkie overdose, Kay-Kay came to the rescue. She called Leona, the woman who owns Landis Lane, and asked if we could have a private consultation after school. Leona took down all my measurements (shriek!) and held fabrics up around my face to see which colors I might look best in. "Black," she said finally. "With your dark eyes and hair, oh, black is so right! So dramatic!" She fingered her pearl earrings, which were the size of eyeballs.

As it turned out, Leona didn't have anything in stock, so she called another small shop in Franklin. By the next afternoon, I had a dress. Not just *a* dress, *the* dress—black strapless with a slit up the front, Empire waist, and hot pink piping on the hem and around the bodice. Mother found shoes to match on the Dillard's website, and Aunt Mary drove all the way to Nashville just to pick them up. Grandma Georgia didn't even care that the dress was black. "You look like a *shayna maideleh*," she said when I tried it on, which means "beautiful girl" in Yiddish.

On prom day, Heavenly Hair was jammed with clients. Miss Bertha was about to lose her mind with so many cell phones ringing, and girls chattering like jungle monkeys, myself included. Richard and Kay-Kay hovered over me, discussing the various hair-style options. Richard wanted one of his intricate up-dos; Kay-Kay wanted something long with lots of curls. "This ain't a *Dallas* rerun," said Richard in that biting, bitchy tone of his (which we haven't heard nearly as much of since Shampoo Drew came along).

"Well, it *ain't* a party for George and Martha Washington either!" Kay-Kay shot right back. Right away, I knew they'd be good friends.

A squeal interrupted the hum of voices. "I love it! I absolutely love it!" shouted Janay Dugger, Hilda May Brunson's niece. Mrs. Brunson was standing over Janay with a video camera, a real one, like on TV shows. She'd rented it and taken a course on its proper use solely for the purpose of capturing every last detail of her niece's first prom.

"Say it one more time, Janay, and look into the camera," Mrs. Brunson ordered.

"Oh. Dear. God. The loss of her virginity will likely be made into a Broadway musical," Richard groaned. Kay-Kay burst out laughing and swatted him with a rolled-up *People* magazine.

"Do that one more time, Kay-Kay, and look into the camera," said Richard, imitating Mrs. Brunson. I got out of the chair and left the two of them acting like fools and slipped off to call Kyle. He picked up on the first ring.

"Hey, Rosie," he said, his voice grinning over the phone lines. "Just so you know, Mama picked out a hot pink cummerbund to match the pink-stripe thing in your dress, but I'm not wearing it. She's pissed, but I went over to Pigg and Parsons and rented a black cummerbund and bow tie myself. I hope you don't care."

"Not at all. Hey, listen, I have a favor to ask."

"Sure, what is it?"

I hesitated. "Um . . . would you mind if I invited Kay-Kay to come with us tonight? I just feel so bad that she's not going."

"But Billy Gardner asked her like five hundred times, didn't he?"

"Yeah, but she doesn't want to go with him. Listen, I don't want you to take it the wrong way. I want to be with you . . . I mean . . . well, like alone and everything. It's just that she's been so good to me, you know? A real friend, and I hate the thought of her sitting home."

The phone line was silent. Dead air. A slow tugging in of breath and then Kyle's reply. "I understand. It's okay. Invite her if you want to."

Shampoo Drew lathered my hair and massaged my temples and neck and shoulders with his smooth magic-man fingers (no wonder Richard was in such a good mood lately). Afterward, I drifted back over to Richard's chair and sat down. "Don't go getting any hetero ideas," he warned. "He's *mine*."

"Don't get your Calvins in a wad. Drew only has eyes for you."

Richard stopped combing out my hair and looked at me. "You really think so?" For once there wasn't a hint of sarcasm in his voice.

"Yep, I really think so."

"I have news," he whispered, glancing over at Kay-Kay, who was absorbed in a brand-new issue of *Hair Trends*. I looked up at him quizzically, and he pressed his finger to his lips. "You're looking at the lead in the next Hope Ferrell video."

"What?"

"*Shhh*. Don't say anything. I'm not telling anybody yet. Drew doesn't even know."

"My lips are locked," I said. *If I had my way, they'd be dead bolted.*

The end result of Kay-Kay and Richard's collaboration was a half-down, half-up coiffure. Long curls at the bottom with the top portion swept up and away from my face. Richard even agreed to Kay-Kay's idea for a fake flower pinned carefully just above my right ear. "The curl's a little tight," Richard explained, "but *don't* brush it out. This way it'll hold through the dancing—and anything else you and big football man might decide to do later." He winked.

I waited until the drive home to ask Kay-Kay about the prom. "Rosie, I swear that's the nicest thing anybody has ever asked me."

"So you'll go with us?" I asked, pulling into her driveway. I rolled down the windows and shut off the engine. The sharp smell of freshly cut grass made me want to sneeze. I fanned away the urge and looked at Kay-Kay.

"Absolutely not, but the fact that you were willing to share your big night with me . . . well, it means more than you know," she said, hugging me tightly. "Besides, Daddy promised we'd order an Ab Cruncher online tonight. He's committed to gettin' back in shape. I'm keeping my fingers crossed it lasts."

"I'm glad about your dad."

"Ever since Florida he's been better. Honestly, I mean, I hate to say it 'cause I don't want to jinx things, but I think he's starting to come out a his depression." Kay-Kay's eyes were shiny with hope, and for the first time since the whole Logan-Marta/Bluebird saga began, she seemed happy. *Kay-Kay has her rah-rah spirit back,* I thought to myself and smiled.

"What?" she asked. "Why are you grinning at me like that?"

"We have a lot to look forward to," I said.

"I *know*! I think about that all the time. I'm so glad I'm not old. I'm glad it's all still out there in front of me, just waiting. You know what the funniest part is?" I shook my head. "I'm starting to feel like there's more stuff ahead now that Logan's gone. The

Bluebirds, too. It's like all those things I wanted so bad were really just gettin' in my way somehow."

Late that afternoon, Mother tried to help with my pre-prom preparations. "Just let me smooth out your foundation," she said, coming at me with a sponge wedge.

"Mother, *please*," I said as patiently as possible, "I need to do this myself." Mother gave me that annoying isn't-it-cute-how-grown-up-she-is smile and slipped off downstairs. I shut my bedroom door, turned up the music, turned down the thermostat, and went to work.

> Step one: Smooth, even foundation with a slightly damp sponge wedge. A hint of under-eye concealer to match my skin tone
>
> Step two: Eye shadow and a touch of dark liner smudged over with powder shadow, some mascara, and a bit of eyebrow pencil (for fill-in only)
>
> Step three: Blush with red undertones
>
> Step four: Lip liner applied carefully—and *faintly*—dabs of lipstick one shade darker than the liner, tissue blotting, and gloss for shine

After I'd finished, I stood in front of the full-length mirror behind my bathroom door. The small diamond studs Mother had given me for my birthday sparkled in the late-afternoon sun. The black dress shimmered, and it was perfect for my Lane Bryant figure—it skimmed the flawed parts, the lumps and bumps of my belly, hips, and thighs, and hugged the good ones: my boobs. Even with the weight loss, Lucy and Ethel (Grandma Georgia's nickname for breasts) were still plump and perky, and I had just the right amount of cleavage, enough to be tempting without seeming downright slutty.

"Rosie!" Mother called up the stairs. "There's not much time, and everyone wants to *ooh* and *aah* over you before Kyle gets here."

"Coming," I yelled back. I waited for the mirror to say something nasty, but it was speechless. So was everyone else when I got downstairs, except for Aunt Mary, of course.

"Why, you just look so cute! Just so cute!" she said, clapping her hands together and flipping the same strand of too-gelled hair off her shiny forehead over and over again (I think her enthusiasm had more to do with the fact that she and Mother had officially made up earlier in the afternoon).

While Mother snapped pictures of Kyle (who was ten minutes early) and me, Grandma Georgia, Miss Bertha, Richard, and Drew stood around gawking. I could tell by the pink in Kyle's cheeks he was embarrassed or nervous or both—not that I blamed him. Richard and Drew stood shoulder to shoulder, and I could tell they were scrutinizing his every detail. I could practically hear the grooming critique going on inside Richard's head: *Dried-out cuticles! A stray nose hair! Razor burn!*

Grandma Georgia kept saying she felt *farklempt*. Miss Bertha just sipped a tall glass of sweet tea as if it were a stiff drink and took the world in over the top of her drugstore half-glasses.

Mother was the only completely nonembarrassing one. Her itchy wig was perfectly in place. She'd dabbed on a little makeup. She took pictures, pinned my corsage, and offered Tic Tacs and tissues for my evening bag. "Just in case you need them," she whispered, and brushed a smudge (probably Grandma Georgia's pink lipstick) off my cheek.

I thought about her own prom all those years ago; more than likely, she was thinking about it, too. Her bravery—then *and* now—made me proud.

When I saw the restaurant's menu board, I didn't know whether to cry or bust out laughing. THE LAMPLIGHTER INN PRESENTS: A NIGHT OF ARTICHOKES.

"What's that?" asked Kyle, pointing to the primitive drawing that looked more like a green pineapple than an artichoke.

"Your first course," said a passing waiter.

"You sure you wouldn't rather go to Frankie's Carhop?" Kyle whispered.

Our opulent table of white linens, glowing candles, and shiny utensils was tucked away in a romantic corner. After we were seated and holding menus, Kyle reached across the table for my hand. "I'm sorry Kay-Kay didn't get a date for the prom," said Kyle, "but I'm kinda glad she's not coming with us."

"I just hate the idea of her sitting home, but she seemed fine with it."

The candlelight illuminated Kyle's broad, handsome face. He smiled at me. I smiled at him. It was a perfectly romantic, heart-stopping, oh-my-Lord-I-think-I'm-in-love moment until the waiter shoved a plate in between us.

"Pull off the leaves and scrape the stuffing off with your front teeth. Don't eat the spikes," he instructed and left.

"Spikes?" asked Kyle, screwing up his face.

A group of noisy prom goers piled through the front door. Her shrew voice stood out among the other normal chattering ones. "Hey, Tara! Check it out. A night of *artichokes*!" Misty cackled. My rabbit heart pounded wildly inside my chest. *It's over,* I reminded myself, wondering exactly how I could make it over if Misty and Tara decided to torture me all night. Maybe I could ignore them on a regular school day, but on prom night, I wasn't so sure.

"You don't really wanna eat this thing, do you?" asked Kyle. "Hell-*o*?" He waved his giant football paw in front of my face. "Earth to Rosie. You're a million miles away."

I slumped down in my seat and turned my head toward the window. In the reflection, I saw the Bluebird group head toward a different dining room. *Thank God,* I thought and sat up straight again.

Our waiter stood in a corner by the kitchen. Kyle's back was to him, but I could see he was giving us the eat-now-talk-later look. Obediently, I tugged off an artichoke leaf and followed the waiter's instructions, scraping the pastelike mixture behind my two front teeth. It actually tasted good, really good, a combination of mushrooms and cheese with a little bit of ham mixed in. I polished off several more leaves (how fattening can a leaf be, after all).

Kyle looked down at his plate. "You think I could get some fries?" he asked.

"The menu's pre-fixed," the waiter interrupted. He stood above us, holding our salad plates. "It's called a night of *artichokes*."

"Even the dessert?" asked Kyle.

The waiter rolled his eyes and smacked our plates down on the table. "I just *love* prom night," he said and huffed off.

Kyle and I zipped through the main course—pasta with crushed tomatoes, red peppers, and artichokes. It was delicious. Just to be on the safe side, we skipped dessert altogether. I didn't want to blow my diet, even if it was prom night, and Kyle was convinced the dessert would have artichokes in it, too.

Kyle paid the bill, and when he wasn't looking, I added a few extra dollars to the tip. I knew why the waiter hated prom night so much (teenagers are notoriously lousy tippers). We climbed into the Suburban, and Kyle leaned in close—full brown-eye-to-brown-eye contact. "Remember that day at the computer table? When you lost control of your chair?" he asked. I nodded. "Well, that was the first day I knew I wanted to ask you out."

"You're kidding, right?"

"No, I'm serious. I liked you then and there."

"Kyle, I was forty-five pounds heavier then and there," I pointed out (idiot that I am).

"Well . . . when you look at a person's eyes or her smile, you can't tell how much she weighs. . . ." He paused, and it seemed like he had something more to say. I wondered if he was anywhere close to *I love you*. I sure was. The words were hanging off the end of my tongue, threatening to let go and make that big leap any second. I resisted, and if Kyle had been about to say the words, he resisted, too.

The Spring Hill High School parking lot was nearly empty. "Looks like we're early," I said.

"Yeah. If we go in now we'll have to mingle with teachers or the prom committee." He grabbed a parking spot in the back, near the tennis courts, and began flipping through his CD collection. Louis Armstrong, Bobby Darin, and Ray Charles flashed by. "You like Ray Charles?" he asked, and went back a page. I nodded. Ray was one of Miss Bertha's favorites, and I knew many of his more popular songs by heart.

Ray's froggy-throated voice filled up the car, and I reclined my seat back a little. "Look at that sunset," I said. Across the late spring sky were streaks of fire orange mixed in with bits of purple, green, and blue. Before I knew it, we were kissing. I'd just reapplied lip gloss, but I didn't care. In Kyle's defensive lineman embrace, I felt small, exposed somehow—as if all *my* spikes were peeled away. And his mouth was so warm, his tongue so inviting. It seemed like all these hard, clutched-up little pieces of me were floating right out the window. Before I knew it, the words *I love you* tumbled out.

It was like I'd dropped a whole drawer of pots and pans. Kyle pulled away and blinked at me. I waited. *Please say it back.* I waited some more. *Please.* Cars were beginning to fill the parking lot, and I could hear music coming from the gymnasium.

"Maybe we should go inside now," said Kyle, his face kind and apologetic.

chapter thirty-six

Girls Gone Wild

On our way inside the gymnasium, Kyle slipped his arm around my waist, but I pulled away. Why had I let the *I love you* slip out? *Stupid, stupid girl!* I hadn't intended to say it. I'd just gotten carried away with the sunset and Kyle's lips and Ray Charles. Somehow I wanted to convey this to Kyle, but there was no way to backtrack now that my *I love you* was out there.

Logan Clark and Marta Pitts were locked in a mutual buttgrabbing embrace over by the giant trophy cabinet. Under the staircase, Tara Waters appeared to be resuscitating the NB I'd tripped that day in the hallway. *Where are the chaperones when you need them?* Kay-Kay had definitely made the right decision. I was beginning to think I should've stayed home with her.

"Wanna dance?" asked Kyle when a song finally came on. The music was so fast it was impossible to find a beat, although what could you expect from a band called Rupture Your Eardrums?

"Okay," I said stiffly, avoiding his eyes. Kyle slipped his arms around my waist and pressed his forehead against mine. He tried to kiss me, but I turned my head to the side, giving him cheek instead of lips. When the song was over, I briskly led the way back to the bleachers.

"Want something to drink?" he tried. I could tell by the way he said it my aloof behavior was making him nervous. *This is not about Kyle*, I heard Mrs. Wallace say. *This is about you, Rosie.*

"Sure. I'll have the punch," I said politely. I felt guilty as I watched Kyle wander off through the crowd. He wore the bewildered, what-just-happened expression of a person involved in an accident, as if he wasn't quite sure what to do next.

Finally, the band took a break. Intermission music crackled through the ancient speakers, and someone jacked up the volume. "Oh, no!" I groaned.

"What?" asked Kyle.

"It's the Bluebirds' theme song," I shouted. Dressed in various shades of blue (a long-standing prom tradition for Bluebirds), the girls scrambled to the dance floor. Tara had pried herself off the NB long enough to grab Misty and jump in the middle of it—all of them sweating and gyrating and shouting out the "We Are Family" lyrics as if Sister Sledge had written the song especially for them.

Girls Gone Wild, I thought, and smiled to myself. This was exactly the sort of thing I would've (under normal circumstances) whispered to Kyle, but not tonight. I finished off my punch, crumpled the paper cup, and shredded it into tiny pieces. I also had a little talk with myself (inside my head, of course).

You don't want some boy saying he loves you just because you said it first. It has to be real.

Yes, but it still sucks that he didn't say it back!

You took a chance, and that's good. Just relax and have fun. What are you? An idiot? Six months ago you wouldn't have even considered this as a possibility—going to the prom with anybody, much less Kyle Cox. Be grateful!

I am. I am grateful. And I love Kyle even if he doesn't love me back.

Then go dance your ass off and try to have a good time.

Okay.

I tugged Kyle to his feet. "Let's go dance some more," I said, and kissed him lightly on the cheek.

"Sure," he said, and let me lead him to the floor.

By the end of the evening, I was certain Rupture Your Eardrums had lived up to their name. My ears rang like the downtown church bells on Sunday morning. Kyle and I walked hand in hand to his car, and the cool night air felt good on my damp skin.

"Let's go to the park," said Kyle when we pulled out of the parking lot. "It's not really time for any after-parties yet."

"Okay," I said, thinking how uninterested I was in any after-parties.

Kyle pulled the blanket out of the back seat and we sat down. "There's no security here tonight," he said. "The city had some cutbacks or something. They had to let the night guy go."

"Did you research this?"

"No. Daddy talks about this kinda stuff every night at the supper table. He's real into local politics. He talks about running for office himself one day, but Mama says the only place Daddy's running is to a ball field to pick up one of my brothers."

"Your mom hasn't been to the salon for a while," I said, trying to make conversation.

"Yeah. She's not much on stuff like that. She always *says* she's going to, but she hardly ever does."

In spite of the chilly temperature, I still felt sweaty from all the dancing. In my mind, I calculated the number of calories I'd burned off on the dance floor. Without warning, Kyle locked his lips on mine and eased me back onto the blanket. His face hung over me like a wide moon. I opened my eyes and watched his eyes flutter behind their tightly closed lids. After a while, I switched my gaze to the inky sky, which was sprinkled with stars. I was trying hard not to feel anything.

"What's the matter?" asked Kyle, drawing back. "What are you looking at?"

"The sky," I replied. I'd insulted his intense kissing, I knew, but something had come over me. I wasn't sure what it was, but everything seemed different now—more reality, less fantasy.

Kyle Cox was handsome. He was a jock. He was even a nice guy. No, he was more than that. He was an exceptional guy, but he didn't love me. Sooner or later, I would have to deal with the fact that the fat girl doesn't wind up with Enormous Strapping Jock Boy in the end. Maybe this was our denouement.

"The sky *is* pretty tonight," he agreed. "So are you," he said, and kissed me again. I thought of the couple Miss Bertha and

I had seen in the park all those weeks ago. I remembered the electric feeling I'd gotten watching the boy knead his girlfriend's bosom like bread dough. I pictured my virginity floating off over the treetops like a bright red helium balloon.

"That's enough," I said, pushing Kyle away. "It's time to go home."

"Home? But what about the after-parties?"

"I'm not going to any after-parties," I said, rearranging my now *very* wrinkled dress. "I plan to start studying for exams tomorrow. They'll be here before you know it, and my mother starts chemo again on Monday. Her lungs are all cleared up now. I wanna spend the day with her. Do something fun to celebrate maybe."

"Oh, well, that's really good. I'm glad," said Kyle, "that your mom's better, I mean." Obediently, he stood and folded the blanket. I tried not to notice the hurt in his eyes.

Crumpled dress draped over my chair, scuffed shoes flung into a corner, Grandma Georgia convinced of a good time, I lay in my bed listening to the hum of the air-conditioning unit. I wondered how Kay-Kay had spent her night. I thought about Logan and Marta. I obsessed over Kyle. The words and images of the day, of the last few months, actually, filled my head. My heart had that two-sizes-too-big-for-my-chest feeling again. "I love you, Rosemary," I whispered. "I love you," I said a second time, because I really needed to hear the words.

chapter thirty-seven

Heart

On the Monday after the prom, I talked Mrs. Wallace's ears off. I probably made her wish she'd never become a nurse practitioner or started studying to be a counselor or ever made her way from Nashville down to Spring Hill. After I'd finished going over the events of the past week—Kyle, Kay-Kay, Mother, Aunt Mary, and I don't even know what else—Mrs. Wallace leaned forward in her chair and studied me. I figured she was deciding which mental hospital to put me in or what kind of psych drug I should take (or whether straitjackets came in my size). Instead, she said, "Rosie, you've made amazing progress. You don't need me anymore."

My mouth fell open, and I stared at her. "What? What do you mean I don't need you? Of course I *need* you! What are you talking about?" Panic pulsed toward my chest.

"Take a deep breath and listen for a minute." She clasped her hands loosely across her lap and leaned back in her chair. Her head was cocked slightly to the side, and she was smiling a little.

"Remember when I told you I was doing a study on the *short*-term effects of counseling?" I nodded. Already, I knew where this was headed, and she hadn't even said anything yet. "Well, *short-term* is the operative word here. You've had several months of counseling, you've lost fifty pounds—"

"Forty-five," I corrected her.

"At any rate, you've made tremendous headway in terms of your weight, your relationships, *and* in your willingness to take emotional risks. Your telling Kyle and your mother that you loved them are probably the biggest signs of how far you've come."

"But my mother was asleep!" I protested.

"You've learned to think your problems through. You've learned to look at life through the eyes of a healthy, smart, self-sufficient young woman. You have coping skills, a brand-new set of them now. And a support network." She stood up, ready to usher me into my life. I knew there was no talking my way back into her ripped vinyl chair once I got out of it.

"I don't know," I said, still sitting.

"You have to trust me on this one. More importantly, you have to trust yourself."

"Wait," I said. "I have something for you." I searched through my purse for the Heavenly Hair gift cards Grandma Georgia had printed up. Her idea was to give a $20 gift certificate to any person who wasn't already a client. I handed the card to Mrs. Wallace. "You can use it on whatever you want. Except for hair products," I added, "and it's good for a year."

"Thank you, Rosie. I'll definitely come by and see you," she said.

On the way home, I called Kyle. "Honey, he's not home," Mrs.

Cox said. "I sure would like to see some a those prom pictures. We took lots of Kyle before he left to pick you up, but I wanna see one of you, too. I heard you were real pretty."

"Oh, well . . . uh, thanks," I said. "I'll send you one."

"Better yet, why don't I make an appointment with your mother. I can see the whole batch then."

"That's a good idea," I replied. I waited, wondering if she would say something, anything at all, about Kyle, but she didn't.

"Well, I'll tell Kyle you called. Bye, hon," she said and was gone. Kyle hadn't called on Sunday, and I hadn't seen him at school all day on account of a field trip to the Parthenon (as in Nashville, not Greece). I drove around for a while and ended up at Heavenly Hair.

The salon is *always* closed on Mondays, so it was odd that the front door was wide open; Mother's car was parked out front, and Miss Bertha's was right beside it. I pulled in the back lot and noticed Richard's and Drew's cars, too. "Nice that there's a party and no one bothered to invite me!" I said out loud.

And it seemed there really was a party. Colorful streamers hung from the ceiling and balloons were taped around the doors and windows. In the back corner, where the magazine rack normally stood, was a brand-new station. For years, Mother had talked about adding another one, but I couldn't believe she'd done it today, and after four hours of chemo. It was slightly smaller than the others, lower to the ground, too, but it matched perfectly.

"Hey, Rose Garden!" said Grandma Georgia. "Come on in! We're having a *simkhe*!" Mother was sitting in her regular chair, sipping a *regular* Coca-Cola. Aunt Mary was perched on a stool beside her, eating peanut M&M's. Richard was giving Drew a manicure, and Miss Bertha was on the phone.

"Uh, it's Monday," I pointed out, as if my family and friends couldn't figure out what day it was.

"Your mama had a brilliant idea," said Grandma Georgia. "Peri's getting out of the nursing home tomorrow, and Willy Ray called up tickled to death, saying he wanted to surprise her and get her hair done."

"There's no way I'm letting her climb from a wheelchair to the regular chair," said Mother. "Not with *her* heart, and we've been needing a station to accommodate wheelchairs anyway. The Quilters are getting up there, too, and well . . . I just wanted to do it." Mother shrugged and grinned at me. It was her real smile, too, not that put-on one she uses just to hide her troubles.

"Well, I got my ticket!" said Miss Bertha, hanging up the phone. "I'm taking the bus to Memphis," she announced proudly. "Reda can't believe I'm coming." She glanced at me over her half-glasses. "What's the matter?"

"Nothing," I lied. *Oh, my therapist just dumped me. My boyfriend doesn't love me, and we haven't talked in two days, but everything else is just fine,* I felt like saying, but I didn't. For the first time in ages, all the people I loved were in a good mood at the same time. I wasn't about to spoil it.

"Kyle stopped by," said Miss Bertha, still looking at me with those probing, experienced-mother eyes.

"Oh, really?" I tried to sound casual.

"I reckon he forgot we were closed on Monday. He left these," said Miss Bertha. She disappeared behind the desk and popped back up again. "Here," she said, handing me a bouquet of roses, not the store-bought kind, but the *real* kind, like the ones that get aphids and grow on stakes in the backyard. Something caught in my throat, and I couldn't speak. "Why is it men never bring flowers unless they've done something wrong?" Miss Bertha flew around the counter and hugged me.

"*I* bring flowers on a regular basis!" said Richard indignantly.

"He does," Drew agreed.

"Y'all do not count!" Aunt Mary snapped. "Of course you bring flowers. That's how come you're gay."

Grandma Georgia rolled her eyes and shook her head.

Kyle's roses were red, and there were little sprigs of fresh rosemary mixed in, too. The whole thing was wrapped in layers of wet paper towels, aluminum foil, and slightly damp tissue paper, and it was tied together with a brand-new shoelace. Judging by the shoelace, he'd done this all on his own.

"Here's the card," said Miss Bertha. I could feel all eyes locked on me as I slowly, fearfully opened it.

Ditto on the I love you.

Kyle

No one made a big fuss about it when I cried, but I cried. It was a little embarrassing, but I couldn't help myself.

As soon as I got home, the phone rang. It was Kyle. I could tell it was him by the way my heart dropped to my stomach and flew into my throat again (even *before* I picked up the phone or glanced at the caller ID).

"Hey, there," he said. "Did you get the flowers?"

"They're beautiful," I replied. "Thank you."

"Did you get my note?"

"Yes," I said quietly.

"I'm sorry I let you hang there by yourself the other night. I was pretty sure I felt the same way, but I didn't want to say it . . . well, you know . . . just because *you* said it. I mean . . . I didn't want you to *think* I was saying it just because *you* said it. I wanted to say it and have you *know* I was saying it because I meant it. You're not still mad, are you?"

"No! I'm not mad. I'm sorry about the other night. But we still had a good time. I didn't ruin your prom night or anything, right?"

"Nah. It was the prom. Other than gettin' to go with you, I wasn't expecting much. And what's a prom without a little drama, right? Oh, and by the way, I'm taking Mrs. Edinburgh's English class next year," he announced proudly.

"Really? And she let you in?" I was shocked. Usually, once a kid dumps Mrs. Edinburgh, there's no getting her back.

"I might've name-dropped," said Kyle. "I told her I'd ask you to help me out if I had any problems."

"What did she say to that?"

"She said if I'd used any name other than yours, she'd have said no, but since it was you, she was willing to give me the chance."

"No way. She didn't say that."

"She did, I swear."

Just as we were about to hang up, there was a moment of strained, who's-gonna-say-it-first silence. I waited. Kyle waited. "I love you," he said finally.

"Ditto," I replied and hung up.

Later that night, I paced around my just-cleaned room. It looked so pretty with its perfect-shade-of-blue ceiling, and I'd even draped a few strands of Christmas lights above the windows just to give things an extra sparkle. On the bureau a candle burned, and Roberta Flack sang "Killing Me Softly" on the oldies station, which I was listening to pretty much exclusively these days. A breeze rustled the lush trees outside my open window, and I could smell rain, distant still, but coming. I could also smell Kyle's flowers, and the hint of rosemary mixed in. Over and over, I'd read and reread the note, then proudly tucked it inside a frame along with one of our prom pictures.

I went to the mirror and stood there a long while. My thighs were slightly pudgy, my face still round and plump, my stomach anything but flat. I thought about something Kyle had said on prom night, about the day he first decided to ask me out. *When you look at a person's eyes or her smile, you can't tell how much she weighs.* The same was true of a person's heart.

chapter thirty-eight

Hope

The salon went crazy when Mrs. McCutchin's new van pulled up to the curb. "Let's go out to greet her!" shouted Hilda May Brunson.

"And give her another heart attack?" Aunt Mary scolded. "We're all staying right here." Mrs. Brunson looked at Aunt Mary sharply and huffed off out the door.

"Well, if she drops dead right out there on the sidewalk it'll be Hilda's fault," said Aunt Mary. I could tell she halfway hoped it would happen just so she could be right.

"So do you wanna go for a ride in my Bug this weekend?" I asked. Aunt Mary was the only one of the 4 Rosies who hadn't been yet.

"I thought you'd never ask!" she said, and put her arm around me.

Since my phone call that day, Aunt Mary and I had been different toward one another—more polite, less disrespectful. At least we were trying to meet halfway. "Do you like my new out-fit?" she asked.

"Yeah, I do," I replied, meaning it. My aunt had developed a crush on some lawyer from Nashville, and his case was on the docket this afternoon. I knew she'd probably gotten all dressed up on account of him.

"Oh, lookie yonder!" Mrs. Ida Harris shouted above the squeal of her new hearing aid. The Quilters, all four of them, had come to celebrate Mrs. McCutchin's return to Heavenly Hair. "I can see her!" Slowly, the van door slid open, and Mr. McCutchin eased his wife's chair onto the lift.

It was as if Miss America were passing right down South Main Street. Every person in the salon went running to the windows, even Drew, who'd never even met Mrs. McCutchin. Her wheel-chair gleamed in the Tennessee sunshine, and a tall neon-orange flag stuck straight up off the back—it was exactly the kind I'd had on my bike when I was little. I glanced down at the wheels of her chair, and there were plastic spoke decorations. *Her boys,* I thought and smiled to myself. Mr. McCutchin rolled her in, and at first everyone held back, afraid.

"Well, y'all don't jest stand there!" she said. "I won't break!" Mother was the first to hug her, then Miss Bertha, Grandma Geor-gia (who hadn't seen her in years), and all the rest, except for me.

Willy Ray grinned from ear to ear and clutched his wife's wheelchair as if she were perched at the edge of a cliff. "Willy, baby, go get them thangs we brought," said Mrs. McCutchin. Mr. McCutchin looked at Mother helplessly, as if to say, *I can't let go of her.*

"Drew, run out to the truck and get the sweets Peri brought," said Mother.

"Now how'd you know I brought sweets? Maybe I brought something else," Mrs. McCutchin teased. Her cheeks had a purple tint, and her breath came in short huffs, just the way I sounded when I tried to talk to Kay-Kay and run up North Main Street at the same time. I stayed on the sidelines, wondering if I should speak or keep quiet. "Now where's Richard? He's the only one that can shave my neck right. No offense, Rose Warren, but he's got the touch."

"I'm right here," said Richard. He moved through the crowd and bent down to kiss Mrs. McCutchin's cheek. "She's all mine now, Willy Ray," he said, and winked, nudging the poor man away.

"I told you he was fresh!" Mrs. McCutchin wheezed. Richard rolled Mrs. McCutchin over to the new station.

"Well, what's this now? We're gettin' mighty fancy around here, Rose Warren."

"It's called progress," Mother replied. "You're the first client that's tried it out. You let me know if it needs anything now."

"Well, I reckon we're going," said Mrs. Harris. "We've got to get a new quilt started. And we don't wanna wear you out, Peri."

"The quilt's for Peri," Mrs. Alcott mouthed. "It was right good seeing you again!" she called.

"Y'all, too," Mrs. McCutchin replied.

The Quilters waved and blew kisses, and the four of them tottered toward the door. I tried not to think about which one was driving.

"I've got court," said Aunt Mary importantly. Her face was pressed close to the mirror, and she was smearing on fresh lipstick.

"I'll walk you up to the courthouse," said Mrs. Brunson. "I need to get a glimpse of this fella you're gettin' yourself all worked up over."

"And I've got to go home and pack," said Miss Bertha. "I'm going to see my youngest daughter in Memphis."

"That's nice," said Mrs. McCutchin. "Do you like them cookies, young man?" Drew was sitting at Richard's usual station devouring one oatmeal raisin cookie after the other, and Mrs. McCutchin was smiling broadly at him in the mirror.

"Oh, sorry. I should've asked first. I'm Drew," he said, dusting the crumbs off his freshly manicured hands and rushing over to meet the woman we'd been fretting over for so long.

"It's a pleasure, Drew," said Mrs. McCutchin. "Next time I'll brang some sand tarts. You like sand tarts?" Drew nodded enthusiastically. "And who are you?" she asked, glancing my way. I looked behind me, but there was no one there. All at once, I realized Mrs. McCutchin meant me. I took a nervous step forward.

"It's me, Mrs. McCutchin. Rosie." She gasped and her hand flew over her mouth.

"Why, you don't even look like yourself! Come over here and let me get a good lookatcha." I went over to her chair and patted her plump shoulder awkwardly. "Oh, darlin', you look so good." She squeezed my hand. "Why, you ain't big as nothin'. Your mama didn't tell me you'd lost so much weight. Oh, Lord, I shore wish't I could. Aw, ain't you so proud, Rose Warren?"

"I am." Mother nodded. "I always was," she added, and smiled at me.

With a light heart, I headed out the door. I had an afternoon study session with Kay-Kay, and that night Mother and I planned to go out for dinner. She was dying to have a steak and a glass of wine before the chemo kicked in and knocked her flat, something she was actually looking forward to. "That's how I know it's working," she confessed.

I pulled into Kay-Kay's driveway, and she came bounding out the door in a pair of sunshine-yellow running shorts, a matching sports bra, and bright white (new, obviously) tennis shoes. "Well, guess what?" said Kay-Kay, leaning into the passenger's-side window. "It came!" she cheered before I had a chance to guess. "The Ab Cruncher came already! And, that's not all. I got a job at Harvey's Gym. I didn't even have to interview. Harvey wants me to start the second school's out. Oh, Rosie! I can hardly believe it! *And* in addition to being paid, I get two new workout outfits a month—this is my first," she said, twirling around to show me all sides, "and if I stay two years, I get a lifetime membership. For *free*! The shoes I had to buy, of course. Harvey can't afford to give those out for nothin'."

"That is *so* great! You'll be right down the street from Heavenly Hair! Hey, we can go to lunch together every day if we want."

"We can do lunchtime weight training sessions, too," Kay-Kay reminded me.

"Great," I teased. "A bonus for us both!" Kay-Kay laughed.

"At least if those Snickers bars start calling out to me from the snack machine, you'll be close by."

"You know your mother really ought to have that thing removed," said Kay-Kay.

"Oh, it won't fit up the stairs, so she just keeps filling it."

"Well, it's always something, I guess. And it's not like you can rid the whole entire world of junk food."

For about an hour, Kay-Kay and I sat on the hard floor in her sparse room and pored over her not-very-thorough English notes. Luckily, I already knew all about gerunds and participles. I'd intended to stay the whole afternoon, but I could tell Kay-Kay was ready to bust out of her skin, so I cut it short. I figured even a little tutoring was better than none at all. Just as I was packing up my books, Kay-Kay said, "Rosie, this summer I want to reinvent myself."

"Reinvent yourself? *How?*" I asked. Kay-Kay Reese was about as perfect a girl as I'd ever seen.

"You know Madonna's always doing that, just totally changing who she is all the time. Just when you think she's all disco sex and dance leotards, she starts living like the queen of England and wearing tweed."

"You wanna wear tweed?" I teased.

"Daddy's always said I could do so much better in school. Sometimes I just flat-out don't try. Like today. I mean, I should study all night long for this test. No offense, but I still don't have a clue about participles, and it's completely *not* your fault, Rosie. It's just I'm too preoccupied with trying out these new running shoes to pay attention." Kay-Kay bit her already chewed-off nails and paced around her small, utilitarian room.

The windows were covered with bland, water-stained curtains, and except for one tattered rug, the floor was bare. There were no pictures on the walls, no fluffy pillows on her bed, no piles of fashion magazines (as I'd so often imagined). Except for a couple of cheerleading trophies, it could've been anybody's space. A few months ago, I'd assumed Kay-Kay's personal life was as perfect as her looks, but up close I could see that wasn't true at all.

"Okay, listen. First, you need to relax a little. Go for your run. Tear it up and then come back and set a goal. Study for thirty minutes, and then jump on the Ab Cruncher. Take a shower. Then study thirty more minutes."

"You think that'd work?"

"I didn't start out running three miles. Remember? I had to work my way up to it. You'll get there."

"You really think so?" I nodded. "You know what, Rosie. Me and you would be a hell of a person put together."

"What?"

"With my determination at the gym and yours in school, we'd be one amazin' girl. *And* we'd have big boobs!" Kay-Kay giggled.

"We'd have big other stuff, too," I reminded her.

Kay-Kay walked me to the door. She threw her arms around me suddenly and squeezed hard. "You don't know how much I've been needin' a friend like you, Rosie."

"Oh, yes, I do," I replied.

"You can drive on the way home," said Mother as she made a left onto the Lewisburg Pike. "I plan to have *two* glasses of wine. I don't remember the last time I had wine! This feels like a celebration somehow. I feel better. You look beautiful. And Peri coming into the shop today . . . well, that just topped everything off. You don't think she was offended at the handicapped station?"

"No! Not at all! I think she was grateful not to have to get out of her chair." Mother rolled the windows down, and I slipped my hair into a ponytail. For a while we rode in silence. Sterling's was twenty minutes outside of town, and on a weeknight, they wouldn't be busy. I was glad. It would be nice to have Mother all to myself for a change.

"So have you and Kyle had sex yet?" The question flew out as if Mother'd been holding her breath.

"No! We haven't had sex *yet*!"

"You're awfully defensive," she pointed out, knitting together what would've been her eyebrows if she'd still had any.

I took a deep breath. "No, we have not had sex," I said again, this time leaving off the *yet* part. Mother kept her eyes glued to the highway and tapped the steering wheel. I could tell she was waiting for me to say something else, to reassure her somehow. "Mother, I can barely face *myself* in the mirror. Does it really make sense that I'd be naked with a boy?" It was the perfect reply, I knew, but I thought about prom night, about Kyle's soft lips and his manly football paws, about the vision I'd had of my virginity floating right over the treetops.

"Well, he's bringing you flowers and taking you out all the time. It'd be normal, I guess, if you did. I'd rather you wait, though. Be sure of each other before you take that step." Mother glanced over at me, but I couldn't look at her. "And you'll have to go to the gyno!" she added, as if this fact alone would be enough to deter any sexual relations. Thinking Mother's little talk was over, I switched on the radio. "You know, I made a lot of mistakes when I was your age," she said, switching it off again.

"I know," I groaned. I hated it when any discussion veered toward teen pregnancy—for so many reasons. I knew *I* was the mistake Mother was referring to, and I didn't much care for starting out that way—this scandalous, unwanted, unplanned, screwed-up-your-mother's-life baby. "Can we *not* talk about this tonight? *Please?*"

"I've been doing a lot of thinking about this," said Mother, "and I want you to hear me out." I sighed and rolled my eyes. *So much for our night feeling like a celebration*, I thought. "I want you to know, *really know*, that you were wanted, Rosie. I *chose* to have you. I never considered any other option, not that I judge people who do. But . . . well, anyway, *I* didn't, just in case you ever wondered. I guess I've maybe been a little too protective of you at times, and I know I worked way too much. Looking back on things, I could've scaled back a little, made more time for you."

"Mother, my weight gain is not your fault. I made a choice to be fat."

"Yes, but I didn't stop you. I saw what was going on."

"You did?" I asked.

Mother looked at me and nodded. "And I didn't do anything about it. I kept telling myself it was just a phase, but deep down I knew it wasn't. I knew why you were eating. I knew it was because you needed me, and I wasn't there for you. I feel terrible about it, Rosie. I just want you to know that. I don't think I can ever forgive myself."

I reached across the seat for Mother's small hand. This was

probably the most personal information she'd ever divulged, at least to me anyway. The wind blew stray pieces of hair into my face, and it stuck to my lip gloss. I peeled it off, only to have it blow back and get stuck again.

"What was it, Rosie? What was it that finally made you lose the weight?" she asked.

I thought for a minute, but it was tough to come up with just one answer. "I guess Mrs. McCutchin started it with that plate full of Christmas cookies that day in the shop. Everybody was standing there staring at me, and I got so mad. And then you wouldn't leave me alone about that stupid treadmill." Mother grinned, and I could tell it made her feel good to be part of my success.

We drove for a while longer, and I wondered where I'd be when the holidays rolled around again. I hoped I'd be at my goal weight by then. I hoped Mother's cancer would be in remission. I hoped Kyle would still love me and Kay-Kay would continue to be my friend. I hoped Drew and Richard would stay together, and Miss Bertha would see more of her family, and Aunt Mary would find a boyfriend. I hoped the Bluebirds would migrate. It was an endless list, these things I hoped for. I thought back to the Emily Dickinson poem I'd read so many months ago—the one about hope.

> Hope is the thing with feathers
> That perches in the soul,
> And sings the tune without the words,
> And never stops at all . . .

More than anything, I hoped the last line was true.

acknowledgments

First and foremost, I have to thank my kind friend and generous mentor, Margaret Meacham, for giving this book to her agent (now my agent, as well) in spite of my protests, and for reading it and being completely honest. Many thanks to Ann Tobias, my guardian agent, for taking so much time with the early drafts of Artichoke's Heart, *for making me work harder, for challenging me and questioning everything, and then for sending it to the perfect editor, Julie Strauss-Gabel. Right from the beginning, Julie understood Rosemary and the story I wanted to tell. Julie guided but never pressed. She encouraged but was never critical, and all the while, she convinced me that I really could do this.*

Along the way there have been exceptional teachers and friends who have in some way, large or small, influenced my writing: Sue Murphy, Harriet Eddlemon, Paige Chamberlain, Joel Glasser, Brooke Blough, Margaret Benner, George Friedman, Scott Allen, Charlotte Locklear, Joy Nelson, and Mary Rozell. Many thanks to John Bradley at Hewitt's Garden and Design in Nashville for his expert advice on Southern gardens. Thanks also to the friends who've offered invaluable support: Anne, Bev, Bonnie, Brem, Diane, Ellen, James, Jamie, Jen, Karyn-Mina, Ken, Kirk, Margaret, Mary-Carroll, Pete, Robin, Stacey, and Tamra.

Special thanks also to my two favorite hairdressers—Sue Ebert and Jill Ruhlman.

Last, but obviously not least, I have to thank my incredible family. Scott, you've been beyond generous with your support and love during this process. Cassie, you've endured years of proofreading, and you'd make a great editor yourself one day. Flannery and Elsbeth, you both continue to bring so much joy and energy to my life.